GUARDING
Suzannah

SERVE AND PROTECT 1

NORAH WILSON

Guarding Suzannah

Cover by Kim Killion, Hot Damn Designs

Book design by Michael Hale, Hale Author Services

ISBN: 978-0-9878037-2-6

Chapter 1

DETECTIVE JOHN QUIGLEY STEPPED inside Courtroom 2, closing the door quietly behind him. One or two people in the small gallery glanced up at him briefly, then returned their attention to the front of the courtroom where a young patrol officer was being sworn in.

Quigg took a seat, glancing around the drab, low-ceilinged, windowless room. *Provincial Court.* Nothing like the much grander Queen's Bench courtrooms upstairs or the Court of Appeal chambers on the top floor. But aesthetics aside, they did a brisk business here. In the fifteen years Quigg had spent on the Fredericton force, he'd been responsible for sending quite a few customers through these doors. Doors that all too often turned out to be the revolving kind, the kind that spit offenders right back out on the street to re-offend.

On that thought, Quigg glanced over at the accused. Clean shaven and neatly dressed, he sat off to the right, beside the Sheriff's deputy. His long hair, drawn back into a ponytail, glinted blue-black under the fluorescent lights. If he were conscious of Quigg's scrutiny, he didn't betray it with so much as a twitch of a muscle. Rather, he kept his flat, emotionless gaze trained on the witness.

"Your witness, Mr. Roth."

At the magistrate's words, Quigg faced forward again.

"Thank you, Your Honour." The Crown Prosecutor adjusted his table microphone and directed his first question to the witness. Mike Langan, the impossibly young looking constable in the witness box, responded, his answer clear and concise.

Over the next fifteen minutes, the prosecutor methodically built his case with one carefully chosen question after another. Constable Langan's manner in the witness box was confident and assured. He referred often to his notebook, which appeared to contain copious, comprehensive notes. Quigg unclenched his fingers and leaned back into his seat. What could go wrong?

Everything.

His gaze slid to the one area of the courtroom he'd so far managed to avoid, the defense table. *Suzannah Phelps.* There she sat, primly erect, all that straight blond hair pulled up into a knot at the back of her head. Even under the black tent-like court robes, she still managed to look model elegant. His pulse took a little kick.

Dammit, why did he do this to himself? He didn't have to be here. He was off today. He didn't have even a glancing involvement with this case, or with Constable Langan.

Because you're a bloody masochist.

"Any questions on cross, Ms. Phelps?"

The magistrate's voice cut into Quigg's thoughts.

"Just a few, Your Honour."

A *few*? Yeah, sure.

"Please proceed."

Quigg glanced at Langan, saw the younger man tense. *Relax man.* He tried to send the thought telepathically. *Don't let her get to you. Don't let her see you sweat.*

"So, Constable Langan, you didn't actually see my client flee the crime scene?"

"No, ma'am. Not from the actual scene. But I did see a man fitting the robber's description running just four blocks from the scene."

"And who provided this description?"

"The shopkeeper."

"And the description was ... ?"

"Native ... er, First Nations individual, average height, stocky build, long black hair worn in a ponytail."

"Were those the shopkeeper's precise words? First Nations individual?"

"Huh?"

"Did the shopkeeper describe the perpetrator as Native? Native American? First Nations?"

"Not exactly."

Quigg sank lower in his seat, suppressing a groan. This was gonna be a train wreck and Langan didn't even know it yet.

"Exactly how *did* he describe him, then?"

"He made it clear that the individual was Indian."

"Those were his words, then? Indian?"

"No." Constable Langan shifted, glancing down at his notebook.

"What were his precise words, Constable?"

Langan glanced at the judge, then back at Suzannah Phelps. "I believe his precise words were, *wagon burner.*"

"Which you took to mean a member of the First Nations?"

"Yes."

Quigg massaged his temple. Ah, Christ, here we go.

"Thank you, Constable."

Her voice was polite, prim, even. Which just served to show that sharks came in all kinds of guises.

Suzannah glanced down at her notes, then back at the hapless witness. "So, Constable Langan, could you take a guess how many males from our Native population would fit that description?"

"Objection, Your Honour. We have eye-witness testimony from the shop owner that the accused is the individual who committed the robbery. He was picked out from a lineup containing no fewer than ten Native men of similar ages and builds."

Finally! An objection from the Crown. Quigg resisted the urge to rake a hand through his hair.

"As my learned friend knows, I could cite dozens of cases where eye-witness identification put innocent men behind bars," responded Suzannah. "And those were cases where the perpetrators' faces were not partially obscured by a kerchief."

"Point taken." The judge leaned forward. "Your objection is overruled, Mr. Roth. You may proceed, Ms. Phelps."

"Thank you, Judge." She turned back to the witness. "Again, Constable Langan, in your opinion, can you tell me how many males of Mi'kmaq or Maliseet descent could answer to that description: medium height, stocky build, black hair?"

A pause. "Quite a few, I would imagine."

"A majority of them?"

"Possibly," Langan conceded.

"Then any Native male observed within a reasonable radius of the crime scene might have fit your description?"

"Maybe. But then again, there aren't a lot of them in this particular shopping district."

Mother of God. Quigg sank even lower in his seat.

"Ah, so my client shouldn't have been there in the first place, in an exclusive shopping district?"

"That's not what I meant." Langan's face hardened. "This particular Native male was fleeing capture."

"Is that so?" She made a show of reviewing her notes. "Was my client running when you first spotted him?"

"No."

"When did he start running?"

"When I cut him off with my vehicle. He was walking fast — I mean, real fast — down the sidewalk, in an easterly direction. I pulled into an alley, blocked him off."

"And then he fled?"

"Yes. He turned and fled back in a westerly direction."

"Were your red and blue bar lights flashing when you executed this maneuver?"

"Yes."

She shuffled some more papers. "Is it conceivable that my client's flight might have been an ingrained response to perceived police harassment?"

"No!"

"No? Constable Langan, are you a member of a visible minority?"

"No."

"Objection!"

The judge held up his hand in the prosecutor's direction. "Overruled."

"Imagine for a minute that you are a member of a visible minority. What might you do if a police cruiser were to suddenly swing into your path like that?"

Constable Langan bristled. "The guy had the money on him. The *exact* amount that was later determined to be missing from the cash register."

"Ah, so now we have a First Nations male, walking where he ought not to, with more money in his pocket than he should have?"

"Money he stole from that shopkeeper at knifepoint!"

Damn, the kid was losing it.

"Ah, yes, the knife." Suzannah flipped the page on the legal pad in front of her. "A knife which bore no fingerprints and which you haven't been able to tie to my client."

"He dumped it down a sewer grate a block from where he was apprehended, two blocks from the scene. He still had the polkadot-ted blue-and-white handkerchief in his pocket. Give or take the coins in his pockets, he was carrying exactly the amount of money that was stolen. He was ID'd by the shopkeeper ... ."

Quigg closed his eyes, pressing a thumb and forefinger against his lids. Inside his head, he heard the theme from *Jaws*.

"Thank you for that summation, Constable, but I think the Crown was planning one of its own." She flipped another page on her yellow pad. "Since you're feeling so loquacious, maybe you can answer this question for me — do you yourself ever carry a handkerchief?"

Langan blinked.

"Would you like me to repeat the question, Constable? When you're off duty, wearing your civilian clothes, do you ever carry one of those polkadotted handkerchiefs? Shoved in a front pocket of your jeans, maybe, or in your coat pocket?"

Five more minutes. That's all it took to completely decimate the Crown's case. Not that Roth surrendered without a fight. He called the shopkeeper and adduced his evidence. Evidence which the defense challenged effectively. But by the time Suzannah fin-ished her summation, she'd planted more than just the seed of reasonable doubt. No one in the courtroom was surprised when the judge pronounced his verdict without even a short recess. *Not guilty.* The prisoner was released.

Quigg stood and slipped out the door as quietly as he'd slipped in.

⁂

Suzannah stood, turning to scan the gallery. The seats had emptied out, apart from her client's two female cousins. Certainly the owner of the gaze she'd felt boring into her back for the last half hour was gone.

"Congratulations."

She turned toward Anthony Roth, whose lean, dark features were wreathed in resignation. Fiercely competitive, he hated to lose, but he was a good prosecutor. He knew his role wasn't to secure a conviction at any cost; it was to get to the truth.

"Thanks."

"And you made yourself a brand new friend on Fredericton's finest, too. Quite a day."

She grimaced.

When young Mike Langan had finally been excused from the witness box, his body language as he jammed on his hat and tugged at his Kevlar vest had screamed exactly how he felt. Suffice to say he wouldn't be joining the ranks of the Suzannah Phelps Fan Club any time soon.

That's how it goes, Suzie-girl. You didn't get into this business to make friends.

"Couldn't be helped," she said lightly. "You know I had to play the cards I was dealt."

"Of course. I'd have done the same thing in your shoes." Roth swept his briefcase from the desk. "Fair warning, though. It'll be different next time we cross swords over this guy."

"There won't be a next time."

His lips lifted in a cynical smile. "Right."

As soon as the Crown Prosecutor moved off, her client moved in. Gripping her hand in a two-handed clasp, he pumped it enthusiastically. "Thank you, Ms. Phelps."

"You're welcome, Leo." Suzannah withdrew her hand. "You still interested in a job at the graphics studio I mentioned?"

He nodded. "Yeah. Yeah, I am."

She plucked a business card from her briefcase and handed it to him. "Give this lady a call. She agrees you have talent, but you'd have to prove yourself."

The card disappeared into Leo's huge hand. "Thanks, Ms. Phelps. This is great."

"And you'd have to stay clean, Leo. You understand?" She caught his gaze and held it. "Squeaky clean. No more altercations with the police."

"I understand."

"I hope you do. You put a foot wrong after this, they'll be watching."

He cast a sideways glance at his cousins. "Gotcha."

"Good. Now get out of here."

He grinned and was gone.

Suzannah turned back to the desk, her smile fading as she began packing her note pads, law books and files back into the big hard-sided court bag.

Dammit, she'd won, hadn't she? Why didn't she feel better?

Made yourself a brand new friend today . . . Roth's words echoed in her head.

"Oh, for pity's sake." She was such a baby sometimes. Shoving the last file into her bag, she glanced around the courtroom. Normally, she'd adjourn to the ladies room to remove her court garb, but she could do a striptease in here today and there'd be no one to witness it.

One tug and the white tabbed collar came off. Then the robe, over the head like a choir gown. She ran a hand over her hair to make sure it hadn't come loose. Satisfied, she folded the robe carefully, stuffed it into a blue velvet sack and pulled the drawstring tight. There. Street ready. She smoothed her pinstriped skirt, slung the sack over her shoulder, hefted her bag and headed for the exit.

Despite the quick change, her getaway was not as clean as she would have liked, however. In the corridor, she ran into Renee LeRoy, half-assed reporter and full-fledged pain-in-the-ass. Suzannah searched her mind for the name of the local weekly Renee worked for, but it eluded her. Not that it mattered. She avoided reading her own press if she possibly could, especially anything *this* particular woman might have to say.

Well, at least this explained the sensation she'd felt of being watched back there in the courtroom. Suppressing a groan, Suzannah tacked on a pleasant smile. "How's it going, Renee?"

The other woman didn't smile back. In fact, her face was set in grim lines more reminiscent of a Russian forward in the '72 Canada/Russia hockey series than a female reporter. As soon as the thought crossed her mind, Suzannah chastised herself. Her dislike of Renee LeRoy had nothing to do with the other woman's appearance and everything to do with her attitude.

"I see your client walked away a free man."

Oh, hell, here we go again. The woman was a broken record. "The burden of proof always rests on the Crown, Renee," she said reasonably. "This time, they failed to meet that burden."

"Thanks in no small part to you."

"Why, thank you." Suzannah offered a wide if disingenuous smile. "I'd be flattered, except I think any reasonably competent criminal lawyer would have secured an acquittal under the circumstances."

The reporter's eyes narrowed. "Doesn't it keep you awake at night, Ms. Phelps? Doesn't your conscience ever bother you, knowing you're helping guilty men go free?"

Suzannah's lips thinned, along with her patience. Was a little open-mindedness from the press too much to ask? "What would *bother me* is to see a conviction entered on the quality of the evidence we saw today. My client deserved to be acquitted. Now, if you'll excuse me, I have a schedule to keep."

A minute later, she descended the steps of the Justice Building and crossed the parking lot. The sun had already begun to dip behind the tallest buildings, casting long shadows. Even so, heat rose from the asphalt in shimmering waves.

All of southern New Brunswick had been gripped in a heat wave since the July 1st Canada Day holiday. Like the rest of her pasty-faced compatriots, Suzannah had welcomed the first real taste of summer. Now, almost three weeks later, she cursed the humidity that made perspiration bead between her breasts before she'd even reached her car.

She thought briefly about stowing her case in the BMW's trunk, but decided that would require too much effort. Instead, she hit the button on her remote to release the door locks. She opened the back door on the driver's side and tossed the garment bag onto the back seat. She'd started to swing the heavy bag into the vehicle when a flash of color from the front passenger seat caught her eye. She lost her grip on the handles, and the bag collided with the car's frame and thudded to the pavement.

Oh, God, no. Not again.

⁂

"Can I give you a hand with that?"

She seemed to just about come out of her skin at his words, whirling to face him. Wide blue eyes locked onto him, and for an instant, Quigg saw fear. Not surprise. Not your garden variety momentary fright when someone startled you. This was real, raw fear. Then it was gone, and she wore her smooth Princess face again.

"Thank you, no. I can manage."

Her voice was cool, polite, completely assured. Had he imagined the blaze of fear?

Bending, she righted the briefcase, deposited it on the car's seat and closed the door. She must have expected him to move on, or at least to step back, because when she turned, she wound up standing considerably closer than before. Closer than was comfortable for her. He could see it in the quick lift of her brows, the slight widening of her eyes. But she didn't step back.

Neither did he.

Damn, she was beautiful. And tall. In those three-inch heels that probably cost more than he made in a week, her gaze was level with his. Throw in all that long blond hair that would slide like silk through a man's hands, and a body that would . . . .

"You're that cop."

He blinked. "*That* cop?"

"*Regina vs. Rosneau.*"

"Good memory." They'd secured a conviction on that one, but her client had taken a walk on appeal. Though in truth, Quigg hadn't minded over much. The dirtball had done it, all right, but strictly speaking, the evidence had been a bit thin. One of those fifty/fifty propositions.

"*Regina vs. Haynes.* That was you, too, right?"

Okay, dammit, that one still stung, although the insult was almost two years old now. Two defendants, separate trials, separate representation, each accused managing to convince a jury the other guy'd done it. Of course, Quigg could take consolation from knowing the noose was closing yet again around Ricky Haynes' good-for-nothing drug-dealing neck. Haynes had since moved outside the city limits, beyond municipal jurisdiction, but Quigg had it on good authority that the Mounties were building a rock-solid case against him.

Yes, he could take some consolation in that. Some *small* consolation. Not enough, however, to blunt the slow burn in his gut right now.

"Keep a scrapbook, do you, Ms. Phelps? Or maybe you cut a notch in your little Gucci belt, one for every cop you skewer?"

Something that looked astonishingly like hurt flashed in her eyes, but like before, it was gone before he could be certain he'd really seen it. Then she stepped even closer and smiled, a slow, knowing smile that made him think about skin sliding against skin and sweat-slicked bodies fusing in the dark, and he knew he'd been mistaken. When she extended a slender, ringless finger to trace a circle around a button on his shirt, his heart stumbled, then began to pound.

"Definitely not the belt thing," she said, her voice as husky and honeyed as his most sex-drenched fantasy. "At the rate you guys self-destruct under cross, there'd be nothing left to hold my trousers up, would there, now, John?"

Then she climbed in her gleaming little Beemer and drove off before his hormone-addled brain divorced her words from her manner and realized he'd been dissed.

Against all reason, he laughed. Lord knew it wasn't funny. Certainly, young Langan wouldn't share his mirth.

Of course, the whole thing defied reason, the way it twisted his guts just to look at her. She was rich. She was beautiful. She was sophisticated. She was the daughter of a judge, from a long line of judges. She was … what? He searched his admittedly limited lexicon for an appropriate term. *Kennedy-esque.*

Meanwhile, his own father had worked in a saw mill; his mother had cleaned other people's houses. Suzannah Phelps was so far out of his league, there wasn't even a real word for it.

She was also the woman not-so-affectionately known around the station house as *She-Rex.* And worse.

Much worse.

Except she hadn't looked much like a She-Rex when she'd spun around to face him, her face all pale and frightened.

Quigg turned and headed for Queen Street, where he'd parked his car. What had spooked her? Not his sudden appearance. He was sure of that. She might not have much use for cops, but she wasn't scared of him.

Maybe it was something inside her car.

He'd reached his own car, which sprouted a yellow parking ticket from beneath the windshield wiper. Great. He glanced up, searching traffic. There she was, at the lights a block away.

What could be in her car to make her look like that? Or was he completely off base? Was it a guilty start, not a frightened start? Hard to say. She'd masked it so quickly.

Damn, he was going to have to follow her.

Climbing into his not-so-shiny Taurus, he fired it up, signaled and pulled into traffic.

Even at this hour with the first of the home-bound traffic leaving the downtown core, tailing her was child's play. As he expected, she headed back to her office. No knocking off early for Suzannah Phelps. She probably put in longer days than he did. Two blocks from her uptown offices, she pulled into another office building's parking lot. Quigg guided his vehicle into the gas bar next door and watched Suzannah drive to the back of the lot where she parked next to a blue dumpster.

Pretending to consult a map he'd pulled from his glove compartment, Quigg watched her get out of the car and scan the lot.

Then she circled the BMW, opened the passenger door and pulled something out. The car itself blocked Quigg's view, but he saw a flash of mauvey/pinky floral patterned paper. Then she lifted the dumpster's lid and tossed the object in. Quickly, she rounded the car, climbed in and accelerated out of the lot.

Quigg watched her vehicle travel east along Prospect. When she signaled and turned into her office's parking lot, he slipped his own car into gear. Thirty seconds later, he lifted the lid to the dumpster.

Flowers? She'd been scared witless by flowers?

More likely by who sent the flowers, he reasoned. Maybe they still had a card attached. Out of habit, he patted his pockets for latex gloves before remembering he didn't have any on him. He wasn't on duty. He had some in a first aid kit in his car, but he wasn't about to dig them out. This wasn't an investigation.

Well, not a sanctioned one.

Grimacing, he retrieved the prettily wrapped bouquet with his bare hands. The florist's paper appeared pristine, undisturbed, as though Suzannah hadn't even looked at the contents. Carefully, he peeled the paper back. Then he dropped the bouquet back into the dumpster.

Holy hell! Long-stemmed red roses. Or rather, what he suspected used to be red roses. Now they were more brown than red. Rusty, like old blood. Dead. Probably a dozen of them.

His mind whirled. How had she known? She hadn't even opened the wrapper.

Because it wasn't the first time, obviously.

Because they'd been deposited in her car, right there in the barristers' parking lot, while she was inside defending Leo Warren. While a commissionaire kept an eye on the lot. While her car doors had no doubt been locked.

No wonder she'd been spooked.

He picked up the bouquet again and examined it closer. No card. *There's a surprise, Sherlock.*

Why hadn't she told him? She *knew* he was a cop.

Domestic. The answer came instantly. Had to be. She knew the source, but wasn't prepared to make a complaint because she didn't want to make trouble for the jerk who'd done this, thereby increasing his rage. How many times had he seen that age-old dynamic in operation?

Except he hadn't expected it from Suzannah. She was too much of a fighter. What could be going on in her head?

Quigg tossed the bouquet back in the dumpster and closed the lid. Climbing back into the Taurus, he sat for long moments.

He should leave this alone. He knew it.

He also knew he wasn't going to.

"This, you dumb-ass, is how careers are ruined."

But she'd called him John. Back there, outside the courthouse, she'd called him by his Christian name. Nobody called him John, except his mother. It was *Quigg*, or *Detective Quigley*, or *Officer*, or even *Hey, pig!* But back there, while her index finger had traced delicate circles on his chest, she'd called him John.

Stifling a sigh, he keyed the ignition and slipped the Ford into gear.

Chapter 2

T HAT DID IT.

Suzannah plunked her champagne glass down with enough force to bring a server scurrying to assure himself of the health of both the Waterford flute and the Chippendale sideboard.

John Quigley. Not only was he here at this exclusive New Brunswick Day bash, but he was standing there beneath the chandelier, flirting shamelessly with the Lieutenant Governor.

Dear God, he was good looking when he smiled like that.

Not that he didn't look pretty good all the time. Not handsome — no one, even at their most generous, would call him that. His face was way too strong. And his clothing always looked so ... disheveled.

She studied him under the brilliant lights. His close-cut hair, a kind of sandy color that was neither brown nor blond, sprang back from a high forehead. His hairline had begun to recede just the slightest bit, but it seemed to Suzannah that it only served to offset the brutally masculine planes of his face, all taut skin stretched over strong bones. Eyes that were more grey than blue, straight nose. Really, really good mouth ....

Her lips thinned as she realized the detour her thoughts had taken. From all appearances, this man was practically *stalking* her, for goodness sake, and here she was mooning over his mouth.

"Another champagne cocktail, madam?"

She didn't lift her gaze from the pair under the chandelier. "No, thank you. I have to be going, actually."

"Then let me fetch your wrap."

She smiled at the server then. "Thank you." Digging a coat check from her tiny evening bag, she handed it to him. He melted away with the grace of a professional who took pride in his job. When she looked up again, her gaze collided with Detective Quigley's.

A third party, an older man, had joined them beneath the chandelier, and was currently monopolizing the Lieutenant Governor. Detective Quigley nodded agreeably at something the man said, but he held Suzannah's gaze for long seconds.

Suzannah's breath stalled in her lungs. Good Lord! She swore she could feel the brush of that gray-blue gaze on the sensitive skin of her shoulders, left bare by the Donna Karan sheath she'd chosen. Then he shifted his attention back to the Lieutenant Governor, who was speaking to him.

Suzannah let her breath out in a rush.

To hell with waiting. She was going in search of her wrap.

Two minutes later, she handed her keys to the valet and pulled her shawl closer around her shoulders. The heat wave still hadn't broken, but with the slight breeze from the river, it was cool enough tonight that she was grateful for the cobweb-thin material.

"Leaving so soon?"

She didn't start at his voice. On some level, she must have known he'd follow her out here. She turned to face him, an odd sense of exhilaration revving her pulse rate.

"Are you following me, Detective?"

Good Lord, was that *her* voice? It sounded way too sexy, too sultry.

"I liked John better."

She felt her face heat at that velvet-voiced reminder of her parting shot the last time they'd spoken. "Answer the question, Detective."

He loosened his tie and undid the top buttons of his white shirt, then cricked his neck one way, then the other. "Ah, that's better. Now, what makes you think I'm following you?"

Her mouth suddenly dry, she swallowed, keeping her gaze on his face, away from the rumpled sexiness of his shirt. What in God's name was wrong with her?

"Hmmmm, let me see — maybe because after not laying eyes on you outside a courtroom until the other day in the parking lot, I'm now seeing you everywhere I go."

He slid his hands in his trouser pockets and leaned back against one of the building's impressive pillars. "Everywhere? Surely not."

"The theater?"

He grinned. "Good play, wasn't it?"

"The exhibit opening at the art gallery?"

The twin grooves on either side of his mouth deepened. "What, you don't take me for a fan of art?"

She snorted. "Of the poker-playing-dog variety, maybe."

He laughed, a deep, surprising rumble that made a sensation flutter in her stomach. Dammit, she was supposed to be lambasting him for trailing around after her. Except it was a little ... flattering.

"Madam?"

She glanced up to see the valet had returned, without her car.

"I'm afraid you have car trouble," he said, handing her the keys.

She closed her eyes, exhaling. "Tires?"

"Yes," he replied.

"Wonderful. Just bloody wonderful."

⚜

She looked so thoroughly disheartened, way beyond what a flat tire should cause. "Relax, Princess." He pushed away from the pillar. "I'll change your tire, have you on your way in five minutes."

"Don't bother," she clipped. "I'll call CAA."

"Hey, I can handle this. Besides, with any luck, I'll get dirt or grease all over me and won't have to go back in there." He indicated stately Old Government House with a nod of his head.

"Thanks for the offer, but I don't have room in my trunk for four spares."

"Four?" He blinked at her. "They can't *all* be flat."

"They can if they've been slashed."

Quigg shot a look at the valet, who nodded a confirmation, then retreated back to his station.

He gripped her elbow. "What's going on, Suzannah?"

Calmly, she removed her arm from his grip. "Nothing that's not par for the course, Detective."

"Jesus, your tires are slashed and you don't even bat an eye-lash?"

She opened her ridiculously tiny beaded purse and pulled out an even tinier cell phone. Seconds later, she was talking to the CAA dispatcher. Cripes, she had the auto association on her speed dial? He listened as she gave her situation and her location.

"Wanna explain what's going on here?" he asked as she tucked the phone away again.

She shrugged, an elegant lift of the shoulder. "Just the cost of doing a little criminal Legal Aid in this town."

"What's that supposed to mean? And why wasn't your first call to the cops, especially if this isn't the first time it's happened?"

"The police." She laughed, a surprisingly grating sound that lacked real amusement. "Yeah, that'd work."

Quigg sucked a breath in through his teeth. "You think *cops* did this?"

She arched a delicate eyebrow. "Congratulations, Detective. I'll bet you graduated top of your class."

"No."

"No? Gosh, with those deductive powers, I'd have —"

He stepped closer. "No, it wasn't a cop who did this."

Her bosom lifted on a long inhalation, but she didn't huff out an impatient sigh as he half expected.

"Look, I've been around the block a few times, Detective. I know I haven't endeared myself to you guys. I also know you stick together —"

"But not like this —"

"Hey, I understand. Really. The blue wall. You're charged with enforcing what amounts to a pretty puritanical code, one that abhors improprieties like drunkenness or lewdness. So you avoid those social situations where you might make a hypocrite of your-self. Then, before you know it, your social sphere includes nothing but other cops."

"Can I just say —"

"It's okay. I totally get it. You put that uniform on, that badge, and it isolates you from your friends, from your community, even from the legal system. Which sets up the us/them solidarity thing.

So when a guy gets a rough ride from me on the stand, of course the rest of you are going to empathize pretty strongly with him."

"Thank you, Dr. Phelps, for that lesson on police sub-culture. But read my lips — it wasn't one of us slashed your tires."

Judging from the exasperated noise she made, the patience she was trying so hard to project had finally reached its limits. "Are you seriously going to stand there and tell me you think every cop on your force is above this kind of dirty trick? That they wouldn't slash a tire or two to get their point across?"

"How could I? I don't even *know* some of the guys, except to nod at them. But I think it's more likely this was done by your dead-flower delivery man."

"What did you say?" Her tone was suddenly sharp.

"I said, this is more likely the handiwork of your FTD psycho, and I'm damn sure *he's* not a cop."

She didn't move, but Quigg felt her withdrawal as surely as if she'd physically stepped back. It was as though she'd pulled her very aura back, drawing it close so it wouldn't brush his.

Whoops. Guess he should have broken the news that he knew about the dead floral offering a little more tactfully.

"You *have* been following me." She intoned the words as though she still couldn't quite believe it.

"Hey, it's not what you think —"

"Spying on me!" She was looking at him now as though he were some kind of particularly disgusting insect.

"You have to call the cops, Suzannah."

Her mouth tightened. "Forget it."

She turned on her very elegant, very high heel and started toward her car, her strides long and brisk. Quigg hurried to catch up. She stopped and whirled so quickly, he had to throw on the brakes to avoid colliding with her.

"One more thing, Detective. You stay the hell away from me or I'll have your ass in court before your head stops spinning."

He almost smiled at that. "Thought you weren't going to call the police?"

"Just stay away from me."

She started off again. Again, he followed, this time at a more discreet distance. He didn't feel like smiling anymore.

"Suzannah, listen, you have to call this in. There's some whack-job out there trying to … hell, I don't know. At the very least, he's trying to scare you."

She'd reached her car and was fishing in her purse again for the keys. Unconscious habit. The Beemer wasn't going anywhere, not sitting at it was with all four rims biting into flattened tires. Realizing the futility of her search, she turned on him.

"*You* are the whack-job, Detective. You're the one who's been sneaking around, following me, watching me—" Her words stumbled to a stop. "The flowers … oh, Lord, was it you? You were there that day, weren't you? You were the one watching me, in the courtroom."

The blaze of light spilling from the mansion's huge windows didn't reach this far down the driveway, so he couldn't read her expression, but he didn't need the visual clues. He could hear the fear-tinged fury in her voice.

"Yes, it was me."

She took a step backward, pressing herself into the car's fender.

He swore, shoving a hand through his hair.

"In the courtroom, dammit. It was me in the courtroom. But I sure as hell didn't put that abomination in your car. I'm telling you, it wasn't a cop did that. And what's more, I think you know it."

He heard her draw a hissing breath. "What exactly do you mean by that?"

"Red roses? Dead ones? Slashed tires? That kind of rage strikes me as pretty personal, the kind of thing a spurned lover might do."

"No."

"Listen, you probably think you're doing the right thing by staying quiet, but it'll come back to bite you, Suzannah. I'm sure he says he loves you, but I'm telling you, men like this—"

She made a frustrated groan. "I don't believe it! You think I know this fruitcake?" Her voice rose on the question. "You think I'm protecting him?"

"Why else would you sit on something like this? It's obviously not the first time it's happened. You didn't even crack the wrapping paper on that posy because you knew exactly what was inside it."

"Omigod, you picked it out of the dumpster, didn't you?"

"Dammit, you looked scared when I approached you in the parking lot that day. I kinda got the idea it was something in the car made you squirrely, something you didn't especially want me to see."

"Of course. And you followed me in the hopes of getting some dirt on me, something to de-fang the tiger." She thumped her purse down on the hood of the car and leaned back against the Beemer's paint job. A shaft of yellow light from the building struck her face. "You are a piece of work, Detective."

He could have set her straight on why he'd followed her, why he'd been there at the courthouse in the first place.

He could also offer his jugular for slashing, but he wasn't about to do that, either.

"You're evading the question. If this isn't a domestic deal, why haven't you reported it? In my professional opinion, that little floral tribute carries a menacing message. And don't tell me it was a cop. A slashed tire maybe, but not this."

"Detective, this has been a fact of life for me since I started practice. Someone slashes a tire here, keys my paint job there, places hang-up calls from a number with blocked caller ID." She shifted so her face was lost in shadows again. "And flowers turn up. Sometimes they're dead roses, sometimes they're beautiful live roses."

He swore, fluently. "Okay, okay, you thought it was us. It isn't. Let's go report it. Right now."

"No."

"No? I'm telling you it wasn't cops."

"Okay, I believe you."

"Then let's go."

"I'm not going to report anything, John."

He was John again, not Detective. That much penetrated his exasperation. "Why the hell not?"

"This is low-level harassment. I haven't had a single direct threat. No one's actually approached me, contacted me or menaced me. There's no way I'm going to go running to you guys, crying about something the investigator will figure I brought down on myself."

"That's crazy."

A big flatbed geared down on Woodstock Road, slowing to turn into the driveway. Her hook had arrived.

"Crazy?" She lifted her chin another fraction. "Crazy would be making a complaint. I have to work inside this system, John. I don't need you guys to like me, but I do need you to respect me."

"Like we wouldn't respect you if you reported this psycho?" Damn, that's exactly what she thought. "You think this is brinkmanship? You can't let us see you blink?"

"Look, if you must know, I *did* report it, the first time it happened. Suffice to say, after that experience, I don't think I'll be doing it again soon. Especially when I can easily afford to replace a few tires."

"But—"

"But nothing." Her voice hardened. "I spend my days poking holes in your cases until they bleed daylight. There's no way I'm going to go to you guys again with something like this. I don't need some fresh-faced young constable telling me I'm overwrought or that I have a persecution complex. And I sure don't need to be reminded that you're busy taking care of the *real victims* my clients leave behind." She pushed away from the car's fender and raised a hand to flag down the tow truck driver. "Thank you for your concern, Detective, but I can take it from here."

Damn her stubbornness.

Despite his clear dismissal, for the next five minutes, Quigg stood back and fumed while the disabled vehicle was loaded on the back of the flatbed. As the driver checked the security of his load, Suzannah turned her attention back to him.

"You're still here."

He gritted his teeth. "You'll need a drive home."

"Thanks, but the tow guy says he'll give me a lift."

Stubborn wasn't the word. His lips thinned. "That so? In that case, guess I'll stick around for the show."

That eyebrow again, arching in elegant inquiry.

"Show?"

"Yeah, the show. If you're planning to climb way up into *that* rig wearing *that* dress, this is something I gotta see."

She lifted her chin. "A cab, then."

His irritation escaped. "Dammit, Suzannah, why can't you accept my help? Someone slashed your tires tonight. That's not something you do with nail clippers or a straightened paperclip. That's something you do with a *knife*. And for all you know, your slash-happy friend could be watching right now, ready to follow you home."

As though unable to resist the impulse, she scanned the parking lot, her eyes searching the parked cars, the shadowed shrubbery, the pools of darkness beyond the street lights on Woodstock Road. When she turned back to him, her expression betrayed a tinge of fear, and considerably more than a tinge of anger.

"Scare tactics, Detective?"

"You should be scared. You should be sitting in a squad car right now giving your story to a uniform. But since you aren't, the least I can do is make sure you get home safe."

Still she hesitated. What was he doing here, trying to help a hard-headed woman who clearly didn't want his help?

"Hell, Suzannah, I won't tell anyone, if that's what you're worried about."

He'd been half joking, but her expression told him he'd hit the nail on the head. She really thought she'd somehow lose face if she sought police help. He bit back his impatience.

"Cross my heart," he said. "I won't breathe a word."

"That's what all the boys say," she murmured, but he could see she was considering it. "Okay," she announced after a few seconds' pause. "You can drive me home. I'll just go tell the tow truck driver."

You can drive me home, in that perfect diction, with that cool-as-a-cucumber, crazy-making tone of hers, as though she were bestowing some frigging prize on him. She turned to dispatch the driver, and Quigg resisted the urge to grind his teeth again.

Man, you shoulda just left this one alone.

⋆⋆⋆

He led her to a late-model Ford sedan.

"There's some stuff on the front seat. Better let me clear it away," he said.

Unlocking the passenger door, he leaned into the interior. She heard him rummaging around. When he pulled back a moment later, she expected his hands to be full of discarded coffee cups and fast-food wrappers, the usual detritus of people who spent a lot of time in their cars. Instead he held newspapers. Lots of them. She recognized the local paper, as well as the Toronto *Globe & Mail* and several more she couldn't identify.

"A news hound, I see."

"Nah, that's just for show. You know, so folks'll think I'm semi-literate."

Her gaze flew to his face. When had she said anything to imply he was less than literate? And what exactly was his problem, anyway? She'd agreed to this escort, hadn't she?

"Gosh, and here I was expecting empty coffee cups and the dried-up remnants of jelly donuts."

"Sorry to disappoint. I mucked the sty out just this morning."

He stepped back to allow her to get in. Once she was settled, he closed her door and rounded the vehicle to slide behind the wheel. He started the car, and waited for her to adjust her seatbelt before he put it in gear. She said nothing as he pulled out onto Woodstock Road and headed east. In the confines of the car, the subtle scent of his aftershave reached out to her. His profile in the dim light cast by the dashboard lights looked somehow softer.

She switched her attention outward, concentrating on their route. He'd continued down Woodstock Road, right through the intersection to Brunswick. Tensing, she realized he hadn't asked where she lived. All the way down Brunswick, under the underpass and onto Waterloo. Her heart thumped a little harder as he drove the length of Waterloo, then swung onto the Lincoln Road.

"You're not even going to ask me for directions, are you?"

He glanced quickly at her, then back to the road. "Would you like me to?"

Of course he knew. He'd been watching her, following her, looking for dirt. "That's an interesting way you have of convincing me you're not the whack-job I should be worried about."

This time when he turned toward her, she caught a definite grin in the shifting light of a street light as they passed under it.

"Nice place you got, but security needs work. Window locks are good, but you could use better one on that front door. And you need an alarm system. You also have to change the lighting on the north side, by the garden gate. What you want is something on the ground that shines up at the house. Last thing the cops need when they're responding to a call is to have to walk straight into a blinding light."

"I can't believe this. You cased my house."

He glanced at her. "I prefer *checked out*. *Cased* has such negative connotations."

She made an inelegant snort, not knowing whether to tear into him for invading her privacy or to admire his honesty. He could easily have pretended ignorance, asking directions, and she'd have been none the wiser.

Lord, was she actually looking for redeeming qualities in a man who'd been shadowing her for the last week? And all because his blunt, masculine physicality called out to some perverse part of her.

Oh, Suz, that's pitiful. It had obviously been way too long. The minute she got to her office on Monday, she was going to find Gabe Courtney's number on her Rolodex and call him. He'd made no secret of his interest when she'd attended the opening of his exhibit last week. She'd actually enjoyed flirting with him. All 6′ 5″ of him. At least until John Quigley had turned up like a bad penny.

"Home again, home again," he said, and she realized he was pulling into her driveway.

She fumbled in the darkness for her evening bag, which she'd made the mistake of putting down in the unfamiliar interior.

Unexpectedly, the dome light came on, and she jerked her startled gaze up to meet his.

Mistake. In the warm, man-smelling confines of the car, a current of awareness arced between them. Quickly, she retrieved the tiny bag.

"Well, Detective, thank you for the lift." Pulse thudding, she turned away and grappled for the door handle.

"Give me a sec and I'll be right behind you."

That pronouncement, delivered in a sexy, gravel-voiced tone brought her head whipping around again. "Hold it right there, Detective. Obviously, you haven't been watching me very closely or very long, or you'd know I'm not in the habit of inviting men into my home even when I like them well enough to accept a first date. Ergo, hell would freeze over before I invite a pushy cop — a pushy cop who just coerced me into accepting a drive, I might add — into my house."

A wide grin split his face, deepening the grooves on either side of his mouth and making a dimple flash on his left cheek. "Not to belittle your considerable charms, Ms. Phelps, but I was thinking more along the lines of a security check. You know, peer into closets, pull back shower curtains, check the windows."

Her face burned. Damn him. "Thanks, but I can handle it." With that, she shouldered her door open and climbed out of the car.

⚜

Quigg cursed under his breath. Damn stubborn woman. She was fumbling with the lock when he caught up with her. Her hand froze on the doorknob and she turned to face him, her pale face cool and impossibly lovely in the porch light.

"I distinctly remember saying thanks but no thanks to your offer to play the big, strong male to my helpless female."

He suppressed a smile. Not very well, apparently, because her lips tightened in irritation.

"Maybe you would care to tell me, what part of *No, thank you* escaped your comprehension?"

There it was again, that haughty Queen of Sheeba tone. Could she get her nose any higher?

"Golly, Suzannah, you're gonna have to use smaller words, maybe some of them there single syllable ones."

She angled her head. "You know, Detective, you behavior is really starting to shade toward stalker."

His face sobered. "You don't believe that."

Did she?

"Just go home, Detective. Or back to the party. I don't need your help."

He felt his jaw tighten. "That's developing into something of a theme with you, refusing help."

"As is your trying to make me accept it." She straightened her spine, drawing herself up to her full height, which with those stilts she called shoes put her cool blue gaze just a hair higher than his. "I don't appreciate being made to look like a weak, frightened woman."

Frightened? Hah! She didn't have the good sense to be frightened. Frighten*ing*, more like it. Not to mention maddening, stubborn and just plain stupid. For a second, he was tempted to throw up his hands and walk away. Then he remembered the obscenity of the dead roses, the viciousness of her slashed tires, and bit back a sigh.

"Look, I just want to make sure the house is empty, do a perimeter check. After that, I'll be on my way."

She looked unconvinced.

"Someone slashed your tires tonight, sweetheart. Since you're too stubborn to call in a complaint, you're stuck with me. My conscience won't let me walk away until you're safely inside and locked down. If it makes you feel better, I'd do it for anyone."

She held his gaze for a few beats, measuring him. "Okay," she said at last. "If that's what it will take to get rid of you, okay."

Turning back to the door, she fumbled with the key some more. Did he make her nervous? The idea brought a rush of male satisfaction, until it occurred to him that she might actually fear him. The spurt of gratification died.

Finally, the lock submitted. She twisted the knob, wiggled her key free and stepped inside. Quigg followed, finding himself in a small entryway dimly lit by two tasteful bronzy-looking wall sconces. She dropped her keys on a gleaming mahogany table, then leaned against it as she slipped her shoes off. She was all grace, all fluid limbs and smooth skin. He caught a glimpse of her bare back in the mirror behind her as she bent to retrieve the ridiculously insubstantial sandals.

"Oh, God, that feels better," she said, her voice conveying that universally female relief at shedding diabolically cruel, indescribably beautiful shoes.

And he was hard as a virgin on prom night.

"You shouldn't do that." His words emerged harsher than he intended.

"Oh, puhlease." She rolled her eyes. "Who are you, now, Dr. Scholl? You're going to lecture me on my choice of footwear? Recommend a sensible flat shoe?"

"Leave your keys on that side table, I meant."

"Oh, that." She nabbed the fat set of keys. "Don't worry, I don't make a habit of it. Now, don't you have some checking to do? I'll go change while you —"

"No. You'll stay with me, at least until I've been through the house."

Wrong thing to say. Or wrong way to say it. Whichever, he could see he drawing breath to scorch him. Before she could blast him, he grabbed her arm and pulled her toward the living room. "Come on. Faster we get this done, faster I'll be out of your hair."

"Finally. Something we can agree on."

She tugged her arm free, but followed him as he made a thorough check of the house. In the last room, a spare bedroom, Quigg spied a door to the attic, a retractable ladder folded up into the ceiling.

"What's up there?" He nodded toward the attic.

"Up there?" She blew out an inpatient breath, lifting a strand of hair that had escaped the smooth twist. "You mean, besides my crystal meth lab?"

He fixed her with a hard look.

"John it's an *attic*. What do you suppose is up there? Christmas decorations, old textbooks from law school, your usual run-of-the-mill junk."

He pulled a mag light from his pocket. "I'll just take a quick look."

"Fine, but I'm going to change."

Since this was the last room to be checked, he didn't object. He'd satisfied himself there were no intruders lurking in the attic and was closing the door when he heard the crash from the master bedroom down the hall.

⁂

Suzannah was picking up shoeboxes, some of which had lost their contents, when John burst into the room, crouched and ready, his gaze sweeping the room. Her heart, already racing, took another jolting leap when she saw his stance. Then she recognized the object he gripped in his hand. Just the bronzed bookend from the desk in her spare bedroom.

"God, I thought you had a gun!"

"No gun." He straightened, his posture relaxing. "I couldn't see packing a piece for the Lieutenant Governor's levy, somehow." His gaze fell on her. "You okay?"

She resisted the urge to press a hand to her heart, which still pounded a painful tattoo against her ribs. "You gave me a fright."

"Guess we're even, then, 'cuz I thought all hell was breaking loose in here." He looked down at the mess on the floor. "Well, well, Imelda. Overcome by the urge to visit with your shoes, were you?"

She reached for a Prada suede number and stuck it in the box with its mate. "Very funny." Ignoring his chuckle, she went searching for the black Stuart Weitzman pump with the funky heel. "I just knocked a stack or two down."

"Stacks? More like towers, I'd say." He tossed the brass bookend onto her bed, then bent to gather up a couple of boxes that still had their contents intact under snug-fitting lids and started stacking them.

"Not like that." She pulled a box from his grasp. "You've just stacked a pair of black flats with beige pumps and brown loafers."

The look he shot her was incredulous in the extreme. "You have a filing system for your *shoes*?"

She lifted her chin, daring him to make something of it. "I can see the concept of organization is a foreign one, Detective, but there's nothing wrong with knowing what goes where. In fact, there can be some bonuses to being a little anal about this stuff."

"Like being able to discriminate between those three pairs of identical black pumps I see lying there?"

She might have argued that the black pumps were nowhere near identical, but instead she drew a deep breath and released it in a long exhalation. "Like being able to say with complete certainty that someone has been in my closet rearranging them."

He stood blinking at her. "Are you sure?"

She nodded. "Positive. There's no way those blue Nickels could have migrated to the top of that stack. I knew right away someone had moved them. That's how I knocked them down, backing out of the closet."

She heard him suck in a breath. "You wouldn't have moved it and maybe forgot about it?"

"No." She shook her head emphatically.

"The front door lock — you fumbled with it tonight. Is it usually sticky?"

"No." A shard of fear, sharp and hot, shot through her as she realized her lock must have been picked. Someone — a stranger? a disgruntled former client? a pissed-off cop? — had stood outside her door, extracted lock-picking tools and proceeded to finesse her medium-security locks. He'd let himself into her house, walked on her Persian carpets, touched her things.

"And no maid? No one with a legitimate reason to be shuffling things around in your closet?"

"Maid?" She lifted an eyebrow. "I'm hardly home long enough to disturb anything."

He shrugged. "Color me skeptical. I couldn't see the daughter of a former chief justice cleaning her own toilets."

"Okay, so I have a woman in to do floors and bathrooms," she allowed. "But she comes just twice a month. As you've already observed, I'm a little compulsive about order."

"Lover?"

"None of your business."

"Right. No lover."

Gritting her teeth, Suzannah bent to retrieve a Gucci sandal, only to have him restrain her by gripping her upper arm.

"Don't touch anything. Ident'll want to go over the whole thing."

Ident! Her stomach did a queer little flip. Police? Crawling all over her bedroom, dusting her shoes for prints. She could just hear them now, joking with each other.

"No. No police." Pulling her arm free, she strode over to the cherry wood dresser, pulling open the top drawer.

"Cripes, Suzannah, if you're right about this, someone broke into your house, spent time in your bedroom. Fondled your shoes, for chrissakes. If that doesn't creep you out —"

"Bloody hell."

"What?"

Just like that, he was there by her side. Clumsily, she shoved the drawer closed on the carefully folded underwear. Underwear that was no longer arranged just the way it was supposed to be.

"Your skivvies, too?"

"Looks like it."

John swore, long and fluently. "Okay, *now* we call the station."

"No, we don't." She clutched his forearm to restrain him, but released her grip quickly, unnerved by the coiled tension she felt in the muscles beneath her fingertips.

"Suzannah, a crime has been committed —"

"Not unless I say it has. Not unless I make a complaint."

"Why the hell wouldn't you make a complaint?"

She felt tired suddenly. Tired and surprisingly close to tears. "We've been through this, John."

"Like hell we have. You need to —"

She put up a hand to stop him. "Okay, say I call the cops. You guys come in, dust for prints, take *my* prints, too. But if this guy picked my lock, you know and I know that he's smart enough to have used latex gloves. And if he didn't take the precaution of wearing gloves, then there's zero chance you're going to match him with someone whose prints are in the database. A criminal wouldn't be that careless."

"But if we apprehend someone later, we'd have prints to match —"

"If you apprehend someone later, I trust it will be because he commits a crime. And if you apprehend him in the commission of a crime, then you'll have ample evidence of said crime without any prints that might be gathered here tonight."

"But —"

"But nothing. If the cops come in here tonight, I'll be no closer to knowing who did it, and your friends down at the station house will have a good laugh. That's just not going to happen, John."

"Dammit, Suzannah. This is no laughing matter."

He shoved a hand through his hair, making it stand up crazily. Improbably, it only made him seem all the more attractive.

"Trust me, I know that. And tomorrow, I'll call a security company to install high-security locks, an alarm system, motion sensors, the whole nine yards."

He swore again, pungently.

"You know I'm right," she said. "Prints would be either non-existent or unmatchable."

"But he got in here."

"Yes, he did, but he won't get in again. I'll see to it tomorrow."

"What about tonight?" he demanded.

Fear swelled in her throat, but she swallowed it down. "He's already been and gone tonight."

"My point exactly. Until you get a decent security system installed, it seems to me he can come and go at liberty."

She couldn't quite suppress a shiver. "He won't trouble me again tonight."

"No, he won't," John said. "Where are your spare blankets?"

It took Suzannah a few seconds to process his words and extract the meaning. "You are not staying here."

He drew himself up, seeming to acquire added height and breadth. "Fine. Have it your way. I'll just call for a squad car to sit on your house tonight."

"You wouldn't!"

He turned to leave.

"Wait." He stopped at the touch of her hand on his arm. Again, she withdrew her hand quickly. "I told you, I don't want the police involved in any way."

"Tough. I can't pull stakeout tonight myself 'cuz I'm back on duty tomorrow, so you'll have to make do with one of the guys from Patrol."

She bit back a curse that would have done credit to a sailor. "Okay, have it your way."

A smile ghosted over those fine, full lips. "You were going to see about those blankets? Since hell will be freezing over tonight, I figure I might need them."

"Anyone ever tell you you're a real bastard?"

"At least once a day," he allowed.

Suzannah strode to the hall, yanked open a linen closet and dragged out a lightweight blanket and a fat pillow, which she shoved into his chest. "Couch is in the living room," she clipped. "Kill the lights and turn the deadbolt before you crash."

With that, she turned and headed back to her bedroom. As she closed the door, she thought she heard him mutter, "You're welcome, Ms. Phelps."

She fumed about it as she stripped off her Donna Karan and hung it carefully on a padded hanger. Damned stubborn, condescending man. Blackmailing bastard. She cursed him as she stood beneath the shower's hot, stinging spray and scrubbed the feel of his electricity-charged fingers from her upper arm.

But when she finally settled down, after fidgeting with her thin blankets like a dog scratching and scraping and readying its bed, she found her fit of pique had subsided. When at last she fell into a light slumber, her last conscious thought was an acknowledgment that it was only his presence downstairs that allowed her to do so.

Chapter 3

"**R**ISE AND SHINE, SWEETHEART."

Suzannah groaned and tried to burrow deeper into the pillows, grasping at the threads of her lovely dream. Hard masculine hands on her body, gravel-voiced words of praise in her ear, hot mouth blazing over her skin . . . .

"Come on, Suzannah. I got a dog at home whose gonna pee on my brand new speakers if I don't get home and let him out."

Her eyes flew open. John Quigley. He'd stayed last night, and now he was in her bedroom. She jackknifed up, the twisted sheets pooling in her lap. "Of course. Go. Yes. By all means." Oh, Lord, she was stammering.

"It's early yet, barely dawn. I'd stay longer, but the dog . . . ."

"The speakers. Right." She pushed her hair back from her face and glanced at the digital alarm. Not yet five a.m. She glanced back at John to find his face had changed, sharpened with an edgy, dark intensity.

Oh, hell! Her nipples thrust sharply against her thin cotton tank, thanks to that dream. A dream in which the man standing by her bed, mere inches away, had played a starring role. For a wild, terrifying second, she visualized herself reaching out to touch him as she might have in the dream, her caress bold, sexual, deliberate. There wasn't a shred of doubt in her mind that he'd answer her need with gratifying urgency.

The idea was scary, dizzying, thrilling, incredibly powerful. Then sanity returned.

She sank back down onto her pillows, pulling the covers up to her chin and burrowing back into her pillow as though to go back to sleep. "Okay," she mumbled through the sheets. "Thanks for letting me know."

"Whoa, whoa. Don't go back to sleep just yet. I need you to throw the deadbolt behind me. It's getting lighter by the minute, but I'd feel better if the bolt were thrown."

Damn. "Okay." She sat up again, this time with the sheets modestly clamped to her chest. "Give me a sec. I'll drag on a robe and meet you down there."

His eyes said eloquently that he wished she wouldn't bother with the robe, but he merely nodded and withdrew.

The moment she heard his tread on the stairs, she leapt out of bed. Damn it, damn it, damn it! She strode into her walk-in closet and yanked a silk robe off a hanger with less care than the garment deserved. Of all the men in her world for her to fixate on, why this one? He was arrogant, pushy, exasperating in the extreme. Too tough, too forceful, too ... yang.

And he was a cop.

So why did her body light up for him as it did for no other?

Chemistry. Random, unreasoning, unfortunate chemistry.

She pulled the robe on, wrapping it around her. Well, she never had been very good at chemistry back in school. And she'd get along very well without it fogging her brain again, thank you. On that thought, she cinched the belt of her robe tightly around her waist and marched downstairs to lock Detective John Quigley out of her house, and with any luck, out of her life.

⊰⊱

Quigg looked at his watch. Four oh five. *Ten minutes later than the last time you checked, stupid.* Exasperated, he reached for his mug and downed the last of his coffee. It was room temperature and bitter, but he didn't even grimace. He was well used to cold coffee. He was in it for the caffeine, a commodity he needed in large doses after a restless night spent on Suzannah Phelps' couch.

God, she'd looked good in that dress. And those shoes. Lying there on her tasteful couch that smelled vaguely of her warm, exotic scent, he'd burned for her. Then he'd come within a heartbeat of jumping her bones this morning when she'd sat up in bed. Warm and tousled and sleep-dazed, she'd looked like his hottest fantasy.

Down, boy. His internal censor clicked on. There'd be plenty of time to play back those images in Technicolor, but not here on the job. *You've got work to do.*

Would Suzannah have replaced that lock yet? Would she have gotten someone hopping on an alarm system? Maybe he should have hung around.

Nah, Bandy would have chewed hell out of his sofa cushions and watered the philodendron, which was dying quite well on its own without any help from that quarter. But he could have gone back after he'd let the dog out, or at some point later in the day. At the very least, he could have made sure she lit a fire under the security guys —

Damn, he was doing it again. Thinking about her.

Resolutely, he forced his attention back to the report he was supposed to be writing. Shouldn't be so hard to focus. This was one of those cases made you shake your head. Man stabs wife. A pretty straightforward piece of business, normally. But this one had a wrinkle. Seems it was an accident. Jimmy didn't intend to stab his pregnant wife at all. He did, however, intend to stab his mother-in-law and his wife just got in the way. And the dumb ass couldn't grasp that he'd done anything wrong. After all, he hadn't meant to hurt *her,* and besides, the plastic surgeon had sewn her up good as new anyway. Even after the serious nature of the charges were explained to him, he'd still insisted he didn't need legal counsel.

Of course, all of this meant Quigg would eventually end up sitting in that witness box giving testimony against this cracker. And given this guy's socio-economic situation, he'd be Legal Aid all the way when he finally lawyered up. Which meant he'd end up with Suzannah, if he had half a brain. And she'd likely be mad as hell they didn't oblige the guy to get legal advice.

"What are you grinning at, old man?"

Quigg glanced up to find fellow detective Ray Morgan standing there holding a tray containing two Styrofoam cups from the gourmet coffee shop.

"Who you calling *old man*?" Quigg pushed his chair back. "Razor, buddy, you're the one with the wife in tow and a mortgage on that picket fence."

Ray grinned. "That just makes me lucky, not old."

Lucky? Yes, Quigg believed his friend was pretty lucky. Grace took some of Ray's rough edges off. She centered him in a way probably no one other than Quigg truly appreciated. "Maybe so," he conceded.

"You, on the other hand, are just old." Ray proffered the tray.

"Go to hell." Quigg accepted one of the coffees.

"No, thanks. Been there once already today."

"Yeah?"

"Remember the Courtenay Equipment break in?"

Quigg pried the lid off his coffee and flipped it into the overflowing garbage can by his desk. "Young offender made off with a four wheeler?"

"That's the one." Ray removed his own coffee and jammed the carry tray into the wastebasket. "It went to trial today, and you'll never guess who the defense counsel was."

Quigg almost choked on a mouthful of coffee. "Suzannah Phelps?"

"The ice princess herself."

"How'd you make out?"

"Kid was convicted. Judge asked for a pre-sentence report."

"So what's the trouble?"

"The trouble, my friend, is that my nice, heretofore pristine goin'-to-court shirt is now permanently discolored from armpit to elbow, thank you very much."

Quigg laughed at the expression on his friend's face. No one would ever accuse Razor Morgan of being a dandy, at least not to his face, but he was a bit of a snob when it came to dressing. Natural fabrics, quality tailoring, the whole nine yards. He'd tried his best to educate Quigg, but that was a non-starter. Anything you couldn't machine wash, haul out of the dryer and drag on didn't make the grade for Quigg's closet.

"Cretin. We're talking Egyptian cotton, here."

"Maybe you should send her the cleaning bill."

Ray snorted. "Yeah, like I'm gonna let her know how bad she made me sweat."

"Did she give you a rough ride?"

"Not really," he conceded. "But you know how it is. By the time they called me, I was second guessing myself like crazy. Did we process the scene properly? Did we get the warrant right? I mean, I *know* the evidence was all gotten fair and square, all our I's were dotted and our T's crossed, but things just have a way of coming undone when that woman's around."

"Man, that's gotta be the understatement of the year."

His reply must have been too vehement, because Ray's face sharpened.

"Not hard on the eyes, though," his friend said casually. Too casually.

Quigg grunted, took another sip of his coffee, aware that Razor was watching him like a hawk.

"Not that you can see much under those robes," he said. "Nice calves though."

Quigg took another swallow of his black coffee. "I suppose."

"You *suppose*? Hell, those are first-class getaway sticks if I ever saw 'em. And unless I miss my guess, I'd say she had a first-class set of —"

"Oh, look, I almost forgot," Quigg grabbed a pink telephone message slip from the jumble of papers atop his desk and shoved it at Ray. "Grace's looking for you."

Ray took the message, but not the hint. "Thanks, but you can't distract me that easily. I want to know what you think the Ice Princess is packing under those black robes."

Unfortunately, Quigg now had a pretty accurate idea. So accurate, the sweat nearly beaded on his forehead at the memory. "I have no opinion."

"Hah!" Ray laughed exultantly. "I knew it! You've got a jones for her."

"Hardly." The denial sprang automatically to his lips.

"You do so. You're hot for Miss Tasty Freeze. God, I don't know why I didn't see it before."

"Grow up, will you, Morgan," Quigg growled.

"Hey, it's cool." Ray lifted his hands, palms up, in a gesture of peace. "It's not like I'm gonna tell anyone."

"It's not like there's anything to tell." This as casual and off-hand as he could manage. Couldn't make too big of a deal out of it or Ray'd know he had him dead to rights.

Ray just grinned, then held up the message. "Must go call Grace."

Great. Wonderful. Might as well take an ad out in the daily paper. Quigg swallowed a gulp of his still-too-hot coffee, grimaced and turned back to his computer screen.

⁂

The sound of the phone ringing unanswered broke Suzannah's concentration. Why didn't the receptionist pick up? She looked at her wristwatch. Right. Past eight o'clock. Everyone was long gone.

Sighing, she plugged in the code for call pickup.

"Castillo and Phelps," she said into the receiver, even as she hit the mouse to scroll through the text on her screen.

"Did you get the lock changed?"

She'd been waist-deep in case law, but his voice dragged her right out. "Detective Quigley."

"John," he corrected. "So, did you get that lock replaced?"

"Yes. The locksmith was there this morning."

"Thought you were in court this morning."

"I was."

"Are you telling me the locksmith agreed to do the job with no one there? Doesn't seem very prudent on his part."

"*Her* part," she said, sitting up straighter in her chair. "And I had my secretary go let her in. Now, was that all, Detective, or did you want to pass judgment on how I conducted myself for the rest of my day?"

A soft laugh. Suzannah felt a treacherous pleasure shiver through her.

"No need. I got a report from Detective Morgan."

"I lost."

"I know."

"My client got a rigorous defense," she felt obliged to say.

"Ray Morgan would agree with you there."

Her lips twitched but she refused to smile. He'd be able to *hear* it, no doubt. "Don't you want to gloat or something?"

"Maybe later."

This time she did grin. "Was that all?"

"What about the alarm system?"

"First thing tomorrow morning, though they tried to put me off until next Thursday. Believe me, I had to pay through the nose for priority service."

"Good girl."

"Well, I figured it was that or put up with flack from you. It seemed easier to throw money at the security company."

"Sorry. Job hazard," he said, sounding distinctly unapologetic. "I just can't stand by and watch people put themselves at risk."

"I don't take risks, Detective."

"John. And I'll bet you're there in the building all alone right now. I'll bet the lights are blazing and the front door's unlocked."

"You'd lose that bet. My secretary always locks up on her way out." Despite the confident words, Suzannah couldn't help casting a glance at the darkened windows. From the passing headlights, she could tell traffic on this west end of Prospect Street was intermittent. Anyone standing out there would be unlikely to be noticed. And they'd have a good view into the building. As John speculated, every light was blazing. She rolled her chair closer to the window and lowered the fabric blinds. "As I've said before, *John*," she paused to give his name emphasis, "I can take care of myself."

"And as I've said before, I can't ignore the threats you've been getting. If you won't go the official route, you're stuck with me."

Suzannah knew a dead end when she encountered one. That's why she was so good at negotiation. Retreat. Approach it from another angle. "What exactly does *stuck with you* entail? What's the bottom line tonight?"

A pause, as though she'd surprised him. Good.

"Minimum? I see you home safely, check the locks, the windows."

"Okay. Done."

"And you'll carry a personal alarm."

"What?"

"You know, hangs around your neck or clips to your purse? Anybody tries to grab you or threatens you in any way, you activate it and it'll raise a helluva ruckus."

"I know what a personal alarm is."

"Good. Get one."

Okay. She could live with that. Sensible precautions for any woman, any time. And once she had them in place, she could tell a certain pushy detective to take a hike.

"All right. A personal alarm. I'll get the security people to outfit me tomorrow."

"Perfect. Now come unlock the door."

She blinked. "Excuse me?"

"The front door. It's locked, remember?"

"You're *here*? Outside my building?"

"For the last ten minutes. By the way, that gauzy window covering doesn't do much good when you've got that much backlighting behind you."

⚜

Quigg grinned as he pulled up behind Suzannah's car at a red light. The way her Beemer had shot out of the lot left no doubt as to her state of mind. Not that her haughty nose-in-the-air routine had left much room for misinterpretation. Damn, this was almost fun, almost worth the aggravation.

Her car surged forward again on green, and Quigg had to nail the accelerator not to get left in the dust. She'd be lucky not to get pulled over before she got home. His smile broadened. That'd be worth serious money, to see how she'd handle flashing lights in her rearview right about now.

His smile faded as he pictured the scene. She'd hate it. Hate that she'd given a cop a reason to pull her over, hate providing fodder for a little station-house gossip. She'd hate that she'd been goaded to recklessness by his yanking her chain.

Most of all, he knew she hated that he'd seen her peer out into the darkness and close the blinds, betraying an apprehension she'd deny with her last breath.

Damn, he shouldn't have rubbed her pretty patrician nose in it. When had he become such a jerk? She was in danger, and he was getting his kicks out of needling her.

Granted, she made it easy. There was just something about that princess act of hers that made a guy want to take her down a notch or two.

Okay, maybe just guys like him.

But not anymore. He slowed and threw his right-hand turn signal on, following Suzannah onto her street. From now on, he'd be a model of restraint. No more baiting her.

By the time Quigg pulled up in Suzannah's drive, she was already out of her car and moving toward the house, her posture regal, head held high on that aristocratic neck. Everything about her whispered wealth and breeding, while her self-assurance announced that she was a woman in control.

Except she wasn't in control of what was happening to her now. Quigg had a mental flash of her pale face in the window at the office before she'd dropped the blind. Damn.

He climbed out of the Ford, pocketed his keys and caught up to Suzannah at the door. Wordlessly, he watched her produce her shiny new house key, insert it in the lock and open the door. He followed her inside, holding the door open a moment to inspect the lock. Good choice. It wouldn't be easily picked or drilled. The floating collar around it made it impossible to get a grip on with pliers. Even an expert lockpick would probably take one look at it and move on to likelier prospects.

"Will it do?"

He closed the door, turning the deadbolt. "Yeah."

She nodded curtly, quite a feat considering she managed to accomplish it without lowering her nose. "Then let's get on with it, shall we? I'm sure you have better things to do."

You got that right, lady, he thought, stung by her cool tone. *There are plenty of places I could go where I'd be welcome. Plenty of places.*

Instead of letting his irritation show, he smiled, his slowest, laziest smile. "It's best not to rush these things," dropping his voice an octave. "No telling what a man could miss out on if he goes too fast."

For the briefest of seconds, something in her answered his blatant sexual innuendo, a flash of naked heat in those pale blue eyes. She smothered it quickly, but not quickly enough to stop the jolt of adrenaline that ripped through him, leaving his heart pounding.

"By all means, Columbo. Take your time."

"You can count on it." Casually, he made his way toward the back of the house to check the other door. He heard her move toward the kitchen.

Columbo? Is that how she saw him? Rumpled, short, middle-aged, with the face of a blood hound and a determination to match?

Quigg moved from room to room, checking the windows. Okay, maybe the image wasn't that far off beam, except the height thing. He was *not* short. Not nearly as old, either. And he sure as hell hadn't imagined the heat in her gaze a moment ago. Hell, every pore and follicle he owned felt like it had been singed by a flash fire. If she thought he looked like Columbo, then she obviously had a thing for Peter Falk —

A muffled exclamation from the kitchen drew his attention. Not distressed enough to send him barreling in there, but definitely annoyed. He finished checking the last window and headed for the kitchen, reaching it just in time to see Suzannah drop something into the garbage and close the lid. Correction, he didn't really *see* her dump it. Rather, he heard it hit the bottom on the plastic-lined disposal unit with a loud thud.

"What's up?"

"Nothing. Just dumping some trash."

Her face looked paler than it had earlier tonight when she'd peered so apprehensively out into the darkened parking lot. He strode to the garbage can. She made no move to stop him, although he sensed she wanted to. He arched an eyebrow at her, and she glared back at him as he stepped on the pedal to lift the lid. Taking his eyes off Suzannah, he dropped his gaze to see what she'd dumped so energetically.

Jesus! Roses. A whole bouquet of them. At least a dozen, he judged. But these ones were fresh, not like the abominations she'd found in her car that time. Perfect red buds, nestled among some ferns and lacy white stuff. Their delicate fragrance wafted up to him.

He lifted his gaze again to meet blue eyes gone stormy. "I take it these long-stemmed babies are unwelcome?"

She clearly deemed his question rhetorical, because she strode to the cupboard and jerked down a bottle of Jack Daniel's. Opening another cupboard, she nabbed two glasses. "Drink?"

He waved her offer off. "Your friend again?"

She nodded, poured a couple of fingers of whiskey into her glass and recapped the bottle. "Apparently, they arrived while the locksmith was working. She brought them in so they wouldn't suffer in the sun." She pushed a note across the counter top.

A quick look at the note verified that the locksmith had indeed carted them inside. Cripes, every man and his dog would have their prints on that vase. The stock clerk, the florist, the deliveryman, the locksmith, Suzannah. Taking a paper napkin from a holder on the counter, he folded it over the rim of the florist's vase and lifted the arrangement out of the garbage can.

"Leave them," she ordered when she saw what he was doing. "I don't want to see them."

"Suzannah, it's evidence."

"Evidence of what? That I've got an admirer?" She took a swig of the neat whiskey, swallowing it without a trace of a grimace. "I can hear the locker room patter already — *Wow, I knew that Phelps broad was a bitch, but calling the cops on a poor bastard for sending her flowers? Wonder what she'd a done if he was stupid enough to ask for a date?*"

"Aw, hell, not this again."

"I won't go to the police with this, John."

He couldn't believe he was hearing this. "What? You said yourself you think it was the same guy. Suzannah, this guy is a serious wingnut. Has it occurred to you what he's saying with the floral tributes? He's showing you he can deliver good or bad, life or death."

He saw the tremor in her hand. He also so how quickly she lifted the old-fashioned glass to her lips to try to hide it.

"He's delivering flowers. That's it, that's all."

"He invaded your damned house."

"*Someone* invaded my house," she corrected. "There are break-ins every night of the week in this town, John. You know that."

"Except this B & E artist didn't help himself to anything. He just fondled your footwear."

Her lips tightened. "By tomorrow, I'll have this nice little alarm system to make sure it doesn't happen again."

"What about the slashed tires?"

She shrugged, took another sip of her drink. "You know my thoughts on that score."

Quigg made a conscious effort not to grind his teeth. "And you know *my* thoughts on it. That wasn't the work of a cop, and you know it." He shoved a hand through his hair. "Why won't you face the fact that some nutcase is stalking you?"

"Someone is sending me flowers. That's all I know."

"Then let's start with that. We'll get prints from the vase."

"And what? Get all the florists in town to give you their prints so you can eliminate them?"

"Okay, then we start with the vase, the arrangement. How hard can it be to figure out where they came from? Once we know that, we can narrow the field down."

"No, we can't."

"What do you mean?"

"John, do you have any idea how many dozen red roses the florists around here send out every day? And that green vase?" She gestured to the arrangement which sat on the counter now. "It doesn't get any more generic than that. *Dozens* of these orders go out every day, from dozens of shops, and every one of them looks the same. A little baby's breath, a few ferns, and presto. They all use the same materials. It's impossible to say where they came from."

"But not impossible to find out which florists delivered to this address."

"None of them have."

He shot her a piercing look. "You've called?"

"Of course I called." She rotated the glass in her hand, smoothing her fingers over the cut crystal. "I'm not being obstructionist here. I *do* want to know who's doing this. But I don't think your inquiries would get any further than mine did."

"We could canvass the florists, see if there's a pattern."

She took another sip of whiskey. "You and whose army?"

"There can't be that many florists."

"Twenty-three in the immediate area. Probably another forty or fifty on top of that if you broaden your focus by an hour's car travel in all directions."

He grimaced. "Okay, what about how they get here? You think he's delivering them personally?"

She cradled the glass in both hands as though trying to warm the contents. "I don't know. He's not using any of the local courier services, at least none that are talking. Could be using a taxi service. There are so many ways he could get the job done. A ten-spot for a wino, a pack of smokes for a middle-school student, a dime bag for a high-school kid."

Quigg narrowed his eyes. "He's delivering them himself."

"Yes." She looked down into the depths of her whiskey. "Yes, I think he is."

"My God, he must be watching you, deciding whether it'll be a live bouquet or a dead one based on your conduct."

"Don't you think that theory has occurred to me?" She lifted her gaze to meet his again, putting her glass down on the counter with a thump. "Though if that's what he's doing, I can't for the life of me figure out what earns me a thumbs up and what earns a thumbs down. There doesn't seem to be any rhyme or reason to it."

"That's because he's crazy," Quigg pointed out. "Which is why you gotta phone this in, Suzannah. This is one weird duck."

"I know you think I'm being reckless, John, but I'm not. Despite my … aversion to relying on you guys, if I thought the cops could make headway, I'd call this in so fast your head would spin. But with all due respect, you guys aren't going to learn anything more than I did, which is zilch. Why would I open myself to ridicule when I know there's nothing to be gained?"

He dragged a hand through his hair. "Jesus, you got a real high opinion of us, don't you?"

"As a matter of fact, I do. I think local police do a very good job, ninety-nine percent of the time." A lone strand of hair had come loose from the elegant twist, and she brushed it behind her ear absently. "But I have a job to do, too, John. I know nobody down there likes me, but right now, they respect me. Some of them are maybe even a little intimidated by me in the courtroom. And that's the way I intend to keep it. I'm not going to put that on the line unless I'm damned sure there's something to be gained."

"Okay, fine, you don't want to go to the cops. Hire a P.I."

"I already have. Several times, in fact. And no joy." She paused to take a sip of her whiskey. "Either the caliber of the private investigators in this town is sub-par, which I doubt, or my friend is very smart. What I've concluded is that if I want to keep a security company on permanent payroll to sit in front of my house, my office and the court house, I can guarantee I'll never get another floral arrangement. Of course, I'll never know who he is, because he's too careful to show himself."

He glared at her. "How do you do it?"

"Do what?"

"How do you make the stupidest folly sound so damned reasonable?"

She smiled, one of those Mona Lisa smiles that made him think she knew something he didn't. "I'm a lawyer."

"Well, hell. What am I going to do now?"

"You're going to finish checking the windows and doors and take your leave," she said. "Then I'm going to lock up behind you, have a late dinner, read some case law I brought home, and go to bed."

"I'm not going anywhere." He held up his hand when she would have interrupted. "And don't even bother to remind me of our agreement. That was before your FTD guy reached out and touched you again. The deal's off. You're not staying here alone until after the alarm goes in."

Her blue eyes cooled. "Let me guess. If I don't invite you to stay, you'll call your buddies and get them to sit on my house all night."

"Or you could pack an overnight case and go to a motel for the night," he suggested in his most reasonable tone. "Or stay with a family member."

"I most certainly am not going to check into a motel in my own town. Can you imagine the gossip? Nor am I going to upset my mother with this."

"Fine. Call your boyfriend, then, and tell him you're coming for a sleepover."

He'd thought her eyes cool before, but only because he hadn't seen how glacial they could get. He was seeing it now.

"I don't currently have what you so quaintly refer to as a *boyfriend*. But then, you knew that already, didn't you, Detective? You've been poking around in my life how long?"

He grinned, which had the effect of producing a dangerous glint in her eyes. "It's always good to have your conclusions confirmed."

"Good? What's good about it, I'd like to know?" She picked her glass up and drained the last bit of whiskey. "For instance, if I had a boyfriend in the picture, you wouldn't be here right now. Or if you were, I'd get him to show you the door." She thumped the glass down on the counter. "If I had a boyfriend front-and-center all the time, I probably wouldn't be getting these stupid flowers in the first place."

She grabbed the whiskey bottle, spun away and stashed it back in the cupboard.

"Of course! That's brilliant. That's just what you need. A high-profile boyfriend."

She opened the dishwasher and stashed her used glass inside. "Yeah, sure. Brilliant." She closed the dishwasher with more force than was strictly necessary and turned to face him. "Let me just jump on the Internet and take care of that right now. Non-smoker preferred. Must have brawn. Brains an asset, but not strictly required. Duties include scaring off creepy stalker types."

"Suzie, honey, your search is over." He grinned at her expression. "You found your perfect candidate."

"*You?*"

His smile broadened. "Me."

Chapter 4

SUZANNAH SIGHED AND PUSHED away from her desk. For the last half hour, she'd been trying to concentrate on the corporate reorganization plan her client needed. Unfortunately, contemplating by-law amendments and share splits seemed to be beyond her right now. Okay, it wasn't riveting stuff at the best of times, but after the events of the last twenty-four hours, she doubted anything could have kept her attention from wandering.

Lord, had she really agreed to a mock affair with John Quigley?

Just thinking about it sent a thrill through her. Of course, that didn't mean anything. She'd had a very similar feeling one time, navigating her way out of Montreal during rush hour. And there was that time she'd been talked into riding a roller coaster at a carnival midway. It was a perfectly natural, perfectly intelligent response to the threat of impending chaos.

When her phone buzzed, a single ringburst signaling an internal communication, she jumped for it. Anything for a distraction. She checked the display. Her secretary.

"I know what you're looking for, Mary Ann," she said into the receiver, "but it's not ready yet. I'm having trouble concentrating."

"This probably won't help matters, then. There's a Detective Quigley here to see you."

Suzannah sat bolt upright. "Is he, now? Well, you just tell Detective Quigley I'll be ten minutes."

"Whoops, too late. He's already on his way back there."

Damn! She hung up the phone just as he materialized in her door frame. She pushed up out of her chair. "John, what are you doing here?"

"I missed you."

Before she could digest that astonishing assertion, he crossed the room, took her face in his hands and kissed her. Thoroughly. Shock held her frozen. By the time her brain caught up to what was happening, she'd already opened her mouth to his invasion. Heat licked through her limbs, her heart thundered, the room spun. Then he stepped back, a pleased smile on his face. Over his shoulder, she saw her secretary standing wide-eyed outside her door.

"I had to come up this way to interview an insurance adjuster," he said, his hands still warm on her upper arms. "Now that I'm here, what do you say we go get a bit of lunch?"

Suzannah craned her neck to see what Mary Ann was making of this, but her secretary had evaporated. She strode to the door. The corridor was empty. Closing her door, she rounded on him.

"What the hell do you think you're doing?"

He shrugged, looking completely normal, as though he were unaffected by the kiss that had just rocked her. "I figured we shouldn't waste any time getting the word out."

"Did I not say I'd take care of dropping the word here?"

"You did," he agreed, "but I couldn't picture private-and-proper Suzannah Phelps just blurting something like that out to her co-workers."

Private and proper? She bristled at the description, ignoring the fact that it was completely accurate. He might as well have called her boring and staid. "So you decided to help me out?"

"Yep."

"Well, that should do the trick," she snapped, brushing non-existent wrinkles out of her suit. Belatedly, she realized it was her composure she was trying to smooth, not the obedient fabric of her favorite St. John Knit. The realization just made her angrier. "And don't expect me to reciprocate. I am not going to traipse into the Station and lay a lip-lock on you."

"Pity," he murmured. "It would do my reputation a world of good."

"It's not *your* reputation I'm concerned about."

"It was a joke, Suzannah." His voice hardened. "You already have my assurance that I won't do or say anything to sully your reputation with the troops."

"The mere fact of our association is going to change their perception of me."

Now his jaw hardened to match the tone of his voice. "Relax, sweetheart. I'll make sure they know you're at the wheel of this relationship. And just think how your legend will grow when this is all over and you can dump me."

"John—"

"Can we go eat now? Because I spent what should have been breakfast walking my dog who'd been cooped up alone all night, and I'm hungry enough to eat my way through the Chinese buffet down the road."

Lunch turned out to be not nearly the nightmare she'd imagined. True to his word, John did eat his way through the buffet. She settled for the salad bar, knowing a heavy carb meal would put her to sleep when she went back to the office to tackle that corporate file again.

Not that she should be sleepy. She'd slept surprisingly well last night despite John Quigley's presence on her couch downstairs. Sure she'd never get to sleep after that crazy proposition he'd put to her — a crazy proposition that she'd accepted, God help her — she'd fallen into the deepest sleep she'd managed in weeks. As angry as he frequently made her, as overbearing as he tended to be, she felt completely safe when he was there.

Okay, dammit, she'd slept surprisingly well *because* of John Quigley's presence on her couch.

Which unnerved her more than she wanted to admit. She didn't need a man around to feel fulfilled. She didn't need a man around to take care of her or shield her from the realities of life. Look where her mother had ended up, widowed at fifty-seven years of age and unable to balance her own checkbook. And all because she'd relied on a man. A good man, for sure. But not a good thing. She'd been ill-equipped to fend for herself . . . .

"Something wrong?"

Lost in her thoughts, Suzannah jumped when John laid a hand on hers atop the table.

"Whoa," he said. "Take it easy."

"I'm not used to being touched."

He arched an eyebrow.

"I mean, without an invitation."

He grinned. "Better get used to it. Nobody is going to believe this relationship if I don't lay hands on you as often as I can. At least, nobody who knows me."

As if she needed a reminder of his physicality. As if she weren't perfectly aware of the male vitality thrumming under that seemingly still, watchful exterior. As if she hadn't felt that pure sexual energy brush her skin.

"Anyone who knows *me* knows how much I abhor public demonstrations." Oh, God, was that her voice? So stiff and stilted. So disapproving. So repressed.

His grin broadened, spreading across his face like the sun dawning. "Honey, that's exactly why they're gonna believe this." He lifted her hand and planted a kiss in her palm.

Her breath caught in her lungs at the brush of his lips. Then she felt his tongue stroke a path of fire across her sensitive palm. Just as quickly, he released her hand. She pulled it back as though it had been scorched, burying it in her lap.

"Just so you know, I'm gonna kiss you before I let you get in that obscenely expensive little car and drive away."

Her pulse took another leap, but she forced herself to pick up her water goblet and take an unhurried sip. He was enjoying this altogether too much, the bastard. No doubt because he saw how much it discomfited her.

She could soon fix that, though.

Quickly, she lowered her gaze to her partially-eaten salad so he couldn't read her eyes. "You know what they say, forewarned is forearmed."

The rest of the meal passed uneventfully enough, but Suzannah had a hard time bringing her pulse rate back down into the normal range. She was too busy thinking about the kiss to come in the parking lot. John didn't seem unduly stirred up about it, but of course he had no way of knowing what he was in for. She allowed herself a smile as she sipped her coffee.

⟡

Quigg was conscious of the eyes watching them as he paid the bill for their lunch. Good. That's what it was all about. The more people who noticed, and the sooner they noticed, the better.

Not that this gig was all bad. Baiting Suzannah almost made up for the aggravation of having to babysit her.

Tucking his wallet back in his pocket, he put a proprietary hand on the small of her back to guide her toward the exit. Together, they strolled out into the parking lot.

After the air-conditioned interior of the restaurant, the heat hit them like a slap, rising in waves from the asphalt. Suzannah's shiny little Beemer was a cream-colored shimmer at the far end of the parking lot. As they neared it, he felt the tension in her mount.

Good enough for her. If she wasn't such a stubborn little miss, he wouldn't have to be here. If she'd just agree to an official investigation, there'd be no need of this pretend affair. If she had an ounce of sense, she wouldn't be getting all bent out of shape right now over having to endure a public kiss in a parking lot. A kiss from a lowly cop.

Yeah, this gig wasn't all bad.

They came to a stop beside her car. He half expected her to fumble for her keys or maybe offer her hand for a formal handshake, but she didn't do either of those things. She just turned to face him, her face carefully impassive.

"This won't hurt a bit." He rested a palm on the side of her slim, graceful neck, using a callused thumb to tip her chin up. Lord, her skin was fine, softer even than he'd imagined. He could feel her pulse, surprisingly strong beneath his palm. "Just close your eyes and think of England."

She did close her eyes, but as they drifted shut, he caught an expression in them that startled the hell out of him. A sensual hungry expression that might lead a man to conclude that she was thinking about something other than the mother country. Poleaxed, he froze in mid-move, his face angled, distance narrowed, lips hovering just millimeters from hers. What the hell was going on here?

Then she slid an arm around his neck and pulled his mouth down to meet hers, erasing any doubt about what he'd seen in her eyes. Her lips were damp, warm, and they tasted tantalizingly of coffee and womanly welcome. Then her tongue, hot and impossibly exciting, probed his lips. He opened for her instantly, felt the electric brush of her tongue against his even as her hand found the tensed muscles of his chest.

Wait, wait, wait, his mind screamed. *Be smart. Pull back. Think about this.*

His body said *screw that noise.* Suzannah Phelps had her tongue in his mouth.

It was a short contest.

He swept his arm around her, meeting her hungry mouth with a hard demand of his own. When she groaned her approval, he gathered her closer. Oh, Jesus, God, she felt like heaven. She splayed her legs subtly, allowing him to press her more intimately against him.

Somewhere in the back of his mind, he knew this was too much, too public, too out-of-control. Then she drew back, pushing against his chest. He released her immediately.

"So, how was that, Detective? Convincing enough?"

Her words held their usual edge, but he heard the husky quaver underlying them. She'd wanted to turn the tables on him but she wasn't as coolly unaffected as she wanted him to think.

Clutching at the threads of his own equilibrium, he forced a laugh. "Hey, you convinced me, sweetheart."

She compressed her lips, which only drew attention to how kiss-swollen they were.

"You know us lawyers. We're all actors at heart."

"Of course."

Her lips thinning even further, she deactivated the car's alarm. It chirped cheerfully. When he heard the electronic door locks release, he stepped forward to open the door for her. She brushed by him and slid into the driver's seat.

"You'll go home at five when everybody quits the building?"

She looked like she wanted to tell him to get his hands off her car. And she really, *really* looked like she wanted to tell him it was none of his business what she did. Instead, she nodded. "I already agreed to that, remember?"

"Just making sure."

She inserted the key in the ignition switch, then glanced up at him. "Do you think I could have my door back?"

"In a minute. I want to talk about what we're going to watch on TV tonight." What he really wanted to see is if she could make that upper lip disappear altogether if she got any more uptight. Apparently she couldn't because it was still in evidence when she replied.

"You don't need to come over, John. The alarm will be installed by then. I'll be fine."

"I'm sure you will. But the objective is to either make this guy cease and desist, or alternatively, to flush him out. And the only way to do that is to convince him you've got a bona fide lover."

She closed her eyes, as though praying for strength. Or maybe counting to ten. Those baby blues were cool as ice chips when she opened them again. "WTN."

"Huh?"

"The Women's Television Network. That's what we're watching tonight."

"Okay," he conceded in his most magnanimous voice. "Between innings of the Jays game, we'll switch over."

Her answer was to start the BMW's engine.

He took his cue and closed her door just in time to prevent her driving off with it ajar.

He glanced around the parking lot. Several heads averted too quickly. Spectators to that clinch, no doubt. Well, that was the whole point of the exercise, wasn't it?

Pasting the kind of smug smile on his face that he figured a guy who'd just swapped saliva with Suzannah Phelps should be wearing, he sauntered to his own car. It wasn't until he merged into the lunch-hour traffic that he let the smile slip.

Dammit, what had he gotten himself into?

Dating Suzannah Phelps was pure hell.

As he waited for the printer to spit out the job he'd sent to it, Quigg leaned back in his chair and reflected on the past week. He'd attended three dinner parties. *Three*, for crying out loud. That was exactly three too many.

Okay, the retirement bash for that crusty old broad from the land registry office had been kind of fun, but for the most part, it had been crashingly dull. Plus he'd spent half his spare time running back and forth to the dry cleaners with his limited wardrobe. The other half he spent listening to fat-cat stockbrokers prognosticating about the post 9-11 economy and artist types bemoaning the dismal level of government support for cultural endeavors.

Did Suzannah enjoy that stuff as much as she pretended, or was she torturing him? He suspected it was the latter. Well, one thing was certain — the nature of their outings was about to change. She'd had it her way for a week. Now it was his turn.

The printer spat out the report he was waiting for. He scooped it up and leaned back in his chair. A casual observer might have gathered he was reading it, but his thoughts were elsewhere. What could he subject her to?

Bowling? Good. Definite plebeian connotations, but not very imaginative.

The local country music bar for some line dancing? Quigg grinned. That'd be perfect, but it would require him to suffer with her. He discarded the idea.

"Omigod, it's true, isn't it?"

The words gave Quigg a jolt. With that eerie soundlessness of his, Ray Morgan had materialized beside Quigg's desk as though he'd stepped out of thin air.

Quigg fixed him with an unfriendly look. "I swear to God, Razor, I'm gonna shoot you one of these days, you keep sneaking up on me like that."

"Well, I'll be damned. It *is* true. I can tell by the look on your face."

Quigg scowled. "That's indigestion."

Ray grinned. "Ah, come on, man. You're not gonna sit there and deny it, are you?"

"Deny what?"

"You're doing Suzannah Phelps! How the devil could you keep that under wraps for a whole week?"

Quigg clamped down on a sudden, uncharacteristic urge to deliver a right uppercut to his friend's chin. "Piss off, Morgan."

Predictably, Ray did not piss off. Instead, he circled the desk to lean on it. "A whole week you've been holding out. I gotta tell you, I'm sorely disappointed."

Hell with the uppercut. He could drop him with a sharp blow to the side of the knee. He'd go down like a sack of concrete. And he'd probably shut up.

Of course, he'd be off work for three months with a ligament repair, which would leave Quigg with an even heavier workload. Plus the guys would know how bad he had it for the Ice Princess.

"What's the big deal?" Quigg leaned back in his chair, the epitome of casual. "When have you known me to run off at the mouth about a woman?"

Ray's jaw dropped. "We're not talking about just any woman here. This is Suzannah Phelps. She-Rex herself. Quigg, buddy, this is the World Series of conquests, my friend. The Stanley Cup, the Masters, the bloody Triple Crown, all rolled up in one."

Well, when he put it like that.... Quigg grinned. "Pretty weird, eh?"

"I'll say." Ray shook his head wonderingly. "Dammit, I *knew* you had a jones for her. Why'd you go all dark horsy on me when I asked you about it?"

Quigg shrugged. "Guess I didn't think it was gonna be a go."

Ray laughed. "From what I hear, looks like it's green lights all the way now."

"And where'd you hear that?"

"Staff room was all abuzz about it. You been elevated to God-like status in some guys' eyes, you'll be pleased to know."

Quigg shifted in his chair. "Don't suppose everybody's thrilled about it."

"The general consensus is you'll slam dunk her when the novelty wears off. The hold-outs kinda warmed up to the idea after that."

Quigg wanted to endorse the locker room speculation, share a laugh with Razor about it. But he kept seeing Suzannah's pinched, anxious face. He'd promised her he wouldn't let her image be weakened by virtue of this association he'd pretty much forced on her.

But who would know? What could it hurt, really?

Damnation.

It would hurt Suzannah.

Quigg sat forward in his chair. "Sorry to disappoint the troops, but that's not likely to happen. Anybody does any dumping, it's liable to be Suzannah."

As soon as the words were out of his mouth, he was struck by how true they felt. *Yikes.*

Not that that wasn't always the case. He'd never dumped a woman yet. At least, not actively. He'd never actively pursued one, either. They just seemed to find him. And when his interest started to flag, they found someone else.

But with Suzannah, if this were a real relationship, he couldn't see his interest flagging. If this were a real relationship and she dumped him, it wouldn't be as a result of a subtle disengagement on his part. If this were a real relationship, he'd be vulnerable.

He glanced at his friend, who was looking at him thoughtfully.

"Wow."

Quigg dragged a hand over his face. "Hey, I didn't say it was *serious.* All I'm saying is that at this particular moment, I can't see getting tired of her in a hurry."

Ray tugged at the cuffs of his perfectly-tailored shirt as he digested that. "You realize Grace'll want to meet her."

An image of Ray's wife sprang to mind, an earnest young newspaper journalist, poised and polished beyond her years and determined to make a name for herself. Yeah, Grace would like Suzannah, and vice-versa. "If you're thinking about a double date, forget it. I didn't even do that in junior high and I'm not about to start now."

"I was thinking more about a backyard barbecue on Saturday afternoon. You know, a couple of neighbors, a couple of the guys, some of Grace's friends from the paper."

A barbecue? Quigg turned the idea over in his mind. Perfect! This was better than bowling, better than line dancing. A real taste of suburbia. Hamburgers cooking on the grill on a too-small deck in a too-small back yard, guests talking and laughing within earshot of neighbors on three sides. Men drinking beer straight from the bottle, women sipping wine dispensed from a box with a spigot.

"Sounds good," Quigg said. "But what about the guest list?"

Ray grinned. "Don't worry. I won't invite anyone she's personally boned and filleted. At least, not recently."

"Much appreciated."

"No problem." Razor pushed himself off the desk and left as soundlessly as he'd arrived.

Quigg linked his fingers behind his head and leaned back in his chair. Now all he had to do was figure out how to get Suzannah to agree to the invitation.

Chapter 5

*W*HAT WAS I THINKING?

That was about the only intelligible thought Suzannah could manage as she sat in the passenger seat of John's car, en route to a cop party. A *cop party*, for pity's sake. It was all she could do to keep from pressing a hand to her stomach to calm the butterflies there. How had she let herself be talked into this?

She glanced over at John, whose attention seemed to be firmly fixed on the road. He was wearing a nice black t-shirt, which appeared to be new, and a pair of jeans which were definitely not new.

She chewed her lip. Was she over-dressed? It was hard to measure by John's apparel. Honestly, the man needed a keeper, someone to dress him in the morning. Still, since she'd opened her door to him twenty minutes ago, she'd been plagued with doubts about the tobacco brown Halston halter dress she wore.

But dammit he'd said casual. He'd said patio party, for crying out loud. So she'd tied her hair back, threaded plain gold hoops through her pierced ears and left her tanned legs bare. That was as casual as this little chickadee got.

Which brought her full circle. What the hell had she been thinking?

You let yourself be railroaded, that's what.

He'd begun by pointing out how uncomplaining he'd been about attending *her* functions. And he had. Not a single groan or eye roll, at least not that she'd caught. Which was pretty remarkable considering she'd dragged him to the dullest, most tedious engagements she could muster invitations for. She'd expected him to decide her social life was far too boring to require such close monitoring.

But he hadn't buckled under the boredom. Night after night, she'd searched his face for evidence of frustration, but all she encountered in his gaze was a quiet watchfulness, a patient, purposeful waiting that put her feminine senses on full alert.

Her mind skittered away from that thought. The last thing she needed to do right now was to add *that* to the mix of apprehensions that had her normally steady nerves vibrating.

She steered her thoughts back to how gracious he'd been about those yawn-fests she'd subjected him to. No doubt about it, she definitely owed him for that. Still, her guilty conscience would not have been enough to secure her agreement to attend this party, and he'd known it. So he'd pulled out the big guns — he'd accused her of being a snob, unwilling to subject herself to his middle-class world.

Her blood heated at the memory of that confrontation. She was most definitely *not* a snob! Granted, she didn't have much experience of that world. But darn it, it wasn't her fault.

She'd been reared and educated among the world's most privileged, moving among them with the ease of someone born to wealth. Rich, spoiled, indulged — she readily admitted she'd been all those things. But she also devoted much of her energy to helping the most underprivileged and socially marginalized of souls. Unfortunately, she had little personal experience of anything in between.

She felt Quigg apply the brakes and heard the turn signal's rhythmic click-*click*, click-*click* as he waited for oncoming traffic to clear. A moment later, he turned left onto a quieter street. The trees lining the sidewalk at intervals were new, tall, sparsely-leafed saplings, which indicated a relatively new subdivision.

"Are we nearly there?" she asked.

"The next block. White bungalow with black shutters, on the right."

Her stomach gave another unaccustomed lurch, and she clutched her bag closer. The driveway was already plugged with cars, so Quigg parked the Taurus by the curb about a half-block past the Morgan house.

She looked over at him as killed the engine and extracted the keys. "Do I look all right?" she blurted.

Something flickered in his eyes. "You'll be the most beautiful woman in the crowd."

Oh, God. She smoothed the fabric of her dress over her knees. It had made her feel so good when she'd examined her reflection in the mirror at home. "I *am* over-dressed, aren't I? Why didn't you tell me?"

He grinned. "Relax, Princess. You look gorgeous. Everybody'll love you. Especially the guys."

She shot him a look that said she'd kill him for this. He merely laughed and climbed out of the car, coming around to open her door for her. With as much dignity as she could command, she slipped out of the car.

"Quigg, ol' buddy, you made it."

Suzannah glanced up to see Ray Morgan wandering down the drive toward them. Eddie Bauer khakis, a black Armani t-shirt and deck shoes. She let a sigh of relief escape. Okay, this wasn't so bad.

"Ms. Phelps," he said, extending a hand. "Glad you could come."

She seriously doubted that, but Detective Morgan's expression looked welcoming enough. Deciding to accept the sentiment at face value, she took the hand he offered.

"Suzannah, please. It'll be a very long evening if I have to answer to my mother's name for the duration."

He grinned. "Suzannah it is, then."

Suzannah felt her jaw go lax. Ray Morgan was a fine-looking man by anyone's standards, but when he smiled that crooked, boyish grin, he was astonishingly good looking.

Quigg cleared his throat. "If you're quite finished pawing my date, I think she could find a use for that hand."

"Ignore him," Ray encouraged. "He's obviously out of practice escorting beautiful women."

She couldn't have stopped the smile that curved her lips if she'd wanted to. The easy way these two men insulted each other was an obvious testament to a deep affection.

"In fact," Ray continued, finally releasing her hand, "the last date Quigg brought to one of these shindigs was a real dog."

Suzannah's smile faltered.

"Ray Morgan!"

The admonishment came from a tall brunette who was making her way toward them across the paved driveway. "You'll have to excuse my husband," she said.

Husband? This had to be Grace Morgan, feature writer from the daily newspaper. Suzannah watched the other woman approach. Slim-hipped, full-busted, fit without being overly athletic. The pretty floral sun dress she wore was off-the-rack, but nothing else about this woman appeared to be. Her precision-cut hair, for instance, was the work of a master, and one didn't achieve skin like that without benefit of regular facials. She was, Suzannah decided, quite beautiful in an intensely feminine kind of way. If it weren't for the warmth lighting her eyes and the quick smile that softened her mouth, Suzannah would have been quite prepared to dislike her.

She reached Ray's side, sliding an arm around his waist. "Before you write my husband off as a complete jerk, I should explain that he's talking about an actual canine."

Realization dawned. "Of course. Bandy."

"Oh, so you've met the mutt?"

"Not yet, but I've heard a lot about him."

Grace's smile widened, showing even white teeth. "That's only fitting, I guess. He's a whole lot of dog."

"That's enough from you, young lady," Quigg growled in mock severity. "You'll scare Suzannah off."

"I think we can safely leave that to Bandy," put in Ray.

"Make yourself useful, Morgan, and put this on ice or something," Quigg said, handing him the bottle of wine he'd brought.

Ray read the label aloud and whistled admiringly. "This, my friend, is a fine Burgundy. We do *not* put leggy red beauties like this on ice. We chill then for ten or fifteen minutes, just to drop the temperature a few degrees."

Suzannah turned wide eyes on John. The vintage Ray had named was one her late father used to favor, and it didn't come cheaply. Had he done that for her?

Quigg shrugged. "Whatever."

Ray just shook his head, muttering something that sounded like "cretin".

Grace ignored her husband, gestured with a nod of her head to the garden gate. "Everyone's back there. Shall we join them?"

Suzannah felt the warmth of John's hand briefly at the small of her back. It was the most fleeting of touches, more reassuring than sexual, but it made her catch her breath. If this relationship were real, it would be exactly the kind of gesture she'd welcome in the circumstances. Reassurance, physical connection, a hint of possessive pride.

But it's not real. It's pretend. And he's very good at this pretend thing.

They passed through the gate on the tall cedar fence. Boisterous voices punctuated by feminine laughter carried to them as the rounded the corner of the small bungalow.

"Hey, guys, look who's here," someone called.

The voices stopped as all heads swiveled in their direction. Suddenly Suzannah could hear the vocals of Matchbox 20's Rob Thomas issuing from unseen speakers inside the house.

I feel stupid.

Perfect sentiment, Rob.

Wrong attitude, she scolded herself. If she gave a damn about popularity, she'd have smeared petroleum jelly on her teeth and become one of those TV weather girls who smiled until their jaws locked.

Still, it was going to be a long evening. She lifted her chin and strode across the small stretch of sun-baked lawn to join the group on the deck.

Two hours later, Suzannah gazed at her own reflection in the mirror in the Morgans' small downstairs bathroom. She didn't really need the facilities, but she did need to fortify herself.

Not that anyone in the small crowd had been overtly hostile. After falling silent on her arrival, the guests had come back to life with a vengeance. Each had welcomed her. Many went out of their way to include her in conversation. But she still felt exactly what she was — an intruder. The false note in the choir. The elephant in the room nobody wanted to mention.

Pulling a gold tube from her handbag, she quickly retouched her lips, though they hardly needed the repair despite the burger she'd eaten. Lipstick was like any other product. If you paid enough for it and used an equally expensive lip pencil under it, it would stand up to anything.

She grimaced at her reflection. None of the other women's lipstick had held up nearly so well, a fact which she was sure each of those women noted. Like the Halston and the Italian sandals, it served to set her apart. Of course, most of the women were cops' wives. They wouldn't have embraced her even if she'd worn a drug store lipstick that disappeared with her first glass of wine.

She snapped her handbag shut with an audible click. Well, there was one person she could hang around who wouldn't give her attitude. At least, not here, not now. Tonight's program required him to be concerned and attentive, and she felt dangerously in need of concern and attention.

A last quick look at her reflection, and she exited the bathroom. She found John on the deck, deep in conversation with one of Grace's male co-workers, a sports columnist, who was expounding on what was wrong with professional hockey. As much as she wanted to sidle up to John, to shelter in his protection, she wasn't about to squash hockey talk. These people already had plenty to reasons to dislike her.

The sun had set, leaving the western sky smeared with pinks and purples, but it wasn't entirely dark yet. Rescuing her half-full wine glass from the table where she'd left it, she made a comment about wanting to see Grace's garden before the last of the daylight faded.

She'd reached the bottom of the steps and had started across the lawn when she was stopped by a male guest. At the brief touch of his hand on her bare arm, she turned toward him.

Bruce Newman. She dredged his name up from earlier conversation. A constable with a decade worth of service, both John and Ray had worked with him. And thank God, Suzannah had somehow managed never to cross-examine him.

"You shouldn't do that," he said, his face stern.

"Do what?"

"Leave your drink unattended like that, then resume drinking it."

Suzannah's gaze dropped to her glass, which held several ounces of the very nice Burgundy John had bought, then flew back to Constable Newman's face.

"A lady should never take her eyes off her drink. You never know what unscrupulous predators are lurking out there. Even a little town like this sees its share of guys putting roofies in ladies' drinks."

Roofies. Rohypnol. Date rape drug. Her heart tripped over into double time, and her muscles screamed for flight, but somehow her brain prevailed. She held her ground. "Thank you," she said, managing to sound normal. "That's very good advice."

He nodded once, then brushed past her to climb the steps to the deck.

Suzannah released her breath in a rush. What was that about? Public safety bulletin or subtle threat? She was certain he must have seen the fear in her eyes, but he hadn't seemed unduly disturbed by it.

Of course, that didn't make him her stalker. As far as most of these guys were concerned, she was the enemy. He'd probably just seen a chance to score a few points off her outside of John's earshot and taken advantage of it.

Or maybe he was just a good guy passing along a friendly warning. A socially-challenged good guy.

Belatedly, she realized she was still standing where Constable Newman had left her. Collecting herself, she continued across the lawn to inspect the beds she'd admired earlier.

The beds were largely perennial, she saw, though the plantings were relatively immature. Happy Shasta daisies, succulent sedums and glorious black-eyed susans in the full-sun areas, tall monkshood, striking beardtongue and leafy hostas in the shady corner.

There, just what she wanted, against the back fence. A stand of heliopsis. She made straight for the cheerful clump of false sunflowers. They were purported to be hardy enough to withstand anything nature threw at them. Hopefully, that included the occasional splash of quality Burgundy, with or without Rohypnol. With a twist of her wrist, she tilted the wineglass, spilling the contents among the hardy flowers.

"You must think me a terrible hostess."

Suzannah turned to find Grace Morgan crossing the lawn to join her at the edge of the flower bed. If she'd seen Suzannah's surreptitious dumping of the wine amidst the heliopsis and the bee balm, she was too polite to mention it.

"Not at all," said Suzannah smoothly. "Your husband said you had something to take care of, something work related."

"I try not to take it home with me too much, but I've been chasing this guy forever for an interview. I might have predicted he'd pick tonight to return one of my many messages."

"Your husband did a credible job of subbing for you, though the men remarked he didn't look nearly so good."

Grace smiled, but it was automatic reflex. The look in her eye told Suzannah the other woman's thoughts were racing. Probably re-running the interview in her head. Lord knows, she'd done that often enough herself, going over testimony.

"Do you realize that in direct discourse with me, you've yet to refer to my husband as anything but *your husband*?"

Suzannah blinked, trying to decide whether or not to be offended by Grace's observation. "Really?" she managed stiffly. "I hadn't thought about it."

"No, I don't imagine you did. But I couldn't help noticing that you didn't call any of the guys by their first names, except for my friends from the paper."

Suzannah blanched. Could that be true? "Really?"

Grace nodded.

"Oh, great," she muttered.

"I wouldn't sweat it. They probably didn't notice."

"Yeah, probably not. It's not like they're particularly skilled at observation or anything."

Grace laughed. Not a chuckle, not a titter, but a real belly laugh. "Oh, I *like* you, Suzannah Phelps."

Suzannah found herself relaxing. "Well, I'm relieved someone here does."

Grace's face sobered. "You'll have to cut the guys some slack. They'll get used to the idea of you and John, but it might take some time to settle. They have enough respect for John that you won't get any flack from that quarter."

Maybe, thought Suzannah. She looked down at her empty wine glass. *Or maybe not.* "I'm sure you're right," she said. "I don't suppose that extends to the wives?"

"Are they giving you a hard time?" Grace said, her expression sharpening.

"Oh, no, nothing like that. They just seem a little ... I don't know ... closed?"

"Tell me about it," Grace said, taking a swig of her vodka cooler.

Suzannah eyed the younger woman. "What do you mean? You're part of the sorority, aren't you?"

"Technically, yes. The guys socialize so much with each other, I couldn't *not* be a part of it, but I think I've been relegated to the periphery."

Out of the corner of her eye, Suzannah noticed John watching her with a quiet intensity from his position on the deck, even as a man from the newspaper talked animatedly into his ear. Ignoring the flutter in her stomach, she switched her attention back to Grace. "I don't understand. Why would they do that?"

Grace smiled. "Actually, I think it's more my doing than theirs. You see, my husband —"

"*Ray*," Suzannah supplied quickly.

Grace laughed again. "See, that didn't hurt, did it?"

"Hardly at all."

"As I was saying, Ray goes out of his way to protect me from the uglier side of what he does, what he sees. The other wives," she gestured toward the laughing group on and around the deck, "I think they sense that, and it makes me not quite one of them.

They always include me, but I always come away thinking there's some secret handshake I don't know."

"Wow, tough crowd."

"Maybe," she conceded, plucking absently at the label on her bottle. "But you know what I think? I think if you and John were to hook up, you wouldn't face that obstacle. They'd give you credit for having been in the trenches yourself."

"Yeah, but they're hardly likely to overlook the fact that the particular trench I'm in is the opposing one."

"There is that," Grace acknowledged, "but it's not insurmountable."

The other woman's tone was so genuine, so earnest, so concerned, that Suzannah felt a pang for the deception she and John were perpetrating. She wished quite fiercely to come clean, but that was out of the question. Instead, she contented herself with downplaying the long term potential of the supposed relationship. "I don't think it's going to be a problem, actually. John and I ... well, put it this way — I don't see it getting serious."

Grace smiled, her face lighting with a gentle amusement that made her seem older and infinitely wiser, when she was clearly Suzannah's junior by half a decade or more. "That's the trouble with this stuff," she said softly. "You never see it coming until it's too late."

⁎

From his vantage point on the deck, Quigg watched Suzannah and Grace, talking and laughing against the backdrop of Grace's flower-lined picket fence. At least he didn't have to pretend to pay attention to Denny White. The copy man had wandered off in search of a more attentive audience, leaving Quigg free to look his fill. And look he did. Damn, she looked good in that too-fancy dress.

Yeah, the dress. He'd watched her carefully, seeing the precise moment when she knew beyond the shadow of a doubt that she was overdressed. Her initial suspicion had been allayed when their hosts had come out to greet them. But Ray and Grace always looked like they stepped straight out of a catalogue. Then she'd met the crowd in the back yard.

She'd tried to make the best of it, he'd give her that, but her manner was too formal, her carriage too regal. To make matters worse, she obviously knew squat about the topics that dominated the ladies' conversation. She couldn't join in the discussions about Billy Bob's latest movie, Enrique's latest music video, or yesterday's episode of Oprah. Her pop culture education seemed to have stopped at "Columbo". Between her natural reserve and the social differences, she'd come across as cool and superior, and she knew it.

Quigg shifted, feeling an unexpected pang.

This was the friggin' plan, man. Payback for her dragging him to those mind-numbingly staid gatherings.

"Would you say we were men of average intelligence?"

From long practice, Quigg managed not to jump as Ray glided up beside him. He turned a reproving gaze on his host. "I'd say one of us is. The other can't seem to remember basic rules of etiquette, such as stealth is not a skill to be practiced in a social situation."

"Okay, but would you say between us we have the combined IQ of at least a garden slug?"

"Razor, what are you talking about?"

"Just answer the question."

"Hell, yeah, I think we're at least as smart as a slug. Though, if you think about it, they can produce electricity, not to mention slime trails —"

"Enough about the snails already. My point was —"

"*Slugs.*"

"Slugs, snails, whatever. My point is, why are we standing here while my gorgeous wife and your beautiful date are standing way over there?"

Damn, Ray was right. As the man who had allegedly breached the heretofore unassailable castle walls, he should be glued to Suzannah. Suddenly, the idea had appeal above and beyond the role he was supposed to be playing. Strong appeal.

"Ray, buddy, that's the most astute thing you've said in recent memory." He drained his soft drink and handed the empty to his friend.

Both women looked up as he approached.

"John, we were just talking about you."

He cocked an eyebrow suspiciously at Grace as he came to a stop beside Suzannah. "Yeah?"

"I was just telling Suzannah what a soft touch you are when it comes to animals."

Ah, hell. "Not this again, Grace. I keep telling you people, I only took the damned dog home because the SPCA didn't have room for him. I'm sure a kennel will open up any day."

Grace laughed. "That was two years ago," she confided to Suzannah, who also laughed.

"Oh, by the way, Grace," he said, "Ray's looking for an excuse to get you alone. He says to ask isn't there something needs doing in the kitchen?"

He had the satisfaction of seeing her face color as her gaze flew to her husband.

"In that case, I'd better run along," she said. "After all, how could I turn down such an eloquent invitation?"

"I like her," Suzannah said, as they watched Grace cross the lawn to join Ray.

"I knew you would."

"You also knew I was dressed all wrong."

Quigg glanced at Suzannah to find she was now watching him closely. He widened his eyes. "Hey, wait a minute, this is me, here, remember? You think I'm qualified to make judgments in matters of dress?"

"What's the story with Bruce Newman?"

The rapid change of subject threw him for a minute, but he wasn't about to complain. "What about Newman? Did he give you a hard time?"

"No."

Her answer was unequivocal, but it was just a second too long coming. He searched her face. "You sure?"

"He was perfectly polite. I just wondered about him, is all. I didn't see his wife here."

"You interested?"

She made a disparaging sound which coming from anyone other than Suzannah Phelps he might have called a snort. "Yeah, like I need another cop breathing down my neck."

Her words were like a scalpel, slipping effortlessly between his ribs. The unexpected pang couldn't have shocked him more than if she'd actually stuck him. He masked it with a smile.

"Hey, sweetheart, you know how to get this cop off your back. Just ride with me down to the station house right now and make a report on your schizophrenic flower boy."

"No." Her answer was automatic.

He shrugged, as though it was six of one, half a dozen of another. "What do you say we get out of here?"

She glanced at the group on the deck. "The party's still in full swing. Won't it raise some eyebrows?"

He closed his hand around her arm to pull her closer, and her gaze flew up to meet his. "Honey, it would raise eyebrows if I don't whisk you away."

Her lips parted on a gasp of surprise, and Quigg couldn't resist skimming his palm up and down the warm silk of her bare arm. He felt her involuntary shiver at the light contact, but she didn't back off.

"I suppose you're right."

Her voice was a husky dream as she made the acknowledgment.

"Kiss me."

"No!" She glanced around to see if anyone were watching.

He sighed. "Then I guess I'll have to do all the work."

Before she could pull away, or maybe before he could reconsider, he lowered his mouth to hers. It was a light thing, the merest brush his lips against hers, but he felt the moist heat of her breath, tasted the temptation. The need to go deeper, past the pleasant taste of her perfect lipstick to the dark secrets of her mouth, surged in his veins. He lifted his head abruptly. "Let's go."

"Let me get my purse."

⁂

Suzannah sat quietly on the ride home, nurturing — despite her better judgment — a small flame of desire.

She should crush it. She knew that. But it was so sweet, and it had been so long since she'd felt anything remotely like this. She glanced at John, who kept his eyes on the road, his face unreadable in profile.

It wasn't real, of course, this feeling he stirred in her. How could it be? She just wasn't the passionate type. Or if there was any passion in her, it was too deeply buried, too thoroughly inhibited to show itself. Except when she looked at him, when she felt that energy that fairly crackled around him, she could almost believe that he might be able to call those buried passions to the surface.

John signaled and pulled over to the curb, the sudden maneuver dragging Suzannah out of her reverie. Before she could ask what was going on, why he'd pulled over on the thoroughfare, she heard the wail of an approaching siren. Twisting in her seat, she saw a fire truck bearing down on them. When it had passed, John signaled and moved back into the roadway.

She settled back in her seat, adjusting her belt. "So, does that make the adrenaline kick up when you hear those sirens?"

He shot her a grin. "Damn straight."

There it was, that jump of the pulse again, just because he'd smiled at her. Would he kiss her again when he dropped her off? Probably not. No audience to impress. Usually, he followed her in for a suitable interval, long enough for anyone watching the house to form their own conclusions, after which he'd leave, whistling and walking with a spring in his step that suggested they'd been doing more than catching up on current events in front of CNN. But maybe tonight —

John swore.

"What is it?"

"That fire truck we saw? I think it was going to your place."

Suzannah grasped the door handle as he cornered hard onto her street. Omigod, the pumper *was* at her house. And a second fire truck and a police car. John pulled up behind the police cruiser. Suzannah released her seatbelt and leapt from the car almost before it came to a stop.

"Oh, my Lord, my car."

John rounded the Ford to join her on the sidewalk. Her BMW was no longer burning, but the acrid smell of smoke still hung in the air and the car was little more than a blackened husk. Water streamed down her driveway into the gutter.

"My car," she said again.

"Stay here," John ordered. "I'll find out what happened."

She grabbed his arm. "No, I'm not going to wait here. It's my car and —"

She was interrupted by a uniformed officer, who approached them with his arm outstretched. "Folks, I'm going to have to ask you to back off."

"Hey, Jules, it's me," John called. "John Quigley, Detective Bureau."

"Quigg?" The officer drew closer. "How'd you get here so fast? They just got the fire out."

"I was with Ms. Phelps. She's the property owner," he said, gesturing toward the house. "And that's her Beemer smoking in the driveway."

The constable's eyes widened. "You're with her?"

"Yep."

Suzannah stepped forward, tired of being discussed as though she weren't present, and extended her hand. "I don't think I've had the pleasure."

"Constable Julian Lambert."

The young constable shook her hand. She thought he might have blushed, but it was impossible to tell with the blue and reds strobing in the deepening dusk.

"Can you tell me what happened here?"

"Well, ma'am, your car was pretty much engulfed when we got here. I understand one of your neighbors tried to put it out with a fire extinguisher, but backed off when he became concerned the gas tank might blow. Funny, they always worry about the gas tank, but nine times out of ten, the real danger comes from the hydraulic stuff blasting off. That's why the firefighters position themselves ahead or behind the vehicle, never beside —"

"Right," said Quigg, cutting off the explanation. "So he backed off and called it in?"

"Got his wife to make the call."

"How'd it get started?" she asked.

"Can't say yet, ma'am." The radio on his belt crackled, and he paused to turn the volume down a notch. "A lot of the car fires we see are electrical, but they tend to be old beaters, not late-model BMWs. I don't suppose you have any reason to suspect someone might want to lash out at you?"

John stepped closer. She felt his tension through the layers of air separating them. Lifting her gaze, she met his. *Tell him*, his eyes said.

"You're right," she said, as though he'd spoken the words aloud. "It's time."

"Ma'am?"

She turned back to the constable. "Yes," she said softly. "Yes, I think somebody might have done this deliberately."

Chapter 6

IT WAS AFTER TEN o'clock before everyone cleared out. An increasingly astonished Constable Lambert had taken her statement, a process expedited by the thorough notes she'd kept in her diary. Dates, times, even the results of her own investigations with the florists. Her burned-out car was towed away for forensic examination. Her neighbors had been canvassed about what they might have seen. Her driveway was mopped up. Finally — *finally* — she closed the door on the last investigator and she and John were alone again.

"There, that wasn't so hard, was it?" John said as she crossed the living room.

"That depends," she said, bending to scoop up the Day Timer diaries she'd left on the coffee table.

"Depends on what?"

She carefully fitted the diaries back in their box. "On whether or not the car turns out to have had defective wiring. If it does, I'll look like an hysterical woman who makes diary notations every time she sees her own shadow."

"Aaarrghhh!"

She lifted her chin. "What?"

"You are one stubborn broad. Did Lambert say anything to lead you to believe he was in any way skeptical about what you had to tell him?"

"Of course not. *You* were here backing me up. What did you expect him to do?"

"His job." John ran an impatient hand around the back of his neck. "Which he'd have done with or without me being here."

His being here.

Time to talk about that. As she'd answered the constable's questions, a dull ache had been growing in her gut, an ache which had nothing to do with the fact someone had probably torched her car. It grew out of the knowledge that there was no longer any reason for John Quigley's continued presence in her life.

She put the Day Timer box back in the corrugated cardboard archive box, aligning it neatly with its mates from previous years. "So," she said, closing the box's lid, "I guess this means you can go, huh, Detective?"

He turned to glare at her. "Go? What the hell are you talking about?"

She stiffened her back. "What do you suppose I'm talking about? Depart. Leave. Go back to your life."

"You think I'm going to leave you alone here tonight after what happened to your car?"

"Yes, I do, actually, but I intended it in the broader sense, as well." She stole a glance at him, only to find his expression had gone blank. Not the usual inscrutable cop face thing he did. It was just ... blank.

She dropped her gaze, rushing to fill the silence. "Come on, Detective, you should be celebrating. You're off the hook. No more babysitting the Ice Princess. Somebody else is on it."

"No."

Her gaze flew back to his face. "No, what?"

"No, I'm not going anywhere. Not until this twisted fuck is rounded up."

The strength of his objection simultaneously thrilled and frightened her. Irritated at her own ambivalence, her tone was sharper than she intended when she spoke. "For heaven's sake, this was supposed to be an either/or thing. Either I reported the harassment or I was stuck with you as my watchdog. In case you haven't noticed, *either* has come to pass, rendering *or* unnecessary."

"Pack a bag."

Had he not heard her? "Excuse me?"

"You shouldn't stay here alone tonight."

"I've addressed that, remember? The alarm system you insisted I install?"

"Much good that will do you if your torch comes back."

She paled. "You think he'd burn my house?"

He made no reply, but she read his answer in his eyes. She shivered. "Do you think Constable Lambert shares that view? That the arsonist might come back and torch my house?"

"The idea probably crossed his mind."

"Then why didn't he say so?"

He rolled his shoulders. "Because he assumed any woman friend of mine would be taken care of. Which is what I'm trying to do, if you'd just cooperate. Now, about packing that bag ... ."

"But I'm not really your ... woman friend," she pointed out. "So tell your buddies the truth, that it was a ruse so you could keep an eye on me. Once they stop laboring under the impression that we're an item, they might even mention stuff like, 'Oh, by the way, you should consider that he might come back with a can of gasoline to torch your house, possibly while you're in it'."

"Yeah, right." He shoved a hand through his hair. "And who's going to tell the rest of the world?"

"What about the rest of the world?"

"There's no way in hell I'm going to be seen as the guy who dumped his girlfriend in her hour of need."

"Read my lips, Quigley. I ... am ... not ... your ... girlfriend."

"Optics, sweetheart."

She squared her shoulders. "Then *I'll* dump *you*."

He snorted. "Think I'd let that happen if you were my woman?"

"I think," she said in her iciest tone, "that it would be beyond your control."

Amazingly, that produced a grin, that lopsided one that crinkled the lines around his eyes and made her heart stutter.

"Shows how little you know," he said. "Besides, I thought you were concerned about preserving the Suzannah Phelps legend."

"What does *that* mean?"

He shrugged. "I dunno. I just figured you wouldn't be too hot to let 'em know you were scared to file a complaint. If I explain about our little deal, the cat'll be out of the bag. And if you thought they weren't too fond of you before, wait'll they hear about your cop-as-stalker theory."

She sucked in a breath. "You wouldn't."

"I'd pretty much have to, wouldn't I, to explain away this mock courtship of ours?"

Oh, Lord, that's just what she needed. Life was hard enough as it was. "Don't do it."

"Then don't try to give me the bum's rush."

She glared at him, and he grinned.

"Hey, it's all about saving face, isn't it? I don't want to be seen as a guy who bails in a crisis. You don't want to be seen as … well, whatever. Hell, I haven't even figured that out. Needy? Vulnerable?"

Needy. Vulnerable. She heard the words he used, but what her mind heard was *human, female.* Is that what he thought? That she was afraid to show she was a normal woman?

Dear god, was it true?

"Pack a bag," he repeated.

She thought about refusing. Of course, he'd probably camp out in her driveway all night if she did.

Without conscious thought, her mind leapt back to the scene in her driveway earlier tonight. The pall of smoke hanging in the still, humid air, the acrid burn of it in her nostrils and throat. The shocking sight of her beloved car, little more than a burned-out husk. The lights on the ambulance, the police cruiser, the big pumper truck blocking the street.

Her heart lurched again. Maybe she was a weak fool, but she didn't want to stay here.

"Okay," she conceded. "I'll pack a bag. You can take me to my mother's."

He massaged his forehead as though a headache had sprung up. "Are you sure you want to drag your mother into this?"

Within the space of a heartbeat, fear snaked around her chest like a steel band, constricting her lungs. "You think he'd go after my mother?"

"I think he's cranked it up a notch, escalated the situation. You can't be too careful."

She blinked, her mind racing. What were the alternatives? "So you want me to pack a bag and go where?"

"My place."

Her heart jumped, but she willed it back under control. "Your place?" Her voice was amazingly composed, considering his suggestion. "What's to stop this guy from following us there? What's to stop him from torching your place as opposed to mine?"

"Not a thing. However, the east view from my living room happens to be the York Street fire station, so I shouldn't think we need to worry too much on that score. And even if he did manage to somehow smoke us out, I'd have my pistol."

Her gaze automatically sought out that subtle armpit bulge she'd noticed so many times, before realizing that it wasn't there tonight. She bit her lip. It sounded good. It sounded safe. Suddenly, it was so incredibly tempting to surrender control, to let him take care of her as he was offering to do.

Which was why she should refuse.

"Why?" she demanded, her voice embarrassingly harsh to her own ears.

"Why what?"

"Why do you want to do this?"

He swore, glancing away. "I told you, I don't want to be seen as a guy who'd —"

"That's a cop-out." That brought his surprised gaze back to hers. "You couldn't possibly give a flying you-know-what about the opinions of the stuffed shirts I've put in your path these last two weeks. And as for your cop friends, they'd throw you a party, maybe declare a new holiday, if you 'dumped' me as publicly as possible. So I repeat, why are you doing this? It's not as though you care about *me*, for goodness sake."

"Who says I don't?"

Suddenly, his eyes burned with a fierce intensity that made her want to take a step back. She resisted the impulse. Barely.

"Dammit, woman, would that be so impossible to believe? Are you so caught up in this court bullshit that you can't see what's in front of your face?"

Her heart seemed to stop, then began leaping painfully against her ribs like a caged thing battering itself trying to escape. "What are you saying?"

He swore, glancing away again.

She waited. Five seconds, ten seconds. "John?"

"Dammit." He lifted a hand to rub the back of his neck. "I like you, okay? I care about you. Call me a masochist."

"Very smooth, Detective." Somehow, the words not only got out through her constricted throat, they sounded normal, gently mocking even.

He fixed her with a glare.

Despite the fact that the words he'd just uttered complicated the situation beyond measure, despite the pleasure/terror they engendered, the decision came easily. Foolishly so, no doubt.

She smiled for the first time since they'd turned onto her street and spotted the emergency response vehicles. "I'll just pack a bag, then, shall I?"

⁂

Quigg parked as close to his house's front door as he could. For about the zillionth time since he'd opened his mouth and let that sophomoric confession escape, he wondered what in hell he'd been thinking.

She moved to open her door, but he put a restraining hand on her arm. "Wait here a sec. I'll just make sure we weren't tailed." He climbed from the car, his eyes searching the street for a few moments, ears straining. Nothing untoward. Well, if anyone had followed them, they'd have to be pros. He'd kept a careful watch on his rearview mirror the whole way.

Satisfied, he rounded the car and opened her door.

"All clear?"

"Yep."

She climbed out, her bag gripped tightly in her hand. "Nice house."

He glanced up at the rambling two-story house. No way he would have picked this monstrosity for a home if his aunt hadn't left it to him. An apartment in a nice, secure building where the neighbors didn't knock on your door and no solicitation was permitted was his idea of appropriate bachelor habitat. "Don't rush to judgment too fast," he said, brushing past her to unlock the door. "You haven't seen the inside."

He could hear Bandy's toenails clicking on the floor as he danced on the other side of the door. "I better go first. The damned dog'll ruin your dress if I don't restrain him."

He pushed the door open. As anticipated, Bandy leapt all over him, whining softly. He bent to catch the mongrel's collar, pushing him back into the kitchen. When he glanced up he saw Suzannah was still standing in the doorway. "Come on in," he called. "He'll be okay in a minute. He just needs to settle down a bit."

She stepped inside and closed the door. Finally Bandy noticed her, a low growl issuing from his throat. She froze.

"Don't worry. That's how he greets everyone. He'll be all over you in a second." He scratched Bandy's neck soothingly.

"That's vastly reassuring."

At her tone, he glanced up to see she had her princess face firmly in place. Oh, great. A damned dog hater. He might have known. Or maybe it was his Bandy's obvious lack of pedigree she disdained. And it *was* pretty obvious. Part Shelty, part junk yard dog. Quigg looked down at Bandy's delicate head, which looked like it had been improbably grafted onto his Sherman tank body, the girth of which was imperfectly disguised by his long silky coat. Yeah, okay, he was butt-ugly, but so what?

"Don't worry, Princess. He may not be best-in-show material, but I can assure you he's flea free. No mange, no rabies, nothing you need to worry about carrying back to your mama's perfumed poodle."

"Appearances to the contrary, I am not a snob." Her posture grew even more ramrod straight, indicating her displeasure, but she never took her eyes off Bandy, who was currently doing his best to crush his own windpipe by straining against his collar. "And my mother did not have a poodle or a Pekinese or any of those toy dogs. We never had *any* kind of dog."

He grinned, finally understanding. "You're scared of dogs."

She took her eyes of the dog long enough to shoot him an evil look. "Anybody would be scared of *that* one." She dropped her gaze to Bandy, who now sounded like he was trying to hork up a tennis ball. "What's wrong with him."

"He'll be okay in a sec. He choked himself in his eagerness to greet you."

"Greet me? He looks more like he wants to *eat* me."

So did his master.

Down, boy.

Quigg cleared his throat. "Don't worry, he just looks scary. He's harmless. Mostly." He knelt beside the dog, who'd recovered from his self-imposed asphyxia. "Even if he did have a mind to bite, he doesn't have the ideal equipment for it. See?" He parted Bandy's soft lips to display an obviously incomplete dentition. Both upper and lower canines on the left side were missing, as well as two incisors on top, leaving a bald patch of pink gum where healthy white teeth should be.

"Oh my goodness, what happened?" She moved toward the dog, her fear seemingly forgotten. Bandy wriggled his stout frame, his fabulously well-haired tail fanning Quigg's face.

"Vet says it was trauma." Bandy started to strain toward her again, and Quigg let him inch closer. "Put your hand right down so he can sniff you," he encouraged. "Once he gives you a lick, you can pet him."

She complied, letting him snuffle her palm before she gingerly patted him on the head. "What kind of trauma?"

"Steel-toed Kodiak to the mouth, most likely. Or maybe a car accident."

He heard her gasp. "Somebody kicked him in the mouth?"

"Somebody kicked him a lot." The memory still had the power to raise his blood pressure, so he paused a few seconds. When he spoke again, his voice was as controlled and matter-of-fact as ever. "He greeted us at the door during a drug bust a couple of years ago, and not in a friendly way."

Bandy sat to better enjoy the stroking she was giving him.

"He didn't think much of your warrant, then?"

Quigg grinned. "About as much as our pharmaceutical dealer did. And if he hadn't flashed those gums at us, he might have got plugged right there."

"Poor dog," she crooned, kneeling. Bandy sidled even closer. "So you took pity on him and brought him home?"

"Hardly. I got the dog catcher to round him up and haul him off to the SPCA."

Her brow furrowed. "How'd you wind up with him?"

He stood to relieve cramped leg muscles. "No takers at the shelter. Everyone wants a pup, and he was already six or seven years old. Behavioral problems to boot, not to mention he needs regular thyroid meds. Who wants to take on that kind of burden?"

"You did." She gave Bandy a last scratch and stood.

"Watch out!"

Too late. Bandy demonstrated one of his behavioral quirks by clawing her leg. She cried out, stumbling backward in her haste, and he caught her. Immediately, Bandy started barking and snapping, his remaining teeth clicking ominously. Quigg stifled a curse. In her fear, she tried to press closer, which only made the dog more frantic. He pushed her away from his chest, but he wasn't fast enough.

"Ow! Dammit, you stupid mutt!" The dog shrank away, but Quigg knew the little bugger would come right back at his ankles if he couldn't keep Suzannah at a distance. He backed away from her. "It's okay." He put up a hand to keep her at arm's length. "He's trying to protect you. He's been socialized to think any human-to-human contact is hostile, even a hug. And with all that squealing you did, he figured I'm the aggressor."

"I did not *squeal*."

He grinned, bending to reassure the still anxious Bandy while she examined her leg. "How is it?"

She straightened. "The skin's not broken, but it's raising a pretty good welt."

"That's another of his quirks. He tends to register a complaint when you stop petting him. I guess I've learned to defend myself. After I fight off a couple of attempted claws, he'll desist. I don't even think about it anymore."

"So, no full-body contact allowed," she mused. Her hair, which had been pinned up in a casual twist, had started to escape. She lifted her arms to release it. "Must be hell on your love life."

He watched her twist all that blonde silk up again and fumble to secure it with the claspy thing. Her uplifted arms did incredible things for her breasts. "It hasn't been a problem for quite a while," he heard himself say.

She lowered her arms, her hands suddenly looking awkward as they plucked at her dress.

Aw, way to go, Quigley. First you say you like her — *like her,* for chrissakes. When had he last said something that asinine? Sixth grade? And now he'd as much as told her he was sex-starved. Way to make her believe she made the right decision coming here, putting herself in his hands.

She was twisting the strap of her expensive purse, now, and looking at the floor, the prints on the wall, everywhere but at him. Well, what'd you expect, Romeo?

He stood quickly. "I've gotta take Bandy for a spin around the block. Will you be okay for a few minutes?"

"Of course."

He reached for the dog's retractable leash and snagged a couple of plastic grocery store bags, which he stuffed in his pocket. "Lock the door behind me. I'll take my keys."

"Okay."

"Bathroom's at the top of the stairs, though I can't guarantee you'll find the seat down. There's beer and cola in the fridge, if you want something cold. Coffee and tea in the cupboard to the left of the stove, if you prefer hot. I'll make up a bed for you when I get back."

"Okay."

"I should be back as soon as Bandy does his business. Ten minutes, tops. And I won't be more than a block away, close enough to keep an eye on the house."

She smiled. "John, it's okay. If I were at home right now, I'd be alone."

No, she wouldn't. He'd be parked a discreet distance from her house with Bandy snoring in the back seat like a lumberjack sleeping one off.

"Okay." He turned to the dog. "C'mere, mutt. Let's get you leashed."

❦

Suzannah sagged against the wall when John closed the door behind him. Had she imagined it, the hunger in those hooded, sleepy eyes as he'd watched her fix her hair? She closed her eyes and saw it again, felt the awareness arc between them. No, she hadn't imagined anything.

She pressed a hand to her chest to try to slow her racing heart. Lord, what was she doing here?

Because he said he cared about her and she believed him.

Because he could offer her safety.

Because she was tired of pretending she didn't want to be near him, close enough to feel the pull of his magnetic energy. Because when he looked at her, she swore she could feel his gaze brush her very skin. Because he made her feel like she hadn't dared to feel since she was seventeen.

Oh, God, she wanted him, more than she could ever remember wanting a man. And he wanted her. She'd known it from the first. But did she have the courage to reach out and take what she wanted? Or would it be the same as every other time? She gnawed her lower lip. Would this precious, sweet desire wither on the vine? Could she afford the price of finding out?

Kitchen. Drink. Now.

❦

Suzannah was nowhere in sight when Quigg let himself back in the house, but he could hear Mark Knopfler's lazy vocals emanating from the living room. "Suzannah?"

"In here."

The volume of the music dropped. He unleashed Bandy, who shot off to find his newest friend. Stashing the leash in its customary place, he followed in Bandy's footsteps.

He expected to find her sitting on his aunt's flowered sofa sipping tea, but instead she crouched by the mantle, scratching Bandy's ears. She stood, but this time, stepped back out of reach before the dog could register a complaint about the cessation of petting.

"Quick study," he observed.

"He made quite an impression."

She picked up an old-fashioned glass from the mantle, took a healthy sip, then cradled it in her hands. Judging by the amber contents, she must have found the bourbon in the cupboard.

"I see you found yourself a drink."

"Umm. Jack Daniel's. My favorite. I hope you don't mind."

"Of course not."

"Care for one?" She gestured toward the coffee table, where the bottle sat.

Strong drink with Suzannah under his roof? A Suzannah who herself had been drinking strong drink? Bad idea.

"Nah, I think I'll have a beer. Be right back." Heart thumping, he retreated to the kitchen. Twisting the top off a Moose Dry, he took a swig, then set it down on the counter. Keep it cool, old man. She's tired, she's scared, and she wants a drink to unwind. Big deal.

He went to the cupboard, extracted a small bag of dog chow and shook some into the empty dog dish. Bandy immediately came running.

She'd also given him *the look*.

Oh, hell.

He grabbed Bandy's water dish, rinsed it under the tap and refilled it. "There you go, buddy."

Okay, no more procrastinating. Suzannah Phelps was sipping bourbon in his living room, waiting for him to rejoin her. And she'd given him the look. The green light. The all systems go.

At least from any other woman, that's how he'd interpret it, but who knew with Suzannah? He had no experience of a woman in her league. Hell, apart from an ill-advised engagement when he was too young to recognize good old-fashioned lust for what it was, he had limited experience of nice women.

Christ in his high chair! He'd just mentally characterized the woman his friends referred to as She-Rex as *nice*.

Okay, not nice, then. Respectable. Socially upstanding. That better described his experiential deficiency. When he did indulge his libido, his style was more the women who hung out at the local watering hole. With them, you knew the score. It was about the badge, and that was quite all right with him. It made it that much easier to gather his clothes in the grey light of pre-dawn and get the hell out of there.

"John?"

Whoops. Time out was over. "Be right there," he called. Then, to the dog, he said, "'Fraid you'll have to stay here, Bandy Man. The lady will probably have to wear slacks for a week as it is."

Closing the kitchen door on a disappointed Bandy, Quigg snagged his beer and walked back to the living room where Mark Knopfler was now husking his way through "Are We In Trouble Now". *You and me both, buddy.*

She smiled when she saw him enter the room. He shot a look at her glass. Eek! Nearly empty.

"This is a great song."

"Yeah." He took a swig of beer. "The whole CD is great."

"Umm," she agreed, depositing her glass on the coffee table beside the half bottle of JD. "Dance with me."

He gripped his bottle tighter. "You think that's wise?"

"Probably not." She strode over to him and plucked the beer from his hands, plunking it on the coffee table beside her drink.

Instant arousal. Just like that, he was hard. She was barefoot, which left her several inches shorter than him. For a moment, he mourned her loss of height. He liked her mouth at the level of his, her eyes able to look right into his.

She moved into him, soft against hard, and his arms went around her. She linked her arms around his neck, the loose embrace somehow effectively cutting off the supply of oxygen to his brain as she swayed against him. Or maybe that was being accomplished by the rush of blood to another part of his anatomy.

"You're not moving," she pointed out.

For pity's sake, he didn't trust himself to move. In the background, Mark Knopfler crooned that it wasn't the music or the wine sending those shivers up his spine. Suzannah swayed against him again, her breasts under the sexy halter dress brushing his chest. Beneath his hands, the bare skin of her back felt like fine, warm satin.

Her hand came up to touch his face and he was lost. Groaning, he went for her upturned mouth, covering it hotly.

She threw herself into the kiss. There was no other way to describe it. Even as he plundered that lush, bourbon-ripe mouth, she plundered right back, giving as good as she got. And all the while, her hands slid through his hair, shaping his skull, pulling him closer.

He lifted his own hands to her hair, finding and releasing the clasp that held it. Then her hair was free, sliding around her shoulders like fragrant silk. He fisted his hands in it and pulled his own head back far enough to break the kiss. She mewled a protest at the loss of contact, but he held her there with a gentle tension on her hair, nipping at her lower lip, grazing her throat, her ear, the corner of her lip. Lord, it was good. He wanted to hold her that way for hours, days, weeks, torturing himself and her with almost-kisses and nibbles, but she was too far gone for that. Using considerable force, she pulled his head down for another hot, open-mouthed kiss.

Any thought of slow, prolonged, torturous kisses was instantly obliterated. He dropped his hands to her breasts, kneading them beneath the slippery material of her halter dress. One tug, he knew, and the whole thing would come off.

Not yet. Slow down. Savor this.

He tried to pull back to look at her, wanting to see the thrust of her nipples through the fine material, but she held him fast. She was like a freight train that wouldn't be slowed. Sweet heaven, she was ravenous. Starved. Wild.

Finally, an alarm bell went off in his head.

Oh Jesus oh Jesus oh Jesus oh Jesus.

He had to stop.

⁂

"Stop."

God, what now? Couldn't he see they needed to do this *right now*, this very moment, while her blood was singing? To prolong it was to risk dousing this sweet fire before it could consume her, and she just might die if that happened. With renewed fervor, she pressed closer, abrading her breasts against him.

He put her away again. "Suzannah, we have to stop."

"No, we can't. Not now."

"Suz, sweetheart, we have to ... oh, Jesus."

She smiled wolfishly at the way his voice broke as her right hand found and cradled the hardness beneath the fly of his jeans. "It doesn't feel like you want to stop."

"I didn't say I wanted to," he gritted. His hands closed around her upper arms, and this time, he succeeded in putting her away. "Dammit, Suzannah, I'm trying to protect you, here."

Protection. She hadn't even thought of that. Could they be derailed for lack of a prophylactic? "Are you saying you don't have a single condom in this huge two-story house?"

"It's not that."

Then what? Was he having second thoughts because of her job? His job? Her blood cooled as another thought occurred to her — could he have sensed her deficiencies already?

Noooo! She was losing it, this sweet, wild wanting. But his breathing was as ragged as hers, his chest was rising and falling like he'd run the hundred-meter dash. Maybe it could still be salvaged.

"Then what is it?"

"The way you're feeling right now, it isn't real."

She struggled to process his words. "Excuse me?"

"I mean, it *is* real. Of course it's real. You're feeling it, right? But it's just a post-adrenaline thing."

"Post-adrenaline thing." She parroted his words.

"Yeah, you know, from the fire. The shock of seeing all those emergency vehicles in your driveway, the danger, the fear. It all triggers an adrenaline dump, the old flight-or-fight response. Except you responded to the crisis with your brain, not your muscles, which leaves your body screaming for release."

Her face felt numb. Numb and tingly all at once. She took a step back, and he released his grip on her arms. "I don't believe this."

"I strong-armed you into coming over here, for your own safety — which I still believe was the right thing to do. And then I spouted off like a sixth-grader with a crush on the prettiest girl in the class — which is also pretty much the case. But dammit, Suzannah, I can't now take advantage of you."

Every breath she drew now seemed to burn her lungs. "Do I look like I feel taken advantage of?"

"Suzannah —"

"And you've never indulged in a bout of sex in the wake of one of these adrenaline rushes?"

"We're not talking about me."

"I'll take that as a yes." The flame was well and truly doused now. It was sheer anger that made her pursue this. "So, did you feel taken advantage of in the wake of those encounters?"

"Suzannah —"

He spoke her name like a warning, but she paid it no heed. "Answer me. Did you feel victimized?"

"Of course not," he growled. "I used those women, okay? And they used me. Mutual using. But that's different."

"How?"

"Someone's threatening you. You're frightened. I'm supposed to be protecting you, not exploiting the situation."

"Bullshit."

His jaw dropped.

"I'm not your charge, John. As far as your employer is concerned, I'm your *girlfriend*. You have no special fiduciary duty. Investigating this case is someone else's job."

"I realize that, but —"

"You wanted to call a halt just now, that's fine. But don't hide behind professional ethics at this juncture."

His face turned thunderous. "What are you talking about?"

"I want to know the real reason you stopped."

He turned away, shoving a hand through his hair. "I told you, the adrenaline ... sometimes you don't make the best decisions. I didn't want you to wake up regretting this one."

"I would think that would fall squarely in the category of *not your problem*. And please don't say you expect me to believe you have objections to — how did you put it? — mutual using."

He whirled back to face her, his eyes glinting dangerously. "What if I do? Huh? What if I object to being your adrenaline tumble? What if I wanted something more? What if I'd rather you didn't look at me like something to be swept under the carpet come morning?"

❧

Quigg heard the echo of his words reverberate in his head. Had he really said that? Suzannah was staring back at him, blue eyes rounded, her reddened, kiss-swollen mouth finally at a loss for words. Just as the silence began to grow intolerable, Bandy scratched at the door.

Stifling a curse, he strode to the door and let the dog out of his kitchen prison. The mutt shot over to Suzannah. She bent to lay hands on him, though it was debatable whether her intent was to demonstrate affection or merely to protect herself.

"Just tell him when it's enough and he'll leave you be, if you use a firm tone."

She glanced up at him, and said, deadpan, "Yes, I see you've mastered that particular command."

He felt a flush climb his neck and lifted a hand to rub it.

"It's okay." She gave the dog a last pat and a firm word, and stood, though she kept a wary eye on him until he wandered over to a throw rug and flopped down. "I guess I kind of jumped on you, there." She turned to look him square in the eye. "You had every right to call me off. It was the smart thing to do."

"Yeah? Then how come I feel like such a dumb ass?"

Her lips curved in what looked like a genuine, if somewhat tight smile. "It's just that I haven't … ." Her voice trailed off and she shrugged. "I don't know. It felt nice. I guess I wanted to hang onto it."

Her words were casual, easy, yet he was left feeling like he'd robbed her of something precious. Suddenly, he had the disconcerting conviction that he was letting some important detail elude him. "Am I missing something here?"

For a second, he thought he saw indecision darken those lovely eyes.

"Suzannah?"

"No." Her lifted her chin, and her eyes were clear as a summer sky again. "You didn't miss a thing, Detective. Now, where am I sleeping?"

He considered challenging her, then discarded the idea. Patience, he was beginning to think, would get him further with Suzannah Phelps than this butting of heads. And patience was his long suit. Or at least it had been until he'd come up against a certain hard-headed defense lawyer. It would be again.

"Spare bedroom," he said at last, in answer to her question. Picking up her bag which she'd left beside the couch, he nodded toward the stairs. "Come on. I'll show you."

He led the way, and Bandy scrambled up behind them, making more noise than a herd of buffalo. "Bathroom," he pointed out as they passed it. Reaching the spare bedroom directly across the hall from his, he pushed the door open and motioned for Suzannah to precede him. He heard her draw in a breath.

"It's lovely."

Quigg put her bag down and regarded the interior with all its wicker and floral fabric and fussy cushions. "I'd like it noted that I had no hand in this. It's my late Aunt Charlotte's handiwork. The only rooms I bothered with are the master bedroom and the TV room, mainly because they're the only rooms I use."

She smiled. "Thank you. I'll be quite comfortable."

Bandy padded in, giving the empty wastebasket a sniff, no doubt in the wistful hope it contained something edible.

"Towels in the linen closet outside the bathroom. Anything else you need, just give me a shout. My bedroom is across the hall." He gestured with a nod of his head.

"Thanks. I'm sure I'll have no trouble."

Get moving, man. You've been dismissed. A flash of what could have been if he hadn't called a halt downstairs ripped through his mind. Suzannah on his bed, under him, as wild and ravenous for him as he was for her.

"I'll leave you, then." He backed out of the bedroom, nearly stumbling over his own feet. "C'mere, Bandy."

Bandy turned languid eyes on him, then promptly leapt up onto Suzannah's bed. Well, scrabbled up might be a better description.

The combined challenges of height, girth and arthritis had left his leaping days behind him. He called the dog again, but it played deaf, circling a couple of times and settling at the foot of the bed.

"Stupid mutt," he muttered, starting back into the room to remove him by the collar.

"It's okay, he can stay," she said.

Quigg held up. "You sure? He snores."

"I'd appreciate the company."

Damn, damn, damn. Don't think about the company she could be keeping.

"Okay." He backed out of the room. "Goodnight, then."

"Goodnight."

He was halfway to the head of the stairs with a drink of that bourbon on his mind when she called his name. He turned back. "Yes?"

"It wasn't about the adrenaline."

The words were still ricocheting around inside his head as, smiling, she closed the bedroom door softly.

Chapter 7

THE NEXT DAY WAS a busy one for Suzannah.

She'd woken at six to a persistent pawing of her leg through the blankets. Bandy. He obviously needed food or water, or maybe to take a whiz. While she was debating what to do, John had stuck his head in the door. At the sight of his leash, her devoted companion of the previous night leapt off the bed and trotted after his master.

In John's absence, she hurried to the bathroom, completing her toilette before he returned with a much happier looking Bandy. She'd taken the risk of putting coffee on herself — did he like it industrial strength or merely strong? — and they danced around each other in the kitchen. John fed the dog; Suzannah edged past him in the narrow kitchen to get to her wheat toast, which had popped. Around and around they circled, the awareness between them as palpable as a third person. Eventually, he'd driven her to work, leaving her with firm instructions not to go home alone. If she needed to go back to the house before end-of-shift, he'd arrange to be there.

She'd since called her insurance company, arranged a substitute car, and attended court to make an election for one of her clients. She closed two real estate transactions (as her partner Vince so often said, you gotta make up that Legal Aid and pro bono stuff somewhere), and called her mother, who'd asked if she were still seeing that sartorially-challenged policeman.

Now, after capping her day with the news that the Crown intended to appeal a recent acquittal she'd earned for a client, she was more than ready to go home.

On that thought, Vince stuck his head into her office. "Quigg's here. Says you're traveling together tonight."

Quigg? *Quigg?* Since when had her partner and John Quigley become nickname pals? "Thanks."

"No problem. Oh, and here." He stepped forward and dropped several files on her desk.

"What's this?"

"DeBoeuf needs to reorganize, incorporate another limited company or two, shuffle some stuff around. I need you to read these files so we can put our heads together over the best course of action."

Gilles DeBoeuf. A charming rogue, and easily the firm's biggest client. Vince had remodeled his kitchen on the last fee he'd collected from the handsome Frenchman for securing a corridor authority for his small trucking company. She picked up the files. "What's our time line?"

Vince grimaced. "Yesterday."

"Yikes." She thumbed through the files. Four of them. "Mind if I take these home? I'm gonna have to burn the midnight oil on these, and Quigg," — she let the name rest there for an extra beat — "hates to see me work alone here after dark."

"Can't say I blame him under the circumstances. Which reminds me, why didn't you tell me what was going on? I mean, I can't believe you didn't say anything."

"Hey, old man, you've got enough to worry about, what with the twins coming and Marly having such a hard time of it."

Vince, whose forty-two year old wife was into the twentieth week of a tricky pregnancy, went for the bait beautifully, launching into a description of Marly's latest tests. Suzannah half expected him to produce a wallet-sized version of the ultrasound images. She was stuffing the files into her briefcase by the time he wound down.

"So," he said, gesturing to her briefcase, "you okay with this? I know Gilles isn't your favorite guy."

"He's an amoral pig."

Vince blanched and she laughed.

"Relax, Vince. It doesn't matter what I think of Gilles DeBoeuf. You're the one who has to deal with him, not me. I just do the grunt work behind the scenes."

"That's my girl." There was no disguising the relief in his voice. "Now, go put your detective out of his misery."

"Misery?"

"I believe Candace was quizzing him about the size of his weapon when I left them."

⚜

John leapt off the leather-covered couch the moment she pushed through the big oak door and into the reception area. Suzannah suppressed a smile at the sight of him. His tie hung askew, and his suit, which she knew for a fact had looked almost passable this morning, was impossibly rumpled. What on earth had he been doing? She lifted an eyebrow. "Rough day?"

His brows drew together. "What do you mean?"

"It looks like you been wrestling alligators."

Following the sweep of her gaze, he looked down at himself, then back up. "I resent that remark. I'll have you know I've been pushing paper all day."

Her smile broadened at his offended tone. "Sorry."

"So, you ready to go?"

"I have my own car, you know. A temporary replacement courtesy of the insurance company."

"Saw it. Thought I'd follow you."

He did, did he? "I don't need an escort every time I leave the building, John."

"Agreed," he said easily. "You can go lots of places without an escort. You can go to court. You can go to lunch. You can go to the Registry Office. In fact, you can go most anywhere there's lots of people around. But you can't go home."

At her station, the receptionist tapped away at her keyboard without missing a stroke, but Suzannah knew the younger woman wasn't missing a word.

"Candace, could you excuse us a moment?"

"Of course. No problem." The tapping stopped, and Candace slipped out of the reception area, letting the heavy door fall closed behind her.

Suzannah swung her gaze back to John, but before she could say anything, he went on the offensive.

"Don't even start with me," he warned. "I told you this morning it's not safe for you to go home alone."

A tendril of hair had escaped her neat French twist, and she pushed it behind her ear with an impatient hand. "Dammit. I hate that I'm scared to stay alone in my own house."

"We'll find the creep. In the meantime, you can stay with me."

Stay with me.

The prospect sounded frighteningly attractive, on too many levels.

"No."

His eyebrows rose, making his forehead wrinkle in a way that was becoming familiar.

"No?"

"Bad enough I let him drive me out last night," she said. "Bad enough that I feel constrained as to where I can go and what I can do. I will not be driven out of my house."

He didn't miss a beat. "Then we'll move in with you."

Her pulse jolted. John, living in her house?

Suddenly, she remembered the scene she'd been trying to banish all day, the memory of the raw yearning that had blazed from his eyes last night just before she'd closed her bedroom door on him. Her parting comment had been meant to make him suffer, but it had backfired on her. She was the one who'd tossed all night, burning with curiosity and something more.

Dear God, it would be the height of insanity to let him move in. Which meant that she must be losing her marbles. Suicidal as it might be, she wanted the danger of being alone with him. Then her addled mind finally registered his use of the plural. "What do you mean, we?"

"Me and Bandy. Unless you want me to kennel the mutt."

A week ago, she might have missed the flicker of shadow in his eyes, the subtle change in his voice. He didn't want to subject the neuroses-ridden old dog to the stress of a kennel situation, but he would if he had to.

"God, no, don't do that."

"Good. 'Cuz he's in the car. It would have broken his heart if I'd dropped him off at the doggie hotel. Shades of the dog pound and all that."

Her jaw dropped. "He's here? Right now?"

"Yup."

"Dog dish, kibble and all?"

"He likes to be prepared."

"What about Bandy's master? Are you all packed for a sleep-over, too?"

He rolled his shoulders, tugged at his already loose tie as though it were strangling him. "I like to be prepared, too."

She shook her head in disbelief. "Am I really that predictable?"

A shrug. "I figured it wouldn't sit well with you, being driven out of your house like that. And there's no way I'm gonna let you stay alone."

Let her stay alone? As usual, his choice of wording could use some work, but she didn't pursue it. This was old ground, and well covered. No point arguing she didn't need his protection, especially when it was looking more and more as though she did. She searched his face, but it held no clue as to how he felt about her decision. "Do you think I'm being stubborn, wanting to go home? Stupid?"

"I'd feel more comfortable with you at my house, no question," he said, lifting a hand to rub the back of his neck. "But at the same time, it might not be a bad idea to show him you're not intimidated. As long as you're smart about it. And bloody careful. That means you don't go there without me. That means we keep Bandy around; he's actually a helluva watchdog. Barks up a storm at the slightest noise. Looks pretty scary, too, if you don't know better."

The same strand of hair fell down again, and Suzannah tucked it back behind her ear. "What are the chances that plan of action — your moving in with me — will just make him escalate his campaign?"

"Pretty high, I expect."

Her eyes widened. "That's what you want him to do, isn't it? Take more chances so your guys can catch him."

"You want it to be over, don't you? You want your old life back?"

Her old life. Life without fear.

Life without a bossy, interfering cop underfoot every way she turned.

He was watching her, she realized, waiting for a response. "Of course I want my life back."

"Then we need him to mess up. And he's more likely to do that if he's a little pissed."

"And moving a man in should do the trick?"

"Moving your lover in," he corrected. "And yeah, I think that'll do the trick, especially if you thumb your nose at him by doing it under your own roof, the place where he threatened you in the strongest terms."

A shiver skittered up her spine, and it had nothing to do with the admittedly aggressive air conditioning in the empty waiting room. She licked lips gone dry. "If this does draw him out, are we equipped for it?"

The strand of hair fell forward onto her face again, and this time it was his fingers that tucked it back in place. She shivered again.

"You want to change your mind?" he asked, his voice pitched low, quiet. "We can stay at my place if you like, lay low. Or you can take a few weeks' vacation and get right out of town, leave the boys to work on it."

"No!" Then, less sharply: "No. I want it over. I don't want to think about it anymore when I cross a busy street. I don't want to jump when I hear some guy gun his engine, or when some old clunker backfires. I don't want to cast backward glances when I'm walking down a deserted corridor and hear footsteps behind me."

"Good girl."

She felt his hand on her arm, warm and approving.

"And to answer your question," he continued, dropping his hand, "I think we're well prepared when this guys crawls out from whatever rock he's hiding under. With your new security system and the beefed-up exterior lighting, you're in a much better position than you were before. And I'll have my radio, not to mention my service weapon."

A gun. In her house. Oddly, the idea wasn't as disturbing as she thought it should be. So much for her pacifist principles. She pushed the thought away. "You're forgetting our biggest asset in that laundry list of security measures."

"Yeah?"

"Bandy."

"Right." He laughed, a throaty chuckle that made her pulse skip a little faster. "Speaking of which, we'd better get going if I want to have any upholstery left."

⁂

An hour and a half later, replete with the pasta Suzannah had prepared, Quigg drained the last of the single glass of wine he would permit himself.

She lifted the bottle. "Refill?"

"No, thanks."

"Are you sure? It's good for the blood chemistry, you know. A red-meat eater like you should probably have a couple of glasses a day just to keep those platelets from congealing. It may even help to ward off cancer."

The benefits of red wine consumption? That's what she wanted to talk about? He was a master himself at avoiding discussions that involved touchy-feely stuff, but this woman took the cake. There were some things you just didn't leave laying out there. Like her bald statement last night that had left him climbing the walls.

"No, thanks," he said. "One's my limit."

She shrugged and topped up her own half-empty glass and put the bottle back down on its pewter coaster. Quigg watched her raise the glass to take a sip, then lift a napkin to blot her damp lips.

"So, what do your tastes run to in television?"

He lifted his gaze from her mouth. "Huh?"

"Vince has got a rush job that's going to tie up my nights for the next while, which means the TV will be all yours, but I only have basic cable. I was just wondering if you'd be able to find something to watch."

He pushed back his chair. "I don't believe this. You're really not going to say anything about it."

"It?" She lifted her chin defiantly, blue eyes glittering. "And what would 'it' be?"

For a wild second, he was tempted to take the glass form her hand, drag her into his arms and show her, graphically and satisfyingly, exactly what 'it' was.

Patience, Quigg, buddy. That's supposed to be the new watchword. And you've already blown it. Don't get her back up any further.

He forced himself to relax, keep his tone low key. "Last night. If I'm going to be staying here, don't you think we should talk about it?"

"Oh, that." She lowered her lashes. "I owe you an apology for that. I guess I wanted to make you suffer a little bit. You know, for turning me down."

"It worked," he said wryly. "But I was already pretty clear on what that was about. What confused me was the other stuff."

She shot him a look, and there was no mistaking the flare of panic in her eyes, though she controlled it quickly.

"Other stuff?"

"Just things you said."

"Like what?"

The words came out casually enough, but he saw her swallow.

He leaned forward, snaring her gaze. "Make no mistake about it, Suzannah — I called a halt because I didn't want us to end up in bed for the wrong reason, not because I didn't want us to end up in bed." Her jaw went slack, but he pressed on. "I still want that, but only if you want it, too. Not out of fear. Not because you had one drink too many. And please God, not as a sort of coin for bodyguard services rendered."

Her eyes blazed fiercely. "I already told you it wasn't about that."

His pulse took a crazy leap. "Good. I didn't think so, but I had to be sure. Which brings me to the next point."

"There's more?"

"You're a beautiful woman, Suzannah. Classy, smart, sexy, sophisticated. Way out of my league. I know that. But for a minute there, when I put the brakes on, it didn't feel like that. It felt like I was depriving you of something you were really stretching for."

She muttered something that sounded like, "Oh, God."

His face burned. "Stupid, I know. I can't give you anything you can't get anywhere, anytime, with a crook of your little finger. But I just can't shake the —"

"Okay, Detective." Her voice broke into his, and suddenly she was on her feet, facing him aggressively. "I'm only going to say this once, so you'd better listen up."

His instinct was to stand, too, but he squelched it. Patience. Going toe to toe with her would accomplish nothing. Instead, he slouched back in his chair. "I'm listening."

"I don't like sex."

He blinked. "Huh?"

"I don't like it. It's ridiculous, awkward, and ultimately unfulfilling. It's my fault, I know. I'm just no good at it."

He heard the words, his brain processed them, but they didn't make sense. That wasn't the woman he'd held in his arms last night. "But —"

She held up a hand to stop him. "I know what I'm talking about, John. It's not like I tried it once and decided okay, I guess sex isn't for me. I do feel stirrings from time to time. I *am* human. And when it seemed like the right thing to do, the natural progression in a relationship, I tried it." She dropped her eyes, twisting the delicate stem of the now-empty wine glass in her hand. "It never got any better."

"I don't believe that for a minute," he said. "The way you kissed me —"

"That's why I was so upset last night. For a few minutes, it felt like I could ... like I might want to ... ."

Her voice trailed off and the room was silent for a moment. When he spoke, his voice was a disbelieving croak. "And you don't think you can get that back? Is that the trouble?"

She colored. "You don't understand."

"No, sweetheart, *you* don't understand." He stood and held a hand out to her. "Come here."

She took a step back. "That was last night. I've changed my mind. I don't want to go to bed with you anymore."

God, she was beautiful. And so earnest. She really believed she was frigid. "Who said anything about bed?" he asked, advancing a step closer.

"Have sex, then." Her voice was tight as she retreated another step.

"Who said anything about sex?" Something leapt in her eyes, and he didn't think it was fear, though she did take another step backward. He smiled. "Don't you want to know if you can recapture the feeling?"

The yearning and fear that chased across her face made his heart squeeze. This time when he reached for her hand, she didn't retreat, possibly because she'd backed herself up against the antique buffet and had nowhere to go.

"Come on, Suzannah, trust me this once," he said. "No pressure, no expectation, just some good old-fashioned necking on the couch." He stroked the inside of her wrist, where her pulse pounded madly, though with fear or excitement, he couldn't say. But she certainly wasn't indifferent.

She chewed the inside of her lip. "I don't know."

"What have you got to lose? If it doesn't work for you, you can tell me to take my hands off you. How's that?"

He was gratified to see her breath come faster, but still she held out.

"I don't get it. What's in it for you?"

He laughed. "Baby, if you still have to ask that when we're done, you can give me a failing grade."

"Won't it be ... frustrating?"

"That's a small price, and one I'll happily pay." Especially since he'd been fantasizing about kissing that prim mouth into a flushed, swollen bloom since the first moment he'd laid eyes on her in the courtroom two years ago.

Still she hesitated.

"I won't let things get out of hand, if that's what you're worried about." Even as he offered the assurance, he prayed for the strength and patience he was going to need to call upon to keep his promise.

"I know."

With those two words and the trust implicit in them, any doubts about his self-control fell away. He'd damned well die of sexual frustration before he betrayed that trust.

He stroked his thumb along the inside of her wrist again, felt the heat of her blood, the strength of her pulse. "So, what do you say?"

"Okay," she said, her voice high and thin. He felt her fingers flex around his. "Okay, let's do it."

Omigod, what had she agreed to?

She'd gone one way to arm the alarm and John had gone the other way to secure Bandy. She'd protested that measure initially, but conceded it was preferable to having their calves clawed to ribbons or their ankles bit the moment they touched.

She was having second and third thoughts when he came to find her a minute later. The misgivings she might have voiced were silenced when he pulled her into his arms and covered her mouth. No thrusting tongue, no full on assault, nothing to make her draw back. Just a long, slow brushing and sliding of lips. The sweetness of it pierced her. At last, he lifted his head.

"Your living room still equipped with that nice soft couch I slept on?" he asked, his breath fanning her face.

"Yes."

He nipped at her lower lip. "And the living room's still through that door?"

She smiled against his lips. "Yes."

With a quick, economical movement, he scooped her into his arms and started toward the aforesaid sofa. Despite herself, she felt her muscles tighten at being swept off her feet. He must have felt it, too.

"Want me to put you down?"

Trust me, he'd said. "Not until you get to that sofa."

His laugh was a rumble she felt go straight to her center.

Seconds later, she found herself sitting on the couch. Somehow, she'd expected him to plunk her down and come down on top of her, crushing her against the cushions, or at least to settle with her on his lap where he could ravish her. Instead, he deposited her on the cushions and sat down beside her, twisting to face her.

"Nervous?" he asked.

"No."

Soft laughter.

"Okay, maybe a little."

Then his hand was on her hair, stroking it lightly. "Can we take this down?"

She lifted both hands to find the clasp, releasing it. Her hair spilled down and John released his breath on a sigh.

"God, I love your hair." He threaded a hand into it, lifting it from her scalp and combing his fingers through to the end. "Gorgeous."

Desire, sweet and potent, stirred in her belly. "Kiss me again."

More laughter. "So impatient." He lifted a strand of her hair to his nose, inhaled, sighed. "There's no destination, no finish line. Only pleasure. Just relax and enjoy."

"I don't know if I can." Lord, was that her voice?

"Try closing your eyes. Stop thinking and just feel," he suggested. "Let me worry about the rest."

She obeyed. The cushions shifted, and she felt his lips, dry and cool, on her forehead. His hand burrowed deeper into her hair to cradle her head. Soft as a whisper, his lips roamed her face, her eyelids, her eyelashes. Somehow, that barely-there contact set up a trembling deep inside. When his mouth finally found hers after long moments, it was only to nuzzle, skim, tease, his tongue a mere suggestion against the corner of her lip. Why, oh why, couldn't all men kiss like this instead of trying to stick their tongues down your throat?

Eyes tightly closed, she savored every fleeting touch, every graze and retreat of his now moist lips. Then, between one heartbeat and the next, something unprecedented happened. She found herself longing to deepen the kiss, to draw his tongue into her mouth, to let her tongue tangle with his. Incredibly, he seemed oblivious of the need growing in her. With studious care, he kept up the torture until finally she clasped his head and pulled him down to meet her lips, opening her mouth in wet, mute supplication.

She felt a shudder pass through him. Then he leaned into her, pressing her back against the cushions, answering her demand with a fierce one of his own.

If the thrust of his tongue weren't enough to drive the last remnants of reason from her mind, the slide of his hands on her body through her silk blouse was. Hard, warm, thrilling, they skimmed her back, her sides, the outside of her breasts. Nothing could have stopped the whimper that rose to her lips.

A shift of the cushions, a cool layer of air against her skin. He was pulling away! She tried to pull him back down, but he resisted the pressure of her looped arms around his neck. She moaned again, this time at the loss.

"Hush," he said, drawing back even further. "I just want to look a minute."

Her eyes, which she'd kept tightly closed to concentrate on the sensations he was producing in her, sprang open. The sight of his face, skin stretched tight over his cheekbones, eyes burning, made her pulse take another jagged leap. Then she dropped her gaze to her breasts, the object of his heated gaze. Against the fine material of her blouse, beneath the seamless cups of her sleek bra, her nipples jutted in unabashed arousal.

"So beautiful."

Mesmerized, she watched the hand at her waist travel upward, pushing the silk over her sensitized skin, across her midriff, up, up .... Then he lifted his hand off her, bringing it back to rest high on her chest, above her breasts this time, fingers tracing the neckline of her blouse.

"Please." The sound of her own voice, the need in it, shocked her. Excited her.

He smiled. "Please what?"

She lifted her hand to his, drawing it down. When his fingers closed around her right breast, she cried out, closing her eyes.

His fingers tightened on the soft flesh. "You like that, baby?"

"Yes."

"Open your eyes."

Powerless to resist his command, she lifted her lids to meet his gaze. Impossibly dark, his eyes glittered with sex and promise and something else. Safety. She was safe here.

"Look how beautiful you are." He drew his thumb across her hardened nipple, dragging a gasp from her. Then his hand was moving again, closing on her other breast, covering the whole of it easily with his palm. Her eyes drifted shut again, the better to savor the feel of him there, only to fly open again when she felt his fingers at the buttons of her blouse.

"I just want to look at you."

Suddenly, she wanted nothing more than his hot gaze on her breasts. Another unprecedented development. By now, her muscles were usually tightening up, an involuntary girding against intimacies to come. But she hadn't lost her faculties entirely. She brought her hand up to still his. "Is this a good idea?"

"Best one I've had all day."

She smiled, and he bent to kiss her again. When he lifted his head a moment later, her senses were spinning.

"What do you say?" The backs of his fingers brushed her breasts through the fabric of her shirt. "We'll stick to your mama's rules all the way."

"Mama's rules."

"Yeah, petting rules. Nothing below the belt, just like back in high school." His fingers slipped to the next silk-covered button. "What trouble can we get into, above the waist?"

"Petting rules?" She'd stopped trying to check his progress. "That's a conversation I never had with my mother."

His hand paused. "I thought every girl had that talk. Every girl I ever encountered, anyway."

"I wasn't every girl," she reminded him. "I was the Chief Justice's daughter. I didn't go parking with boys."

His eyes widened. "Never?"

"Never."

He worked the next button loose. "Did you want to?"

She thought about the tangle of emotions she'd been in high school. She thought about Burke Wheeler, leather-jacketed, cigarette-smoking bad ass. She remembered the excitement in the pit of her stomach when she thought he was going to ask her out, the disappointment when he'd walked right past her to loop an arm around her more buxom friend's neck.

"What I wanted or didn't want was immaterial. Nobody was going to risk my father's wrath by asking me out."

He unbuttoned the last button and pushed her blouse open. When he spread his hand on her flat belly, she drew her breath in sharply. He smiled, then bent to kiss the tops of her breasts above her bra.

"What do these rules say about the removal of bras?"

She felt his smile against her skin.

"That kinda depended on the dexterity of the guy," he said.

She sucked her breath in again as he smoothed his hand around and up her back. "And were you particularly dexterous?"

His reply was to pop the clasp on her bra.

"Oh!"

"Ummmm." He bent to push her bra out of the way to catch her hardened nipple in his mouth.

Susannah's world careened out of control. There was nothing left but the hot, wet tug of his mouth on her breast and the pulse of need it set off in her belly. By the time he'd ministered to both breasts, she was all but mindless with wanting him. Mindless enough that she wriggled into a semi-prone position, pulling him down with her. For a second, she gloried in his weight pinning her to the cushions and the evidence of his arousal against her lower limbs.

Then he pulled back. She groaned a protest, but he scooped her up into his lap and pressed her head close to his thundering heart. Over the next minutes, with soothing words and calming hands, he gradually brought her back down again.

❧

Quigg inhaled, breathing the subtle scent of her hair. He couldn't quite identify it, but it smelled great. Something exotic, like grape seed extract or green tea. Some organic thing or other. He might not know what it was, but he doubted he'd ever forget it. It was imprinted indelibly on his brain.

As was the taste of her, red wine and woman and passion.

Passion. God, did she really think she lacked it?

She lifted her head. "Thank you."

He'd restored the bra over her breasts, but it was still unfastened, her shirt still hanging open. Yet it wasn't her delectable body that drew his gaze. He was more interested in what was written on her face.

Gratitude. Peace. And her body. Even now, it felt relaxed and boneless, as though she'd melted against him. It made the ache in his groin seem a small price to pay.

"My pleasure. Or couldn't you tell?"

"I could tell. I guess that means you get a passing grade." She laid her head back down on his shoulder and his arms came around her easily, as though they'd done this a hundred times. How'd it come to feel so natural, so fast? The thought gave him a little bit of a jolt. Time to move.

"The History Channel."

She pulled back. "Huh?"

"You asked me what my TV tastes ran to. I like the History Channel. And police dramas. And baseball. Which means I should be able to keep myself occupied while you work."

"You're going to dump me off your lap to watch reruns of *NYPD Blue*?"

She said it jokingly, but he saw the ghost of a shadow in her eyes. Could she really not know how badly he burned for her?

"Baby, I'm not doing it because I want to. I'm gonna do it because I said I would. And to score points for my super-human restraint."

She smiled. "Well, okay, then. When you put it like that."

So saying, she pushed away from his chest, levering herself to her feet. Suddenly, his arms felt empty, bereft. Instead of releasing her hand, he hauled her back down again. Surprised, she fell onto him, into him. Oh, Lord, it was sweet, to catch the laughter on her lips, feel her sigh her pleasure against his mouth. Minutes later, heart pounding just as hard as before, he set her away again.

"Damn, woman, I've gone and missed the first fifteen minutes of my show. Sipowicz'll have it all wrapped up without me."

She laughed, and this time there were no shadows in those baby blues. They glowed with a new light as she untangled herself and stood up. Her clothing was all askew, her mouth as kiss-swollen as he'd pictured it in his hottest fantasies, but somehow she managed to retain that proper, regal dignity that was so much a part of her. A treacherous tenderness unfurled in the vicinity of his heart.

"Suzannah?"

She glanced up from fixing her blouse.

"This was just a taste. There's lots more where that came from."

She blushed and it was all he could do not to haul her down again. Fortunately, he knew his own limits. If she landed on the couch with him again, she wouldn't get up for a long while.

"Here." She picked something up and flipped it at him. His hand shot out in time to keep the object from hitting him in the chest. The remote control for the television. "Don't keep Andy waiting. Lord knows he probably can't solve the case without your armchair advice." With that, she collected her briefcase from the table in the hall and disappeared.

Grinning, he pointed the remote at the TV, clicked the power button and found *NYPD Blue*. Did she have him pegged or what? Shifting to adjust his still-aching groin, he sprawled back to enjoy the show.

Seconds later, he heard the clicking of toenails on hardwood floor. Bandy. Poor bugger. He'd forgotten him. Suzannah must have liberated him from the kitchen. Automatically, he lifted his hands to shield himself as the dog sprang up onto the couch, but the mutt still managed to land one foot — and a good quarter of his weight — dangerously close to Quigg's groin.

Quigg swore. "Miserable mongrel. I don't know why I keep you around." Bandy gazed at him lovingly. Quigg cursed again, but settled a hand on the dog's ruff, stroking the silky coat as he turned his attention back to the television.

Chapter 8

SUZANNAH WAS DEEP INTO case law when her phone rang. Absently, she picked the receiver up. "Suzannah Phelps."

"Hey."

John. "Hey, yourself."

"You taping this conversation?"

She leaned back in her chair. "No. It's not set up yet."

A sigh. "You promised."

He'd wanted her to let the cops put a tap on it, but as a criminal defense attorney, she'd had to draw the line at that. She'd agreed to a tap on her line at home, reasoning that if she got a call from an incarcerated client, she could tell them to clam up until she got there to discuss the situation in person. She could hardly do that here at the office. As a compromise, she'd agreed to run her line through the dictating equipment so she could record a conversation at the flip of a switch.

She rolled her shoulders to ease the tension that had built up there from too many hours at the same task. "The tech guy is coming this afternoon to do it."

"Good." A brief pause. "So, I guess this means we can talk dirty."

A little jolt of excitement spiked her pulse. "I guess we could if we were so inclined."

"What are you wearing?"

That was his idea of talking dirty? "Some detective you are. You saw what I was wearing when we left the house."

"Yeah, but I didn't see what you were wearing under it."

Just like that, she was hot. All he had to do was pitch his voice low and raspy. She didn't think it would even matter what he said, especially if those eyes were on her. She closed her eyes and reproduced that look he gave her, all banked heat and patience. She swiveled her chair toward the window, oblivious of the view. "Maybe I'll give you a little preview at lunch."

"You'd let me look down your blouse?"

"Like it would be the first time that happened."

"Damn the bad luck."

"What?"

"I can't make it for dinner. That's why I'm calling. Trial went into a *voire dire* and I'm stuck here until they get back."

That's right. He'd said he had a jury trial. Local businessman on a decade-old sexual assault charge. She squelched her disappointment. "Sounds like you've got your hands full."

"You know how it is, these hot-shot criminal defense attorneys from Upper Canada. Gotta justify that fat fee somehow."

Frankly, she was inclined to agree with John's assessment, but there was no way she'd tell him so. "You are such a cynic, Detective," she said, careful to keep the smile out of her voice.

He snorted. "Like you're the original Pollyanna."

She didn't try to hide her smile this time. "So that's why you called? To stand me up for lunch?"

"No choice about standing you up, I'm afraid, but I'd like to send a stand-in."

Suzannah tipped her chair forward so fast her elbow connected painfully with the desk. She transferred the telephone to her other hand, grimacing as she shook the pain out of her left arm. "You want to send a stand-in?"

"Yeah. Ray Morgan."

John's sidekick. His image came instantly to mind, as impeccably pressed as John was carelessly rumpled. "That's not necessary."

"Not to look down your blouse or anything. Just to keep you company."

"No."

A pause. "No?"

"I don't need a cop to babysit me over dinner, John."

"Hell, Ray's a friend. He'd be doing it as a friend."

"Your friend is a cop."

"Suzannah . . . ."

"I've gone as far as I care to go by filing a complaint."

"Well, of course you filed a complaint. Any person with two clues to rub together would —"

"Hey, I agree," she overrode him. "And I don't regret it for a minute. But that doesn't mean I'm ready to have the entire force think I'm scared to cross the street for a burger without a police escort."

She heard his sigh loud and clear through the receiver. "Order in, then."

Not so long ago, the command in his tone would have gotten her back up. She knew now that he was motivated by genuine concern, abetted by an overdeveloped sense of protectiveness. She might even have complied to alleviate his anxiety. But today she just couldn't.

"John, I've been hunched over this desk for three hours. I need a stretch, some fresh air and a change of scenery."

"You're walking?"

She rolled her eyes. "The whole block and a half."

"Take somebody with you."

She glanced at her wristwatch. Ten to twelve. In all probability, Vince would have just left and Candace would be just getting back. "Okay," she agreed.

"Got your alarm with you?"

Her gaze automatically went to the small gadget she'd clipped to her purse. Sacrilege to ruin the clean lines of the Prada, but it was better than wearing it around her neck as John had wanted. "Yeah, I've got it," she said. "Any more orders?"

"Yeah. Talk dirty to me."

She laughed. "I wouldn't know how."

"Sure you do. I'd give you a demonstration, but I'm standing at a public pay phone in a crowded hallway. Wouldn't want to draw a crowd."

A crowded hallway in the Justice Building. Her lips curved in a wicked smile. She might not be very good at it, but she might never get another chance like this one. "Well, there is this one fantasy . . . ."

"Yeah? Go on."

He did it again, dropped his voice to that register where it seemed to shiver right through her. "Not a fantasy, really. More of a wish."

"One we can make come true?"

She closed her eyes. "Easily. And you wouldn't even have to move a muscle."

"Sounds ... intriguing. Care to elaborate, counselor?"

"I was thinking it's my turn to get under your shirt this time."

Background voices surged and receded. Then John's voice in the receiver, lower and more gravelly. "I think that could be arranged."

"Good. Because my hands seem to have developed a will of their own."

"Yeah?"

"Mmmm. You see, they've got this bone-deep need to touch warm skin. Your chest, your back, your shoulders." Voices again in the background, this time very close. She pictured him angling himself away from the others.

"Sounds wonderful."

"When these hands are finished with you, Detective, I expect to be able to sculpt a three-dimensional model with my eyes shut."

He swore softly.

"Problem, Detective?"

"Witch. I think you know what my problem is."

She laughed. "You asked for it," she reminded him.

His answering laugh warmed her all the way through. "I guess I did, didn't I?"

"Goodbye, John."

"Wait! Don't hang up. I can't walk away from the phone."

Her grin broadened. "I recommend calling the local radio station. Maybe they'll spin a special request for you."

Fifteen minutes later, as she popped the lid off her taco salad, she was still smiling at the mental image of John staring in disbelief at the dead receiver in his hand. Life was good.

Beneath the table, her cell phone buzzed from inside her purse, its ringer muted. Swiveling in the chair, she groped awkwardly for the bag. It rang twice more before she managed to open the bag and retrieve the slim phone. She turned away from the crowd and flipped the phone open, pressing a hand to one ear to drown out the lunch-hour din.

"Suzannah Phelps."

No reply.

"Hello?"

There were muffled noises in the background, but nothing else; no breathing, no caller carrying on a second conversation.

"Hello? Are you there, caller?" she repeated.

Again, no reply.

Shrugging, she snapped the phone shut and slipped it back in her purse. This time, she parked her bag on the table for quicker access if it rang again, and returned her attention to her meal.

Half way through the salad, she started to feel a little giddy, though not unpleasantly so. All this thinking about John, she supposed. She picked up her diet cola and drained it. There'd be hell to pay tonight for their little phone conversation. The sweetest kind of hell. He'd insist she make reality of the mind-pictures she'd conjured.

Suddenly, in the middle of a busy fast-food family restaurant, at the height of the lunch hour, she was fully aroused. Her face felt flushed, her breasts tingled and her body ached. Tonight was too far away.

What if she were to meet him at the Justice Building? Maybe she could whisk him away when he finished his testimony.

Her breath came hard at the thought. Pushing her tray out of the way, she grabbed her purse and headed for the door. Briefly, the faces around her seemed to swim together. She blinked twice, and everything came back into focus.

Her eagerness to reach John suddenly struck her as funny. She laughed, drawing a few curious looks. God, she'd better shut up or the lunch time crowd would think she was drunk! Carefully, she made her way through the parking lot. Three more steps and she gained the sidewalk, except as she walked, the concrete slabs beneath her feet seemed to undulate, making her stagger.

Good God, she *was* drunk! But how? She hadn't consumed anything even mildly alcoholic.

Finally, fear penetrated her confusion. Going hot and cold at once, she glanced back toward the parking lot. Cars, faces, clothing … everything blurred. She tried to gauge the respective distances to the restaurant and to her office. The restaurant was a little closer, but if someone had doctored her drink or her food, they must have done it back there.

Why hadn't she listened to John?

Then she heard it, brisk, purposeful footsteps approaching from behind. Heart tripping, she lurched into motion again. She had to get to her office. A man's voice called her name. Instead of turning, she broke into a run.

The voice called her name again, much closer, shouting for her to stop in a tone so commanding she almost obeyed. She was so close now, her office building just across the street, but with her pursuer closing in, she'd never be able to cross the busy four lanes. She could hear his breathing now, close behind her and knew she wouldn't even have time to reach one of the commercial businesses on the north side of the street.

This was it. Her only choice was to turn and fight, hope someone came to her rescue.

The alarm! She was carrying a personal alarm. Why hadn't she thought of it sooner? Fingers clumsy, she fumbled for and found the electronic gadget attached to her purse. Seconds later, the air was rent by the high-pitched, intermittent shriek. It was the last sound she heard before she sank to the sun-warmed sidewalk in a dead faint.

⚜

Quigg burst through the doors of the ER. Ignoring the stares from the crowded waiting room, he strode to the triage station. "Suzannah Phelps. Where is she?"

"Are you a relative, sir?"

He flashed tin, saw the nurse's expression change. "She was brought in a couple of hours ago."

Hours ago. He gritted his teeth. No one had told him until after his testimony was out of the way. Couldn't have him rushing off before cross. Intellectually, he understood the decision, but dammit, he didn't have to like it.

A moment later, an orderly led him to one of the many curtained treatment areas fanning out around a busy nurses' station, but he didn't need the direction. He could hear Ray Morgan's voice coming from the last bed from the end. Thanking the orderly, Quigg stepped into the cubicle.

Whatever he'd expected to see, it wasn't a fully dressed, perfectly normal-looking Suzannah slipping her shoes on as though she were ready to walk out the door.

"Suzannah?"

"John!"

She looked like she was going to get up, and he moved into the room to restrain her with a hand on her shoulder. "You okay?" The question came out gruffly.

She lifted a hand to cover his. "I'm fine now, thanks to Detective Morgan."

"Ray," Razor corrected.

"Ray," she amended, glancing in his direction. Then she turned back to face Quigg. "Thanks for sending him."

"Don't thank me too fast." Ray's voice laced with self-disgust. "All I managed to do is nearly chase you into traffic."

Quigg dragged his gaze away from Suzannah's to give Ray a sharp look.

"I was late getting there." Ray grimaced. "They've got Smythe Street dug up for repairs. With the detour, time I got there she'd already started back on foot. I could see she was having trouble putting one foot in front of the other, so I went after her. But by then, she'd figured out she'd been slipped a mickie, and seeing as I was chasing her, she concluded I was the perp and ran."

Quigg blanched. No one had told him the details, only that someone had spiked her drink and she'd been rushed to hospital.

Now it was Suzannah who grimaced. "I finally remembered the personal alarm and triggered it just as Det ... just as Ray caught up to me. Then I passed out." She gave Ray an apologetic smile. "I gather he had to flash his badge for every suspicious merchant and passer-by until a patrol car arrived."

"No problem," Ray assured her. "You did exactly the right thing, triggering that alarm. Right, Quigg?"

"Right." He caught her gaze and held it. "Though not going to lunch alone would have been my first choice."

She groaned. "Please, no lecture, John. I got the message loud and clear."

Maybe. But there'd still be a lecture. Later. "So, what'd the bastard slip you?"

She swallowed, as though to ease a tight throat. "Rohypnol."

Quigg swore, tightening his fingers on her shoulder. Rohypnol. A benzodiazepine, ten times stronger than Valium. *Date-rape drug. Roofies. Rope.* The street names for the strictly illegal drug ripped through his mind. As did the drug's effects — intoxication, decreased resistance, and in high doses, blackout. In extremely high doses, coma and death. At as little as five or ten bucks a pop, it was gaining chic with the high school crowd as a cheap drunk. Not to mention its popularity with a certain segment of the male population who weren't averse to a little sexual assault, provided the victim couldn't dredge up the details afterward for a successful prosecution.

"They did a full tox screen on me," she continued, "but Ray tipped them to look specifically for Rohypnol and GHB."

"Good call," Quigg said. They didn't usually screen for Rohypnol on a standard tox screening.

Ray shrugged. "Instant intoxication. Seemed a good bet."

Quigg forced down the bile rising at the back of his throat. It must have been a pretty massive dose to knock her back so quickly without the extra kick of alcohol. He put an arm around her shoulder and drew her close. She slipped an arm around his waist and hugged him back, pressing her face into his shirt. No doubt she thought the gesture was meant to preserve the fiction of a relationship for Ray's benefit, but Quigg knew better. He did it simply because he couldn't *not* do it. After a few seconds, he drew back.

"Well, you look okay now."

She smiled. "Amazing what a little stomach-pumping will do for a gal."

Of course they'd have pumped her stomach. Standard drill. Guess he'd wanted to spare himself the mental picture. "Any idea as to how he did it?"

"I got a call on my cell phone just as I sat down to eat," she said. "I had to fish around under the table for my purse, then I think I turned away to shield the phone from the noise when I answered it."

She pushed a stray strand of hair behind her ear in a gesture so familiar, it gave him a strange ache in his chest.

"All I can figure is someone must have swapped drinks while I was preoccupied with the phone."

"And the caller's identity?"

She lifted her shoulders in a shrug. "No one on the line."

Quigg flicked his gaze to Ray.

"We're already on it, but I think we're going to find it was placed from the pay phone in the vestibule of the restaurant. The receiver was found to be off the hook."

"Prints?"

"Wiped clean."

"So, what's next?"

"We're canvassing everyone we can find who was there at the time. Maybe someone will remember seeing someone walk away from the payphone, leaving the receiver off the hook."

"Show Suzannah the list of people interviewed," he suggested. "Maybe she'll see a name there that jogs something."

Suzannah inhaled sharply and come to her feet. Quigg reached out to steady her, but she didn't seem to need it.

"You think he was among the interviewees?" She asked. "Your guys might have actually talked to him?"

"Certainly possible," said Ray. "He was definitely in the restaurant to make the call and to switch drinks. But he could just as easily have been waiting outside for you. Or maybe he was inside but left before the troops got there."

"It couldn't hurt to have a look at your client list for the past few years," Quigg added.

"I can't give you my client list. That would —"

"Just the criminal cases," Quigg interrupted. "Especially guys who got sent up despite your defense and who are out now."

"He's right. It's a matter of public record anyway," Ray put in. "We could look it up ourselves, but I expect it would be quicker and easier if you just give us the information yourself."

"Okay," she agreed. "Anything more for me?"

Quigg looked at Ray, who said, "I got a statement, and she's undertaken to give us a list of clients she's represented on criminal charges, with outcomes. I think we're done for now."

Quigg turned to Suzannah. "Anything you can think of we should be pursuing?"

Something flickered in her eyes, and she cast a sideways glance at Ray. "No, nothing."

Damn. There was something, but she wasn't about to say in front of Razor. "Then I guess we're good."

"In that case, do you think we could go home, now?" she said.

"You're cleared to leave already?"

"Yes."

Ray cleared his throat. "Okay then. I'm out of here." He shrugged back into the jacket he'd taken off earlier, straightened his tie. "FYI, you'll see a lot more patrol cars in your neighborhood, Suzannah. Hopefully, you can rest a little easier."

Suzannah looked from Quigg to Ray and back to Quigg again.

"What?" said Ray, picking up on the silent exchange. "What'd I miss?"

"Suzannah's a little concerned it might disadvantage her in the courtroom if she requests anything over and above," he explained for Ray's benefit. Then, for Suzannah's benefit, he assured her there wouldn't be a cop car sitting on her house, just stepped up patrols in the area.

She looked to Ray for confirmation and he held up three fingers. "Scout's honor. No special treatment. We'd do the same for anyone in this situation."

Suzannah picked up her purse. "Okay, let's go."

Ten minutes later, Quigg helped her into the passenger seat of the Taurus. Rounding the car, he climbed in himself, then turned to her. "Okay, what is it?"

Her eyes rounded. "What's what?"

"Don't bat those eyelashes at me, Suzannah. You were withholding something back there. You know it, I know it, and Ray Morgan sure as hell knows it."

"He does?"

Her face paled and Quigg felt like a real bastard.

"You don't do as many interviews as he's done and not pick up when someone is holding back."

"Why didn't he press me?"

Quigg shrugged. "Who knows? Because he knew I knew and figured I'd get it out of you, maybe? Because he knows you had a rough afternoon and he's not as big a bastard as I am?" He keyed the ignition and the Ford's motor jumped to life, but he didn't put it in gear. "I'm sure I'll hear about it tomorrow. In the meantime, don't try to change the subject. What were you hiding back there?" He nodded in the direction of the hospital.

"You don't want to hear this."

He tried to catch her eye, but she'd dipped her head. Did she really think she could say something that would shock him? "Honey, unless it involves necrophilia, I've probably heard it."

She bit her lip. "Remember me asking you about Constable Newman at Ray and Grace's barbecue?"

"*Goddammit.*"

"See?" Her eyes flashed at him. "I told you you wouldn't want to hear this."

He took a deep breath, forcing the sick feeling in the pit of his stomach down. "It's okay. Go on. I'll let you finish."

She trained her gaze directly ahead as she spoke. "I'd left my wine glass unattended for a few minutes, and when I came back to reclaim it, he made a point of telling me I shouldn't do that, that anyone could come along and spike it. That even in little old Fredericton, Rohypnol was not an unknown commodity."

Cripes. "Maybe it was a friendly warning."

"Maybe."

"Did you get a bad vibe off him?"

Her brow creased. "I don't know."

"You don't know? Suzannah, either you did or you didn't."

"Okay, I did." She turned to look him square in the eye. "But it was more like he wanted to jerk me around just a little, score a point or two off the Ice Princess. But now … ." She shrugged, letting her words tail off.

Quigg swore softly. She dropped her gaze to her hands, which were clasped in her lap, but not before he glimpsed something in her eyes. Resignation? Was that it?

Ah, hell. She thought he'd dismiss her concern, take Newman's side automatically.

Which he would have done a week ago. Which he *should* do even now. The realization sent a shock through him.

The unspoken code pretty much demanded his first loyalty had to be to his fellow officers, and for good reason. Cops counted on other cops for effective backup when a situation went sour. The minute you broke with that code was the minute you could stop feeling like that backup would be there for you a hundred percent. How far down this road was he prepared to go?

His gaze shifted to her face, but she seemed to be engrossed in a study of her hands. She'd pinned her hair up in one of those casual dos, exposing the slim, vulnerable line of her nape. He placed a hand over hers and her gaze flew to his face.

"I'll look into it," he heard himself say.

"Thank you."

Two words. A simple thank you. But there was nothing simple about the charge of emotion that rocketed through him as their gazes met, clung.

How far down the road was he prepared to go? Is that what he'd just asked himself? God help him, maybe he'd already passed the point of no return. Dragging his gaze away, he gunned the motor, put the car in gear and reversed out of the parking space.

⁂

The ride back to her place was accomplished in silence. Occasionally, Suzannah stole glances at John. In profile, his face looked dark, hard, remote. But for a few seconds — seconds which had stretched out like eons — she'd seen the stark need in his eyes, as deep and frightening and inescapable as her own.

The time had come.

Her heart took a leaping bound in her chest at the realization. The balance had been slowly shifting over these past weeks, bringing her to this moment. The moment when the need to have this man, to possess and be possessed by him, outweighed the fear.

⚜

Bandy greeted them ecstatically at the door, his stout body waggling with the swishing of his tail. Suzannah bent to bestow an enthusiastic petting before Bandy decided he had to demand it.

"You be okay for a few minutes if I take him out for a spin around the block?"

She straightened to see John standing there with Bandy's leash. He'd ditched his jacket and tie and rolled up the sleeves of his hopelessly creased shirt to reveal strong, tanned forearms. *Patience, Suz.*

"Of course. I've got some calls to make. Vince made me promise to call when I got home."

He bent to clip the lead on Bandy's collar. "Lock up after me, and arm the alarm," he instructed, using that authoritative tone she suspected they must teach in the academy. "I don't want to hear any protests about it being broad daylight, either."

"Don't worry. I may be stubborn, but I'm not stupid. I've just seen what can happen in broad daylight."

A muscle flexed in his jaw. "I won't be twenty minutes."

Suzannah locked up behind him as instructed, then called Vince. He'd been shaken when she'd called him from the hospital to explain why she'd gone AWOL. She'd had to be very forceful to prevent him canceling his afternoon examination for discovery and rushing to the ER. Her assurance that John was with her now and would continue to stay with her until this lunatic was caught seemed to go a long way to calming him down.

Once Vince was settled down, she called her mother. Thankfully, Elena Phelps hadn't heard about her daughter's visit to the

ER, and she wasn't about to hear it from Suzannah. Rather, they talked about the party Elena was planning to host for her closest friend's fifty-fifth birthday.

Hearing John and Bandy return, Suzannah wound up the conversation with her mother. John was carrying a takeout bag from the local sub place.

"Hope you're hungry," he said, handing her the bag.

They sat down and ate their subs at the table under Bandy's wistful gaze. Her stomach was in such a knot that she couldn't manage much more than a quarter of the foot-long sandwich, but she noticed John had no trouble downing his. Afterward, Suzannah cleared away the remains of their meal while John put down food and fresh water for Bandy.

"So, what's on for tonight?" he asked.

Us, I hope. Her pulse took a little jump. "Nothing."

He shot her a look. "Thought you had a rush job for Castillo."

She grimaced. "The clock's still ticking on that one, but I told Vince it'd have to wait. I just couldn't see getting my head into a corporate re-org after the day I've had."

"I can understand that. Why don't you make an early night of it?" He picked up the TV remote from the coffee table and flopped down on her couch. "I'm sure I can find a ball game."

As her heart thundered in her chest, he calmly pointed the remote at the television, which sprang to noisy life. He adjusted the volume downward, flipped to the sports network.

Dammit, this was supposed to be easier. She'd imagined them sinking on the couch together, possibly him sliding an arm around her. Even she could have taken it from there. Instead, he seemed to be doing his damnedest to get her out of the room.

She wet her lips. "I'd rather do what we did last night, but without the stopping part."

The remote control clattered to the floor. Cursing, he leaned over to pick it up, depositing it on the coffee table again. "I don't think that's such a good idea."

She'd been prepared for any number of reactions, but not this one. He'd all but promised her endless kisses, endless sweetness. "Why not?"

"Why not? Suzannah, someone slipped you a colossal dose of Rohypnol just hours ago."

What did that have to do with anything? "Thank you for reminding me, but they emptied my stomach."

"Not before it went to work on you." He picked up the remote again, this time to kill the drone of the TV. "Rohypnol is a powerful intoxicant, a profound disinhibitor. I just don't think it's smart to —"

Understanding came on a wave of anger. "Oh, no, you don't."

"Huh?"

"You don't get to use impairment as an out. They gave me an antagonist in the ER."

He lifted an eyebrow. "Which in English means ... ?"

"Something to counter the Rohypnol. The worst that can happen is I might get sleepy when the antagonist wears off."

"Okay, but it's still been a helluva day. You had a scary experience —"

Her eyes narrowed. "Go to hell."

"Excuse me?"

"That's another cop out, and you know it."

"Like hell it is." He surged to his feet, the sudden movement eliciting a low growl from the dog.

"You think cops are the only people who know what an adrenaline burst is?" She fisted her hands at her sides to keep them from trembling. "What do you think it's like to cross-examine a witness before a jury when a man's fate hangs in the balance? What do imagine is happening inside when I'm sitting there trying to look composed while the jury is filing back into the courtroom? What in hell do you think is coursing through my veins when the foreman stands up to read his verdict?"

"Suzannah —"

"Forget it. I know what you think runs through my veins." She laughed harshly. "I'm the Ice Princess, right?"

"If you'd just shut up for a minute —"

"The truth is you're scared. Scared of me. Scared you don't have what it takes to melt —"

Quigg silenced her the only way he knew how — by grabbing her and covering her mouth with his. He felt her shock in the stiffness of her body as he held her head fast and kissed her the way he'd been dying to kiss her since last night. Then he felt something else.

Teeth. Pointy ones. Biting into his ankle.

"Ow!" He broke away from her, knowing it was the only way the damned dog would stand down. "Stupid mongrel." He bent to catch Bandy's collar.

"Don't hurt him."

"I'm not going to hurt the mutt. I'm just gonna lock him in the kitchen. I don't intend to have him gnawing on my leg while I'm making love to you."

She was still standing where he'd left here, a hand pressed to her mouth, when he came back from securing the dog.

"Now, where were we?"

She dropped her hand. "You don't have to do this."

"*Have to* is not the way I'd characterize it."

"I goaded you." Her words coming out in a rush. "I'm sorry. I know you're not scared of me. Not scared of anything. I was just angry. You don't have to prove a thing."

Scared? Hell, he was petrified, but not for the reasons she thought. He was scared there'd be no pulling back after this. One taste would never be enough. He put those thoughts aside. "You're right there. I don't have anything to prove."

He took her hand, the one she'd touched to her mouth, and pulled her closer. Her eyes widened, and he could see a pulse leaping at the base of her neck.

"So you can go back to your baseball game," she breathed.

"Not in a million years." He stroked the inside of her wrist, watching her pupils dilate.

"Okay, *I'm* scared," she confessed.

He smiled then. "Oh, ye of little faith. Did I show you nothing last night?"

"We don't have any condoms."

His smile broadened. "Yes, we do. Or rather, I do."

"How very forward-looking of you."

He didn't mistake her testiness for anything more than it was, an expression of her fear. "Sweetheart, I've had it bad for you since you stood up two years ago and tried to shred the case I'd spent months building. You think I'd move in under the same roof with you and *not* bring condoms?"

"Remy Rosneau," she murmured. "I lost that at trial."

"And had the conviction overturned on appeal, despite the fact I know the guy touched that girl."

She bristled. "I notice the Crown didn't take it to the Supreme Court."

"I didn't say you didn't earn the reversal on technical merits, I said he was guilty as hell. Now, are we gonna stand around talking about this all night or are you gonna let me kiss you again?"

He had the satisfaction of hearing her breath hitch as he pulled her close again.

"Two years?" she asked.

"Two years."

The confirmation was breathed against her lips, which parted softly, giving him the merest taste of her. It was part familiar comfort, part exotic mystery. Part sunshine, part sin. And one hundred percent, full-moon-howling sexy.

He pulled back a fraction, wanting to look his fill of that glorious mouth before he tasted it again, but she clutched at his shirt front, pulling herself up on tiptoe to preserve the contact. He got the message. *More. Now.*

Lightheaded, he stroked her parted lips with his tongue, lingering on the sensitive tissue just inside her lower lip. From last night's petting session on the couch, he knew she liked that, liked the long, slow prelude to a deeper, more intimate mating of tongues. Suddenly, he wanted to give her that slow, sensual trip. He wanted to carefully stoke her desire, make her dizzy with pleasure. Digging deep, he ordered his thundering heart to slow. *You can do this. You can be as patient as she needs you to be.*

Then she released his shirt front and slid her hands up to grip his head, kissing him back, pressing her breasts against his chest like she couldn't get close enough. In that millisecond, his good intentions were blasted away by a tidal wave of urgency.

He tugged the tail of her blouse out of her skirt and pushed his hands under the fine material to sweep across her back. Lord, she felt good, like satin. Warm, smooth, soft. He let his hands roam lower, gently squeezing the sweet curve of her butt under the taut fabric of her little skirt. That brought a harsh sob to her lips. The low, sexy sound nearly ripped the lid off what remained of his self-control.

Pushing her backwards, he guided her to the couch. She went down, pulling him with her, onto her. Her body was warm, solid, and impossibly exciting beneath his. Way too exciting. Damn, he had to slow this down.

He pulled back slightly, which she took as license to tug his shirt free, her fingers fumbling with the buttons as she worked them loose. Then her hands were skimming his chest, sliding around to clutch at his back.

"Now, John." She arched against him, her body moving restlessly against his arousal.

He groaned. "Not yet, baby."

"Yes, *now*." Her hands went to his belt, undoing it. "I don't want to lose this. I don't want to start analyzing everything. Please. I'm ready now."

He gritted his teeth against a surge of desire that threatened to swamp him. "Maybe," he managed, "but I'm not."

At his words, he felt her go still. *Oh, hell.* She thought he wasn't *ready* ready, as if she wasn't sexy enough to make him instantly hard. As if he hadn't been ready forever. "I mean, I *am* ready. So ready, I can hardly stand it. But the condoms ... they're upstairs. We have to go up there."

He pulled back to look at her. Her pupils were dilated with desire still, but he also saw trepidation there. Cripes, did she seriously think this desperate, clawing need was going to go away if they pressed pause long enough to get to the bedroom?

Maybe it would, for her.

The thought whispered through his mind, just loud enough to make itself heard over the pounding of his pulse. To be on the safe side — God, it would kill him if she changed her mind now! — he decided not to give her a chance to lose the buzz.

He levered himself off the couch. "C'mere, baby."

She accepted his hand. As soon as she came to her feet, he pulled her into his arms. More mind-melting kisses. More slipping and sliding of material as he worked his hands over her body with increasing urgency. Finally, he brought his hands around to her shirt front. Making quick work of her buttons, he pushed the fabric aside to expose her small breasts cupped in impossibly delicate white lace. He put a few inches' distance between them so he could properly appreciate the view.

"Beautiful."

The word emerged as little more than a croak, but it seemed to work for her. Or maybe it was the stark desire in his eyes that he made no attempt to hide. Whatever the reason, she closed her eyes, arching her body in silent supplication. *Touch them,* her posture implored. Touch *me.*

He did, running the very tips of his fingers lightly over the gentle swell of flesh above her bra. When she moaned for more, he cupped her breasts fully, rasping his thumbs over her tautened nipples.

She came at him then, her mouth seeking his, her hands roaming his back. Minutes later, he pulled away, his pulse thundering as though he'd just run a rabbiting suspect to ground, and led her to the base of the stairs.

"You first," he said. "I want to watch that sweet a ... um, skirt of yours all the way up."

"John!"

So, she hadn't lost the power of speech altogether. He grinned. "Okay, I'll go first. But try to control yourself."

At the first landing, he stopped. "Okay, you're doing way too good a job controlling yourself." She laughed, but the sound died when he pressed his lips to hers. He pressed his body to hers, too, pinning her against the wall. With hands that were embarrassingly close to shaking, he raked her skirt up so he could caress the sensitive mounds of her buttocks through one less layer of clothing. She gasped, another one of those crazy-making, sexy sounds, and suddenly he forgot he was doing this for her. When he slid a hand between her silk-encased thighs to cup her intimately, it was all for him.

Oh, Lord, she was hot. Even through her underwear, he could feel her moist heat. Hiking her skirt up further, he dropped to his knees and pressed his mouth to her silk-covered sex. She made a shocked, strangled noise, and for a heartbeat, he thought she might push him away. She twined her fingers into his hair, but not, he realized, with the intent of stopping him. She was just hanging on, her whole body trembling like an aspen in the breeze. He stood, dragging her quickly up the rest of the stairs. At the top, he paused.

"Your place or mine?" he asked. "Bear in mind, the condoms are in my room."

"Your room."

Clothes started to come off as soon as they hit the bedroom. Fingers fumbled, hands trembled as they helped each other out of their clothes until they stood naked beside the bed.

Sweet heaven, she was beautiful. Her breasts were even better than he'd imagined, and he'd spent some considerable time imagining them. The areolas were small and surprisingly dark against her pale skin. Her nipples, tightened with arousal, jutted out in frank, silent invitation. The need to push her down and cover the slim, toned length of her body with his screamed in his blood. But first, he owed her the words.

He pulled long strands of blonde hair, which had long since come out of its fastener, forward to frame her breasts. "You are so incredibly beautiful," he breathed.

"I don't want you to be disappointed."

He blinked. How could she still think along those lines? "Are you planning to change your mind?"

Her breasts lifted on a deep breath. "No."

"Then it's not even a possibility."

"I never know where to put things."

"Where to put things?"

"You know, elbows, knees."

He smiled. He couldn't help it. "Darlin', long as your arms are around me, everything'll be where it's supposed to be."

Before she could obsess any further about it, he guided her down onto the bed. She scooted to the middle with an alacrity that betrayed her nervousness. Thank God he hadn't let her entertain a single lucid thought on the way upstairs or she'd be a basket case.

On the other hand, it was no hardship distracting her from her anxiety. Following her down onto the bed, he used his mouth and hands and all the patience he could summon to bring her to a fever pitch again.

When she cried "Now!" again, he obeyed. Taking a condom from the night stand, he tore the wrapper off and sheathed himself smoothly. Her arms came around him in welcome as he settled between her parted thighs. Despite her readiness, he felt tension grip her again. *Oh, baby, please don't leave me now.*

He covered her mouth again, kissing her, long and hot and deep until she writhed under him again. Then, urging her legs wider, he slid home with a strong, controlled thrust.

Dear Lord, she was so tight! The only thing that would feel better than being buried in her silken heat would be to pull out and do it again. And again. And again. Fast and hard as a piston. Somehow he found the strength to hold his hips still as he looked down into her face. Her eyes were closed, and she'd caught her lower lip between her teeth.

"You okay?"

She lifted her lids. Her eyes looked a little dazed. Dazed was good, he decided.

"Suzannah? Did I hurt you? You're so tight . . . ."

"Oh, no," she breathed. "It's actually . . . very nice."

Very nice? No woman had ever characterized his lovemaking with such faint praise before. His ego would have been dented but for the knowledge that *very nice* was probably the high water mark for her. Time to raise the bar.

"I'm going to move now. If anything gets outside your comfort zone, tell me and I'll stop."

Her reply was to rock her pelvis against him. *Good answer.*

Watching her face, he withdrew almost completely, repeating the full penetration. This time, she arched up to meet him.

"Good?"

"Yes!"

He stroked her like that for a while, long and slow and deep, until she communicated her need for more with the thrusting of her hips. Picking up the tempo, he rocked into her. He felt her shift her position slightly to maximize the friction against the center of her pleasure.

He reached between them to open her folds still further. "That's right, baby. Rock it, now. Rock against me."

She did, and he felt her building excitement in her every breath, in her tightening muscles. *Oh, soon. Please make it soon.* "Lock your legs around me now," he urged. She complied, gasping her pleasure. With each thrust, he felt her tension coiling tighter, higher, and she was making noises now. Small, quiet, polite noises. It was so *Suzannah.* And sexier than anything he'd ever heard before.

Suddenly, his control was gone. He let go of all thought of technique and just pounded himself into her, rocking the bed until the headboard started banging the wall.

Fortunately, it seemed to be what she needed. He felt her orgasm coming at last, her internal muscles gripped him with astonishing power. Then it hit her. He thrust deep and stilled, pinning her to the mattress as she rode it out. In the silence of the bedroom, her quiet sobs made him want to weep. When her contractions had quieted to mere tremors, he resumed moving. A few more thrusts into her pulsating, impossible tightness and his own climax slammed into him.

He lay there in the sweet cradle of her thighs, his heart echoing the thundering of hers, thinking, *Man, you are in so much trouble.* Fortunately, he felt way too good to worry about it.

Chapter 9

I GET IT. *I finally* get *it.*

Suzannah lay there, cradling 185 pounds of trembling man in her arms and finally understood. This was what all the fuss was about. This was what drove people to the extremes she witnessed time and again, in courtroom after courtroom.

Oh, she'd *known* on an intellectual plane. But that kind of knowledge was not the same as this bone-deep knowing.

He stirred and she released the handful of hair she'd been clutching so he could lift his head. He gazed down at her, his hair sexily tousled, face flushed. Even now, his brown eyes scorched her.

"You okay?"

She smiled at his husky question. "You could say that."

He rolled away and off the bed. She let him go reluctantly, missing his warmth and weight more than was reasonable or prudent, and he disappeared immediately into the bathroom.

Suddenly she was assailed by the demons of doubt. Just because it had been great for her didn't necessarily mean it had been great for him. Did it?

Oh, God, what if it had been awful for him? Was he going to step into the shower, wash every last trace of her from his skin?

Before her insecurities could balloon any further, he was back. Wordlessly, he scooped her up, flicked the covers back and placed her on the cool sheets. Seconds later, he crawled right in beside her, gathering her close.

The condom, she realized. He'd gone to dispose of it. Relief made her giddy.

"I thought you were going to turn out to be one of those fastidious types. You know, jump into a scalding shower and scrub off the top layer of your epidermis."

As soon as the words were out, she could have bitten her tongue off. They too accurately captured her own reaction to her last ill-judged foray into the bedroom.

"Hardly. In fact, I may never wash my right hand again."

"John!"

More laughter. More silly talk, which led to silly kisses, which led to serious kisses. Long, languorous, sweet kisses. This time, there was ample opportunity for exploration, and Suzannah took full advantage of it. Using her hands and lips, she explored his face, his neck, his shoulders, his chest, and in a feat of great daring, she laid hands on his prodigious arousal. She would have liked to taste him, too — thrilling tongues of fire licking through her veins at the mere thought — but she lacked the courage.

In any event, her hands seemed to be quite sufficient for the job. He endured her ministrations with obvious pleasure, but eventually he turned the tables on her. With tremendous skill and infinite patience, he subjected her to a similar erotic torture. Finally, when neither could stand another second of foreplay, he sheathed himself again and brought them both to a quick, shattering climax.

Afterward, they lay spooned together beneath the covers.

"Damn. I gotta get up."

She felt his sigh stir the hairs on the nape of her neck. "So soon?"

"Can't you hear that?"

She tensed and lifted her head, listening intently. "I don't hear a thing."

"Exactly." He rolled out of bed, fished a pair of jeans out of the drawer and hauled them on. "Bandy's either asleep or up to no good. I'm betting it's option B, especially since I didn't stop to feed him."

"Whoops. Better rectify that." She sat up, sheets clutched to her breasts, and watched him dress.

"I will. Right after I walk him." He dug a clean t-shirt out and hauled it over his head. "I'll arm the alarm on the way out and let myself back in with my key."

The alarm. Locked doors. Stepped-up police patrols. Back to reality. A reality that included a faceless stalker. But for a while, in this virtual fortress they'd created, she'd felt safe enough to momentarily forget the lunatic who stalked her.

Or maybe it was John's arms that made her feel so safe.

Veering away from that thought, she watched him poke his feet into battered runners and lace them up.

She should get up too, but this was *his* room. She'd have to go down the hall for a change of clothes. Despite the fact he'd already explored her body intimately, she felt oddly shy about walking around naked in front of him. Of course, she could always drag the sheet off the bed and warp it around her, but that would only underscore her ridiculous modesty. Which meant she was stuck here until he left. God, she was such a prude.

A strand of hair fell forward, and she pushed it back behind her ear. "Spaghetti okay for dinner? I want to make it something quick so I can tackle the work Vince gave me."

He straightened, nabbed his keys from the top of the dresser and stuck them in the pockets of his jeans. "Spaghetti sounds great, but why don't I make it? That way, you can get straight to work and just take a break when it's ready."

She grinned. "You're going to cook for me?"

"As often as you like. As long as the menu is spaghetti. Or a nice rib eye on the grill. I can do that, too." He crossed to the bed, grasped her face and kissed her, a quick, hard kiss. "Back soon."

She heard him cross the landing and jog lightly down the steps, heard him talking to Bandy, heard the dog's nails clicking excitedly on the hardwood floor. She smiled, picturing perfectly the way the stout dog would be wriggling as John tried to clip the lead to his collar. She could get used to this.

Except she'd better not.

Her smile faded.

The threat to her safety was the sole force bringing them together. Well, that and a strong physical attraction. The former would be removed when her stalker slipped up, which he was bound to do soon. The latter, the chemistry between them, would run its course quickly, too. After all, they were such an unlikely couple.

She chewed her lip. Their relationship had to be costing him with the other guys. It was one thing for him to let them think he "doing" the She-Rex. Quite another for them to know he'd moved in with her and was making her safety a priority.

Of course, no one from her social circle was taking a terribly positive view of the relationship, either. She'd actually overheard two male friends speculate that she was "slumming" with the rough-edged detective and would soon weary of it. Her girlfriends, on the other hand, did not speculate behind her back. They were completely upfront about her delicious choice for a walk on the wild side. Her own *mother* believed much the same, for goodness sake. Only Vince was genuinely glad of the relationship, and that was because he figured John would keep her safe. Beyond that, her partner probably shared the consensus opinion that this was a case of opposites temporarily attracting.

Annoyed with herself, Suzannah threw the covers off and leapt out of bed. It didn't matter what anyone thought. Picking up her skirt, she shook it vigorously.

It didn't matter, either, that it wasn't a forever thing. She snatched up her blouse and located her underwear under John's shirt. She was quite capable of enjoying it while it lasted, after which she'd file it away with other pleasant memories, like the three weeks she'd spent in the Dutch Antilles last year.

Marching to her own bedroom, she tossed her clothes on the bed, strode to the bathroom and turned on the taps. Adjusting the water temperature, she flicked on the shower, stepped under the spray and let it soak her hair.

She wasn't Sleeping Beauty looking for a handsome prince to come along and cart her off to some happily ever after. She was a modern woman. A *sophisticated* woman.

Squeezing shampoo into her hands, she worked it briskly through her hair, then leaned back into the spray to rinse the rich lather away.

She certainly wasn't one of those girls who imagined themselves in love just because some guy came along and gave her an orgasm. Not even for a mind-blinding, soul-shaking orgasm.

No, this girl was going to grab as many of those orgasms, enjoy as many laughs, as she could. But she'd keep her head and heart a proper distance from danger.

Satisfied, she stepped from the shower and grabbed a towel.

❧

Seven hours later, Suzannah woke to the certain knowledge that she was alone in her bed.

She certainly hadn't been alone three hours earlier. She smiled at the memory.

John had fed her as promised, then left her in peace to work on the DeBoeuf files while he watched the Yankees and the Rays. As she worked, she caught the occasional muttering from the TV room, often about the dubious collective IQ of the umpiring crew. She'd worked until the idea of peeling his clothes off and making love to him on the couch in the flickering light cast by the television totally destroyed her concentration. It had taken another few minutes to work up her courage to actually do it.

When she entered the room, something exciting was obviously happening on screen, because he barely looked up. She rounded up Bandy and secured him in the kitchen, giving him a new rawhide strip to keep him preoccupied. Heart pounding at her own audacity, she'd run upstairs to fetch a condom from his supply in the spare bedroom. Then she went back to the living room. He did tear his eyes from the action this time, specifically when she knelt in front of him, slid her hands under his t-shirt and instructed him to lift his arms so she could haul it off.

He complied enthusiastically, then tried to reciprocate by removing her silk knit tank top, but she forestalled him, making it clear that it was *her* turn this time. He'd leaned back into the cushions readily enough, smiling in a wicked, sexy way that threatened to steal what remained of her breath.

In the flickering bluish light, she knelt between his knees and explored his chest, his arms, his shoulders, the vee of fine hair arrowing down his abdomen to the waistband of his jeans. He protested not at all when she undid his belt and slowly, carefully, drew down his zipper. And when it came to getting the worn Levis off, he was downright helpful. When she ran her nails up and down his hair-roughened thighs, she had the satisfaction of seeing his erection leap. And when at last she laid hands on that supremely male part of his anatomy, he almost came out of his skin. But that reaction was nothing compared to the sounds he made when she replaced the caress of her hands with her mouth.

Incredible. Never had she felt such feminine power, or such a deep arousal. Gasps of pleasure, broken words of praise, hoarse entreaties. When he warned he could stand no more, she handed him the condom. As he sheathed himself, she shed her own clothing and climbed onto his lap. He tried to stall her, insisting she needed attention to make her as ready as he was, but she wouldn't be slowed. Gripping him between her thighs, she sank down on his thrusting hardness, impaling herself, dragging a sigh of delight from both of them. Pushing him back into the cushions, she rode him, lifting, sinking, gyrating, as he filled his hands with her breasts. Within minutes, she felt his climax coming in the harshness of his breathing and the tremor of tension rippling through him. Incredibly, it was enough to trigger her own orgasm. As her flesh contracted around his, he gripped her hips and surged into her to find his own release.

Afterward, when their heartbeats had returned to normal, he'd killed the TV with the remote. He scooped her up, carried her to the kitchen long enough to liberate Bandy, then on up to her bedroom. With infinite gentleness, he laid her on the cool sheets and climbed into bed beside her. Blissfully exhausted, she'd fallen asleep cradled against his solid heat.

Now, with her digital clock reading almost 1:00 a.m., his side of the bed had grown cold. Had he gone back to his room? Lots of people — including herself, normally — couldn't stand to share a bed for actual sleeping. Curiosity getting the best of her, she threw the covers off and pulled on a silk wrap. Beside the bed Bandy raised his head briefly, sighed loudly, then went back to sleep. Suzannah stole down the hall to the spare bedroom. In the moonlight, she saw that his bed was empty, though he'd obviously remade it at some point. Unease prickled along her nape.

Moving into the room, she checked the bathroom, which was also unoccupied. Had he gone downstairs in search of food? Probably. They'd eaten fairly lightly, especially considering their exertions.

She made her way downstairs. At the first landing, she could see a faint glow of light, but it came from the direction of her study, not the kitchen. Frowning, she descended the rest of the steps and glided to the open doorway of her study. There he was, reclined in her chair, bare feet on her desk, reading.

"Hey," she called, her voice husky from sleep. "What are you doing up?"

He started. "Whoa!" He swung his feet and stood. "Didn't see you there."

"I missed you." She moved into the room. "What are you doing?"

"Reading. Police stuff." He dropped the material on the desk, almost furtively it seemed, then skirting the furniture to intercept her. "Best cure in the world for insomnia."

"Couldn't sleep?" He'd come so close she had to tip her head back to look at him. Even in the dim light cast by the banker's lamp, she saw his eyes darken.

"I won't sleep easy until this bastard's in a cage."

Her heart twisted in her chest. She'd been sleeping like a baby and he'd been down here worrying. About her. And once again, she'd slept like a baby *because* he was here, worrying about her.

"He'll screw up soon." She slid her arms around him. "I can feel it."

He closed his arms around her, tucked her head under his chin. "You're right. And the boys will be right there to pop him when he does."

She pulled back a few inches. "Think you can sleep now?"

"Yeah." He sounded surprised. "Yeah, I think I could."

⚜

"So, does she know?"

Quigg glanced up from the coroner's report he'd been reading. Ray stood there, coffee in hand, looking like a GQ model. Only the subtle bulge under his arm marred the lines of his suit. "Dammit, Razor, could you give the rest of us a break?"

Ray grinned, loosening his tasteful, impeccable, unwrinkled, unstained tie. "Hey, blame it on Grace."

Quigg snorted. "I'd like to, but you always looked like that, even when you were dressing yourself."

"So, does she know?"

Back to that. Quigg played dumb. "Does who know what?"

"Does Suzannah know you hired a private dick to sit on her?"

"No, and there's no reason why she should."

Ray parked his butt on the side of Quigg's desk. "Must be costing a pretty penny."

Quigg shrugged. "Hank owed me one. And you know she wouldn't stand for the cops sitting on her, even if the brass would approve that kind of deployment." He leaned back in his chair. "Now, what can you tell me about Suzannah's case? Learn anything at the fast-food joint?"

"Nothing very helpful. The drinks there are self-serve, from a fountain. Someone must have doctored a drink, then swapped it for Suzannah's. Be easy enough to do. Suzannah says she got a call on her cell phone. The switch probably took place when she turned away to dig her cellular unit out."

"The call?"

"We confirmed it came from the pay phone in the vestibule of the restaurant. Receiver was wiped clean."

"Security cameras?"

"Pointed at the cashiers and the lineup. Nothing trained on the area where Suzannah was sitting. We'll have to get her to view the tapes and ID everyone she recognizes. 'Course, our guy is no dimwit. He might never have entered the camera's range. He probably nabbed an empty beverage container from one of the tables — lots of people don't bother to dump their own garbage when they're finished — and refilled it at the fountain with whatever she was drinking."

Quigg's gut tightened at the mental picture of Suzannah's stalker following her through the self-service soda fountain, maybe just feet away .... "He might not be dumb, but he's getting impatient, taking chances. He'll screw up."

"No question."

"What about the Rohypnol? Any leads there?"

"'Fraid not. Not surprisingly, nobody's being real forthcoming about who they might have sold some roofies to. Guy at the tat parlor tells me it's mostly adolescents who use it."

Quigg shook his head. "Damned stuff put you in a coma if you wash it down with a couple of beers, and kids can buy it with their lunch money." He yanked at his tie. "Have we looked at her client list?"

"Yeah." Ray shoved a sheet at him. "As far as I can tell, there's no one loose who has reason to fault her for her defense. And definitely no one behind bars who's got the kind of bling to go after her from inside."

Quigg scanned the list, stopping at the fourth name.

"Halliday?"

"Convicted, sprung and born again. He's now a lay minister in Brockville, Ontario."

"Denton?"

"Deceased. OD's his second week outta prison. Guess he coulda benefitted from a community-based methadone maintenance program."

"Rosneau?"

"Nah. He was acquitted on appeal. Remember? You were fit to be tied."

"Yeah, I remember. But I also remember he was a pretty creepy proposition. We popped him for touching a minor for a sexual purpose."

"Yeah, I know, but the guy never turns up again in our database. And you know pedophiles. They *will* re-offend."

Jesus. Maybe Rosneau was innocent after all. Maybe Suzannah was right. Maybe he'd been doing this too long .... He shook off the thought. "Okay, what about the flower shops? Still nothing?"

"Nothing," Ray confirmed. "The particular arrangement he favors is too generic. Every blessed flower shop makes the same one. Same roses, same ferny stuff, same green glass vase. But Stevie came up with an idea that might help in future, presuming our perp continues to communicate via this live posy, dead posy routine."

Of course. "Mark the vases to discriminate between shops."

"It'll have to be on the inside of the vase, of course, probably below the water line. Something real discreet. Even at that, I'm not sure this guy wouldn't find it."

Quigg rubbed his forehead. "What about Suzannah's friends?"

"We're looking at 'em. Along with dumped boyfriends, dweebs she might have blown off in high school. Hell, we're even looking at other lawyers she might have embarrassed in the courtroom. You name it, we're trying it."

"There's one avenue you haven't tried."

Razor shot him a look. "What's that?"

Seeing no way to sugarcoat it, Quigg just spit it out. "Remember that barbeque you invited us to?" At Ray's nod, he continued. "Bruce Newman made a comment to Suzannah about leaving her drink unattended. He made specific reference to Rohypnol."

"Whoa, whoa, whoa, just a minute." Ray surged to his feet. "You're not suggesting Bruce is our stalker?"

"I'm saying Constable Newman made a direct comment to her about the possibility of getting Rohypnol slipped in her drink."

Ray's eyes narrowed. "A legitimate warning."

"At a cop party?"

"Anywhere, anytime. As a matter of practice, a woman shouldn't leave her drink unattended, *period*." Ray's hands disappeared into his pockets to jangle the coins there, a sure sign of agitation. "Maybe Newman just wanted to get a rise out of her," he said. "Just because she never disemboweled him personally on the witness stand doesn't mean he might not want a little payback for the grief she's caused some of the guys."

Unlike some people, Newman knows how critical it is to be tight with the boys. The unspoken message hung between them.

Quigg sighed. "Look, for what it's worth, I think you're right. That's what Suzannah thinks, too, that he was just trying to throw her off balance, make her uncomfortable."

"Then what's the problem?"

"The problem," Quigg said, "is that if a civilian had made that remark so proximate to the assault, we'd be all over him."

Ray swore, but it was an acknowledgment of the truth of Quigg's assertion.

"Look," Quigg said, "I'm not asking you to investigate New-man. I'll look into that angle myself. I just wanted to give you a heads up."

"This won't make you any new friends."

"No kidding?" Quigg resisted the urge to rub at his right temple to quiet the nerve that had started jumping there.

"You know, it was one thing when the guys thought you were just doing her. There was a certain level of . . . I don't know . . . approval there, a little of that *give her one for me* mentality."

"Cripes, Razor."

"But this is different. This is —"

"What if it was Grace getting menaced? Huh? Wouldn't you pull out all the stops, do whatever you had to do?"

Ray blinked. "So it's like that."

Ah, hell. Quigg rubbed the tic-ticking nerve at his temple. "I don't know how it is."

"You'd better figure it out soon."

"What's that supposed to mean?"

"Hey, I like Suzannah. If you two are gonna have a happily-ever-after, great. We can double date on Fridays. The guys'll come to accept the situation eventually, and it will all have been worth it. But," he said, "if she chews you up and spits you out after we've collared her number one fan, you're gonna be left with one helluva hard row to hoe, my friend."

"You're not telling me anything I don't already know, Razor. Might as well save your breath."

"'Kay. But can I ask just one more question before we leave the topic of Suzannah Phelps?"

Quigg suppressed a sigh. "Would it do any good to say no?"

"Not really."

"Then fire away."

"She got anything to do with you looking to be a desk jockey?"

Quigg scowled. "Who said anything like that?"

Ray rolled his eyes. "Gimme a friggin' break, here. You leave a book like *The Complete Preparation Guide for Police Sergeant Exam* laying around, a highly-trained investigator like myself might hypothesize that you're gonna take a run for Sinclair's job when he finally takes that early retirement he's been talking about."

Trapped. That's how he felt. Cornered.

Hell with it. It was time Ray knew, anyway. Past time. "Okay, you got me. I'm busted. Satisfied?"

"Not yet. You didn't answer my question. How much does Suzannah figure into your decision? She want to get you off the streets? Into a higher income bracket, better social circle?"

"She doesn't know." But she'd come damn close to knowing last night when she'd caught him reading some study material. Even now, the thought of her knowing made him weak at the knees. This whole business of wanting to be ... what? — something more? — for her made him more vulnerable than he was ready to deal with. Besides, what if he didn't make the grade? How humiliating would that be? No, much better she didn't know.

"But she does factor in there somewhere?"

Quigg shifted under that damned all-seeing gaze. "What's wrong with wanting to further my career? I got a few years on you, if you'll remember, junior."

"Not a thing, if you're doing it for the right reasons."

"I'm satisfied with my reasons."

"Good." Ray dug car keys out of his pocket. "By the way, you'll make a great sergeant."

Great. Ray was going out. Quigg was off the hook, for now.

Then Ray's phone rang. He nabbed the receiver. "Morgan."

Quigg went back to perusing the coroner's report, but his concentration was fractured again when Ray swore. One look at his friend's face and Quigg didn't have to follow the clipped, one-sided conversation to know he'd caught something hot. Anything that called for the forensic identification team was smoking. "What's up?" he asked, when Ray hung up, his stomach taking a queer dive at the look on his friend's face.

"It's Suzannah. Our guy just made a move on her."

Chapter 10

QUIGG LEAPT UP, SENDING his chair reeling backwards on its casters.

"Relax, she's okay," Ray said. "Rattled, but okay."

"She was going spend the whole morning in the Record Office doing some kind of search. Hell, I made sure she got there myself, checked it out. The place is quiet as a friggin' library. And Vince was gonna pick her up at lunch time. She swore she wouldn't set foot outside the building until Vince came for her."

"Happened right there at the Record Office. Our guy slipped into the building, followed her to the washroom, which is a little bit removed from the records area."

Quigg swore. "Did he hurt her?"

"No, didn't lay a hand on her, but it sounds like she hurt *him*. I'll have to get the details, but I gather she stabbed him."

Quigg's knees went weak. "Stabbed him."

"Uh-huh. With a ballpoint pen. At which point he fled."

Another wave of stomach-turning fear. Quigg sagged against his desk. "She had to fight him off, hand to hand? Dammit, why didn't she use the personal alarm?"

"I have no idea. But Quigg, buddy, this could be the break we've been looking for. We've got physical evidence. *Blood*."

Quigg grabbed his coat. "I'm coming with you."

"Fine by me."

Suzannah couldn't stop shaking. She was safe here in the employees' break room with a constable posted outside the door. She knew she was safe, but it didn't seem to matter. She regarded her reflection in the mirror over the kitchenette's sink and despaired. Her eyes looked huge and haunted, her face pinched and frightened. God, she had to get this trembling thing under control before Ray Morgan showed up. Bad enough to look like an emotional basket case in front of the young patrolman who'd responded ....

The door to the staff room flew open and John burst into the room, followed by Ray Morgan.

"Are you okay?"

She met burning brown eyes. "I'm fine."

It was all she could do to get the words out before he crushed her in a bear hug. Twenty-four hours ago, she might have thought the gesture was intended as much for Ray's benefit as for hers, but she knew better now. This was real. It had to be.

"Oh, baby, you scared me."

"Scared me, too."

"I wouldn't have left you here if I thought there was any risk."

"I know."

Ray cleared his throat and John released her.

"Think you could answer some questions for me?" Ray said.

Suzannah brushed her hair back and took a deep breath. "Of course."

They sat, she and John on the couch and Ray in a worn chair. For the next half hour, she related the details, reliving the ordeal. She'd almost finished the title search Vince had sent her to do — a multi-million dollar corporate mortgage transaction, he didn't trust it to the title abstractors they usually used — when the two coffees she'd had throughout the morning drove her to seek out the washroom.

The sound of her own footsteps had echoed hollowly as she strode down the abandoned corridor. However, soon after entering the washroom stall, she'd heard the room's door open and close. She was instantly gripped by a sense of disquiet. Yesterday's experience fresh in her mind, she groped for her personal alarm, only to realize she'd clipped it to her briefcase which she'd left in the main records area. She never carried a purse when she carried her briefcase, and it never occurred to her to lug her briefcase to the washroom.

Telling herself she was letting her imagination run away with her, that there was no one out there lying in wait to pounce on her, she straightened her suit. But no matter how she tried to steel her spine, she couldn't bring herself to open the stall door. Humiliated by her fear but still frightened, she decided to out-wait the other patron.

Then a hand a come up to grip the top of the stall door. She screamed, a small, involuntary reaction. But he didn't try to kick the door in or rip it off, or any of the dramatic things she envisioned. Rather, he held it firm as though to trap her, to make her aware that she was cornered, at his mercy.

"Who are you? Why are you doing this?" she cried.

"Because you owe me," came a hoarse whisper. "Because I want you to suffer like I've suffered."

She owed him? What did that mean? If she only had her alarm. It had scared him away once. She blinked. Maybe it could scare him away again.

"I'll activate my alarm!"

"Nice try, but I know you left it out there."

Oh, shit. He'd been watching her! "I'll scream."

"I know you will." The voice held genuine pleasure, no fear. "But I'm willing to bet no one can hear you from here over that noisy air conditioning unit. And I didn't see many females who are likely to come along and disturb us."

God have mercy, he was right. Was she going to die here?

Or was he just trying to terrify her some more?

And omigod, he was wearing latex surgical gloves.

Her hands contracted into fists. A weapon. She needed a weapon. Her hands flew to the pockets of her lightweight suit. Yes! A pen, shoved in there absently and forgotten.

Before she could rethink her decision, she drew the ballpoint pen from her pocket, lifted her arm and drove the pen point as deeply as she could into the flesh of the back of his hand. He yowled, part pain, part anger, and cursing her viciously, jerked his hand back. She heard him rip paper towels from the dispenser.

"This isn't over, bitch."

Then the door opening and closing behind him.

She waited a few heartbeats, until she was sure her legs would bear her, then let herself out of the stall. Heart hammering against her ribs, she pulled the washroom door open and risked a look up and down the corridor. Just as deserted as before. Taking a deep breath, she raced straight to the Registrar's Office.

Now, here she was.

Quigg breathed a word that was usually a profanity on his lips, but it sounded more like a prayer this time. Then he took her hand and squeezed it. Tears burned the back of her eyes.

"Okay, a few questions, if you're up to it."

This from Ray. She turned to face him, nodded, felt the reassuring squeeze Quigg gave her icy fingers. "Of course."

"Did you get a glimpse of him at all, or just the hand?"

"Just the hand."

"What'd it look like?"

"Through the surgical glove? Clean, I guess. Blunt fingers. I got the impression the nails were on the longish side, maybe. Like he might enjoy the occasional manicure." She watched him make a few scribbles in his notebook which must have meant something to him.

"Caucasian?"

"I think so, but the latex may have influenced that impression."

"How tall, do you think?"

"Not exceptionally tall. Not tall enough for me to see the top of his head over the stall's door when he gripped it." At the memory, her fingers flexed in Quigg's grip and he gave her a hand an answering, reassuring squeeze. "Of course, I don't know how far away he might have been standing, or whether or not he might have been crouching down …."

"It's okay. We can work with that." Ray made another henscratch, then looked up at her again. "What about his voice?"

She thought for a moment. "It's hard to say. He talked in a harsh whisper, like he was disguising his voice. At least until I stuck him with my pen. He dropped the whisper then."

"Don't suppose you recognized it then?"

"No." She shook her head. "His words sounded thick, guttural, but I think it was rage that made his voice that way. I have no idea what his normal speaking voice might sound like."

"Anything else you can think of?"

"Just that I can't figure where he came from. I mean, I really didn't feel at risk here with so many legitimate people milling around — abstractors, lawyers, articled clerks — but I was ... I don't know ... *aware* of comings and goings. I swear I didn't sense anyone out of place. And he had to have been lurking, watching me," she pointed out. "He knew I'd left my alarm with my briefcase."

She saw Ray and Quigg exchange a glance over her head.

"Could you identify everyone who came and went?"

"Oh, yes," she replied. "The men, anyway. A few women came and went, but I didn't take particular note, although I could probably name most of them if I thought about it. As for the men, if I can't dredge up all their names, I certainly know who they're affiliated with. Names wouldn't be hard to get."

"Good. Include Record Office staff, too. Hell, include the Pope if he happened to hobble past. Your mother, your neighbor, your old law professor. We need to look at everybody, okay? *Everybody.*"

She nodded. "Okay."

"I'll need you to produce a list of those people for me, everyone you can remember. And I'll need a statement."

"I'll produce both, list and statement, and send them down to you." Anything to wind this up.

"That'll work."

God, she needed to crawl onto John's lap, feel his arms tighten around her, lose herself in his heat. "Are we done for now, Ray?"

"*You* are. I'm gonna go get a progress report from the forensic investigation team." Ray closed his notebook and secreted it in an inside pocket of his suit. "By the way, great work with the pen. Nothing like blood and tissue."

On that cheerful note, he left.

⚜

As soon as the door closed behind Ray, Quigg did just what he'd been longing to do. He scooped her up to straddle his lap, crushing her within an inch of cracking her ribs. Still, it wasn't close enough, safe enough.

"You left your alarm on the damned brief case."

She pulled back, reached between them and lifted the gadget from between her breasts, suspended from a thin nylon cord. "It's around my neck, now. I'll wear it all the time, I swear."

"Great. Glad to hear it." He lifted it over her head and laid it aside. "But it has to come off for a minute, 'cuz I plan to kiss you until this fear goes away and we don't need that thing going off by accident."

With that, he enfolded her again, kissed her, muttered reprimands for her carelessness, gratitude for her safety, praise for her courage. And all of it punctuated with urgent kisses and touches meant to reassure — who? him? her? — that she was safe, whole.

Only when passion threatened to overcome good sense and morality laws did he pull back. Even at that, all he did was lift her so she was sitting in the more conventional sideways fashion on his lap. Her soft bottom was a torture, but one he couldn't bear to deprive himself of just yet.

"This can't go on," he muttered into her hair.

"I know. Someone's bound to walk in."

He laughed. "Not that. Though we do have to cool it. I meant this stalking thing. It can't go on."

She lifted away from him to search his gaze, her own eyes bright and brilliant as gemstones. "I'm all for that, but how do you propose to stop it?"

"Let's think about this." He settled her more comfortably against him. "It's the bottom of the ninth. Bases are loaded —"

"Baseball? You're turning to baseball for an answer to my nightmare?"

Her expression made him smile. "Sweetheart, baseball has all the answers. Now, are you going to let me think?"

"*Baseball?*"

"Okay, they've got home-field advantage. It's bottom of the ninth, and you've got a slim one-run lead that you have to preserve."

"Wait a minute. Why does he have home-field advantage?"

"Because he knows who his opponents are, but we don't know him."

"And why do I have a lead?"

"Because he hasn't caught you yet."

She shivered, delicate but unmistakable. "Okay."

"All right, back to the game. If you can shut 'em down in this last at bat, game's over. You win. But it's not going to be easy. Bases are loaded. The count is full, three balls, two strikes."

"So he's the batter and I'm the pitcher?"

"Correct. He's the guy with the big stick who can hurt you. You're the one who has to out-think him."

"Great," she muttered. "So, what do I do?"

"Bases loaded with a 3-2 count, he's sitting dead red on a fastball."

"So I throw him a curve ball?"

He shook his head. "He knows you can't afford to miss with a breaking ball. If you do, game's over."

A frown pleated her brow. "So I throw him a fastball?"

"Hell, no. He'd be all over that."

"And God knows my slider is rusty."

He grinned. "Smartass."

"Okay, coach, what do I do?"

"Throw him a change-up."

"Huh?"

"Something off-speed. Same arm action as a fastball, same plane of delivery, but you take a little off. He's sitting on a heater, thinks he's gonna get it, and then wham, he's way out in front of it, off balance. At your mercy."

"That's all well and good, but what are we going to *do*?"

He barely heard her words, her voice drowned out by the turbulent rush of thoughts colliding, coming together. Of course!

"Come on." He spilled her off his lap and leapt up. "We have to find Ray. I have a plan."

⚜

It was harder than she thought it would be. Hard to kiss John goodbye and watch him load Bandy into the Taurus and drive away.

Hard to be alone in her own house, even with the alarm armed. In the silence, the ticking of her kitchen clock was oppressive. She stole a casual glance out the window. There it was, the cable TV van she knew housed four officers. Four highly-trained members of the emergency response team.

Taking a deep breath, she went directly to her study, turned the computer on and settled to work. Or rather, settled to pretending to work. Not that she didn't have plenty to do — the DeBoeuf files Vince had given her still sat on her desk like a reproval, but no way could she concentrate with her nerves twanging like this.

Forty-five minutes later, it happened. A scratching at her side door, so faint she'd have missed it if she hadn't been straining for it. Then the alarm, shrill and piercing.

She ran to the living room to see a man pelting down her driveway, a blur of black clothing and speed as he turned onto the sidewalk. Then the doors of the van flew open. Flak-jacketed and armed, the ERT team hit the pavement running.

"Stop! Police!"

Suzannah heard the shouted command even from inside her house, even with the intermittent squawking of the alarm, so there could be no doubt the suspect heard it too. All he did was glance back once, then sprint faster. Another command to stop, accompanied by a warning that shots would be fired. Still, the suspect raced on, zigging and zagging, making a desperate bid for the cover of the deciduous woods at the end of the street. Then a cruiser, its lights strobing, pulled onto the street blocking his escape route. Officers sprang from both sides of the car, taking separate beads on the suspect from behind the cruiser's doors.

The suspect surrendered then, throwing his arms up in the air. She saw him mouth something, but he was too far away now for her to hear. She saw the suspect put his hands on his head, fall to his knees, stretch out on the pavement, following commands she couldn't hear. Then the ERT team fell on him.

She'd watched scenes like this play out a hundred times on television, but the reality was different. Despite herself, she gasped at the violence of it.

No, not violence. That wasn't the right word. The whole operation was controlled, professional, textbook. But the speed and efficiency with which it was handled, the force and authority behind every action, brought the reality of it home.

Suddenly, she realized the alarm was still bleating. She hurried to the panel and killed it, then went back to her post at the window.

This is what John does, she thought as she watched the handcuffed man being carefully stowed in the back of the cruiser. Oh, not the tactical SWAT team thing. But he *was* trained to take a suspect down like that. She'd known it, of course, but there was knowing and then there was *knowing*.

Then John was back, his car screeching to a stop on the street. Parking haphazardly, he jumped out, slammed the door and rushed toward the house. She met him halfway. There on the lawn, in full view of the neighbors, a half dozen cops and any number of other onlookers, she flew into his arms.

"It's over," he said, clasping her tight. "You're okay. You're okay."

She clung to him. "Thank God you're here."

"You'll have to go downtown, now."

"Will you come with me?"

"Of course."

She allowed herself to be helped into the passenger seat of John's car, where she waited a moment while he had a word with Ray Morgan. Then John joined her in the vehicle.

As soon as his door closed, she said, "Do you think we pulled it off?"

He grinned. "Hell, *I* was sold, and it was my plan. R.J. did a helluva job, don't you think?"

Constable R.J. Barnett, on loan from the Saint John PD for the purposes of today's performance, lest a local officer be recognized. Suzannah had never met the man, but she had to agree he played a great felon. "I knew it wasn't for real, but I thought my heart would pound right out of my chest."

He leaned over, gripped her head and kissed her once, hard. Was that for real or was that for their audience?

"Now we gotta finish the sell-job for the media, in case our man missed the live show." He fastened his seat belt and shot her a glance. "Ready for Act II?"

Just the thought of Act II made her stomach flip. "Ready as I'll ever be."

⁂

Within two hours, the arrest was all over the news. By the next morning, all the television stations had footage of the 'suspect', identified as Richard Sherwood, being escorted into court, where he was quickly remanded to the forensic psychiatric facility in Campbellton for evaluation. Footage of Suzannah saying how grateful she was to finally have the year-long ordeal of her stalking over. Then the payoff question, planted with a friendly reporter:

"So, what does this mean for your romance with Detective Quigley?"

She faced the unblinking eye of the camera. "Romance?" Looking as cool as her Ice Princess persona under the hot lights, she let an amused smile curve her lips. "I guess Detective Quigley and I were better actors than we thought."

"So the two of you were never romantically involved?"

This from Renee LeRoy, who looked just as disapproving as ever. Some things never changed.

"That would be rather bad for business for a criminal lawyer, now, wouldn't it?" Renee's lips didn't twitch, but laughter rippled through the rest of the press. "Sorry. I didn't mean to be flip. No romance here, I'm afraid. Detective Quigley was merely posing as my boyfriend to try to get the drop on my stalker. As you can see, it worked beautifully. Now if you'll excuse me, I'm going to celebrate my freedom by taking a week's vacation, starting right now."

"Nothing special planned? No romantic getaway?" The same obliging reporter.

"No getaway, romantic or otherwise. After this ordeal, I'm just planning on rediscovering privacy and the joys of solitude."

Smiling, she pressed her way past the media scrum. Half way to her car and not quite out of sight of the media, John stepped from behind his vehicle and grabbed her arm.

"No romance, huh?"

She'd been expecting it, had helped choreograph it, but his sudden appearance took a lift out of her. She tried to pull her arm free, per the script, but the words she said were the wrong ones, for his ears only. "Do we really have to do this part?"

"'Fraid so, sugar."

"But I just told the world there's nothing between us."

"And now we're gonna make them believe it."

"John —"

"Suzannah, there's a very good chance he's here right now, watching this from the sidelines. Now look at me like I'm a bug just crawled out from under a rock."

She looked down pointedly at his hand.

He released her elbow. "Oh, very good. Now give it to me with both barrels."

"All right, Detective, but remember, you asked for this," she muttered. Drawing herself up to her full height, she turned her haughtiest look on him. "I think you must be confused, Detective," she said, allowing her voice to rise. "That was just pretend, make believe. But it's all over now."

"Suzannah, we had something special. Don't ruin it."

The anguish in his gruff voice sliced into her. *It's not real. It's not real.* Suzannah closed her eyes and repeated that refrain a few times. Then she took a deep breath and opened her eyes. "Something special? John, you were my bodyguard. Self-appointed, I might add. I didn't ask you to do it. And all we *had* was a plan to flush out my stalker. It worked. I'm grateful. End of subject."

"But Suzannah —" He grabbed her arm again.

Oh, God, this was hard. Only a handful of the onlookers who'd drifted closer to listen in on the exchange would know the truth. The rest would take her cruel disdain at face value. She tasted bile at the back of her throat and knew she was in danger of throwing up. Finish it quickly.

"Look, I'm sorry you got the wrong idea, but now that I'm no longer in danger, there isn't any *us.* Got it?"

This time, he did more than just release her arm; he practically shoved her away. "Got it." Wheeling, he walked stiffly away.

She adjusted the sleeve of her jacket, lifted her head and marched toward her rental.

Close curtain on Act II. Just please, God, let it be the last one.

Chapter 11

QUIGG LEANED BACK IN his chair, twisting a coin absently in his hand as he waited for Suzannah to answer the special cell phone he'd given her.

On the third ring she picked up, her voice breathless. "John?"

"Where'd I drag you from?"

"I was upstairs napping, but I'd left the phone downstairs."

"Keep it close," he instructed. He hated not being there to help her endure the waiting. He couldn't even be part of the surveillance team holed up in the adjacent houses. He had to be seen to have removed himself from the role of Suzannah's guardian. It helped a little to be able to talk to her occasionally. "How you holding up?"

"Great."

"Baby, you are such a lousy liar."

"Okay, I'm a wreck. It was hard enough sitting here for the staged version. The real thing is killing me."

He flinched at her turn of phrase, knew by the quality of the silence humming between them that she'd caught the echo of her own words. He rushed to offer reassurance.

"Hey, this is gonna be a cake walk. Our boy thinks we're preoccupied with the suspect we collared. He thinks surveillance has been dropped and that you and I are splitsville. He believes you're defenseless, and that's what's gonna sink him."

"I know. It's just ... wearing." A pause. "John, what if he doesn't make a quick move? What if he delays for weeks? How long can your guys sit on my house?"

Her question would have scared hell out of him if it hadn't already occurred to him. But it had, and he'd thought it through. "He'll make his move, couple of days, tops."

"How can you be so sure?"

"Three things." He shifted the cell phone to his left hand to accept a sheaf of messages a clerk was handing him. He sifted through them quickly. Dammit. A break in his biggest case. Looked like the scumbag's secretary-slash-lover was ready to dish the dirt on her boss. Seeing surveillance photos of said boss renewing his wedding vows with his wife after promising he would divorce her must have done the trick. Quigg suppressed a groan. A month ago, he'd have given his left testicle to nail this guy, but the timing really sucked.

"Three things?" Suzannah prompted.

"Yeah, sorry. Someone just handed me a message, but I'm back again." He turned away from the pink message slips. "Number one, his attack on you at the Registry Office. He made personal contact for the first time. He promised a reckoning soon. With that action, he's taken it to a new level, the penultimate level."

"Good ten-dollar word, Detective."

He heard the fear edging the sarcasm in her voice. "I actually know quite a few of them," he said mildly.

"Okay, what's number two?"

"Number two is you fought back. You inflicted an injury on him. He won't let that lie for long. From what he said to you it's always been personal, he always intended to make you suffer, but I'm willing to bet your striking out at him has taken that desire for revenge to a whole new level of urgency."

"And number three?"

"Number three, you drew blood."

"I thought that was number two?"

"No, I mean the blood itself. DNA. And unless he's fallen off the edge of the earth, he knows by now that we have a suspect in custody. He'll act before we have a chance to realize we apprehended the wrong man."

"But DNA tests take forever," she protested. "Even if you put an urgent rush on it, it's going to take weeks. That's pretty common knowledge."

"True. But blood typing doesn't take any time at all. And everybody knows that, too."

A short silence while she digested that. "You're right. Thanks. I feel better."

"And I'd feel better if I were there with you."

"Me, too. I missed you last night."

Her voice had turned husky, taken on that tone that made his groin tighten. "Ditto."

"I'll be so glad when this is over."

"We should take some vacation, go somewhere." The words were out before he had a chance to consider how he'd cope if she declined.

Silence stretched for a moment, then her husky voice again. "I'd like that."

She'd said yes. He grinned. Then the clerk came back bearing another message slip. He glanced at it quickly. "Look, Suzannah, something's breaking here, a case I've been working forever. I hate to hang up, but I gotta go."

"Of course."

"I'm just a phone call away. I'll keep this cell on me. And you're in good hands with Ray."

"I know."

"And the ERT team's top notch. They drill for this stuff all the time."

"I'm not scared. Just nerved up and anxious to have it over. Don't worry about me. Besides, I have work to do. I still haven't done a tap on that corporate re-org Vince gave me."

Quigg grinned. The last time she'd tried to tackle that project, she'd abandoned it in favor of having her way with him on the couch. He was probably the only man in the world who got hard at the words 'corporate re-org'.

They said their good-byes. Quigg's lingering smile faded as he picked up the latest message from Letitia Wood. Time to go talk to her. He grabbed his jacket, marveling at his good luck. When would men learn not to mix business with pleasure? Stupid to be dipping his wick at the office, but doubly stupid to do it with a personal assistant who knew his business so intimately. Hell hath no fury and all that jazz.

⚜

Suzannah hadn't held out much hope that she'd be productive, but as it turned out, work was just the antidote against anxiety that she needed. And just as well she had lots of it, for nothing happened all day.

She finally put the files aside to make a solitary supper of crusty French bread, some excellent Brie and a glass of equally excellent Cabernet-Shiraz. Because they'd told her it was necessary to show herself outside, she'd taken her meal on the patio. Then she'd gone out to her backyard beds and cut flowers. After filling three crystal vases with dramatic arrangements of Asiatic and Oriental lilies, she'd sat out for another half hour pretending to read the latest Grisham novel.

She'd felt terribly exposed, but not because she feared her stalker would take her out with a rifle. That would be too impersonal and anonymous. He'd want her to know who he was and why he was extracting this revenge. No, she felt exposed because she knew there were countless eyes on her the whole while from behind slitted blinds.

It was a relief to go back inside. Amazingly, she lost herself in work again until John's call at ten o'clock.

He'd had a productive day, too, he said. They were inches from nailing a guy he'd been dogging for a year and a half on money laundering charges. They had documentation, bank records, the modus operandi, the whole nine yards, but they'd have to move fast on this guy. The file was in the Crown Prosecutor's hands right now, but if word leaked, he'd take his millions and flit.

She'd used her free hand to shut down the computer as he'd talked, then walked through the house shutting off the downstairs lights.

"Where are you now?" she asked as she climbed the stairs. "Home?"

"No, I'm in my car, monitoring my radio."

"Where?"

"Far enough away not to be noticed. Close enough to get there in minutes."

"Good." She flipped the light switch in her bedroom and the bedside lamps came on.

"You're perfectly safe, you know. Just because it's dark doesn't mean —"

"I know. Infrared technology. Ray explained. If someone approaches the house, they'll see him as clearly as if it were high noon."

"Pretty much. You know, I should hang up, let you go about your nightly routine. If he's watching —"

"Already did it as we talked. I'm in my bedroom now and all the lights are off." Silence on the line, but she felt the surge of awareness, thick and sexual and breath-stealing. She blushed, not wanting to even think about sex while all those infra-red eyes were trained on her house. Quick, something else. "Is Bandy with you?"

A pause, then he followed her change of subject. "Yeah, he's in the back seat. Snoring like a wino sleeping one off — whoops."

"John?" No answer. "John!"

"Stay put, Suzannah. Something's happening."

No sooner were the words out when she heard shouts outside. It was over in what seemed like seconds, the real thing much faster than the staged event.

"They got him, Suz!"

"Thank God!" She heard his car's engine roar to life in the background.

"Ray's coming in to get you, so don't whack him with a candle-stick. I'm on my way."

The cell phone went dead just as Ray's voice called from down-stairs. She raced down the steps and would have plowed right by Ray in her need to see the man who'd been making her life so miserable for so long. But Ray grabbed her arm.

"Careful. Broken glass and wet tiles."

She looked down to see a shattered green vase on the floor of her sun porch, water everywhere. Perfect long-stemmed red roses — a dozen of them, she knew — lay strewn across the Italian tile, their delicate fragrance making her stomach clutch. "I want to see the bastard."

Seconds later, with Ray by her side, she stepped onto her flood-lit front lawn to confront her tormentor. Cuffed with one officer holding each arm, he hung his head, the picture of misery. Not so cocky, now, you sonofabitch.

"Turn him toward the light," she requested, moving closer. The officers obliged, but they needn't have. At her voice, the man's head whipped around.

Shock collided with her cold anger, ripping a layer cleanly away. "Geoffrey?"

He hung his head. "I'm sorry, Suzannah. I didn't mean to scare you."

"Didn't mean to *scare* me?" she repeated weakly. Then stronger: "How do you think I felt every time I got one of your rotten floral tokens?"

"I'm sorry." Geoffrey hung his head again, and this time he was crying like a child.

John materialized beside her. Suzannah realized she hadn't even heard his car arrive. He squeezed her elbow and she looked at him blankly, still in the throes of shock.

"You know him?"

She blinked at Ray's question, then pulled herself together. "Geoffrey Mann. He's an abstractor. He does title searches at the Record Office. Vince and I both use him. But you'd never meet a more mild-mannered, shy man."

Ray nodded at the officers, who removed Geoffrey to one of the cruisers that had pulled up at her curb. Suzannah blinked to try to dispel the unreality of the situation.

Was it really over?

Geoffrey Mann? Shy, tongue-tied Geoffrey? She turned to John. "He'll get a psychiatric evaluation?"

"No question."

John wrapped an arm around her and she went into his embrace.

An officer came up the walk, conferred with Ray, then strode off again. Ray's radio crackled and he turned the volume down. "We'll leave Mann's car for the evidence unit, but there's a tidy stack of florists' bills on the passenger seat," he said. "I'm betting they'll match up nicely with the dates in your diary, Suzannah.

If we can get him to roll to this, we probably won't even need to execute a costly DNA warrant."

She released her breath. "So it's over."

"It's over," Ray confirmed.

"Good," John said, "'cuz I want to take the lady home."

She glanced up at John, whose eyes glittered beneath the lights, then back to Ray. "Can we?"

"It's gonna be lit up like Christmas around here for a few hours and you sure won't get any sleep." Ray looked around, came to a decision. "Sure. Why not? As long as you're prepared to come in tomorrow morning with your box of monthly diaries."

"Of course." Suzannah glanced back at the house. "Do you need access to the house, or can I lock up?"

"Just the sun porch. You can lock the main door."

"Do I need to worry about mucking up prints?"

"Nope. Our guy was wearing white gloves."

"White gloves?"

"Yeah, soft white ones. You know, like the butler might wear to polish the silver if you lived at Tara."

Soft white gloves, not thin surgical latex. Suzannah shivered again. Had he meant to use those gloved hands on her? Would Dr. Jekyll have become Mr. Hyde? Would he have whispered her supposed transgressions into her ear as he choked off her air supply with velvet-sheathed hands?

John tightened his arm around her as though he'd felt her shudder. "Come on. Let's get you out of here."

Suzannah declined his help, needing to assure herself that her legs still worked and that she could manage on her own. Quickly, she threw some things in an overnight bag, collected her purse and locked the house, not bothering to arm the alarm. It had done its job.

They'd strung crime scene tape already, she noted, as she joined John and Ray in her driveway. The second time in so many days her lawn had been cordoned off. But this time, thank God, without the crowd of onlookers. Her immediate neighbors had been persuaded to pack their campers and take impromptu holidays with their families. That's how they'd slipped the surveillance team and equipment in, under cover of packing coolers and fishing tackle and a hundred other things, a hundred trips in and out of the respective houses. In all the hubbub, who would notice if some of the guys who went in failed to emerge again?

"Wait'll the media gets wind of this," said Ray, obviously on the same wavelength. "Two stakeouts netting two stalkers in two days."

"Yes, we better get that sorted out." She slid under John's arm and he pulled her close. "As far as I'm concerned, the sooner we explain the first arrest was a ruse to draw out the real stalker, the better. I'd prefer not to be viewed as an irresistible stalker magnet."

"I'm not in charge of communications, but I can't see them waiting long. I expect the Department's just as keen as you are to correct the record." Ray pulled a stick of gum from his pocket and folded it into his mouth. "Now, are you guys gonna get out of here, or do I have to run you off?"

"Try and stop us." John started steering her down the driveway, but she pulled back.

"Ray?" she called.

He'd turned away to speak to a uniformed patrolman, but turned back toward her.

"Thank you," she said. He started to shrug it off as just doing his job, but she waved him off. "Look, I know I didn't make it especially easy. As John alluded a couple of days ago, I wasn't crazy about accepting the Department's help." As she spoke, she was conscious of John's gaze on her face, his hand on her back. Both made her feel warmed to the core. "I really didn't think this guy was much of a threat. Worse, I didn't think you guys would think he was, either, although John tried to tell me." She grimaced. "I guess I was too worried about how it would look to the rank and file, my filing a complaint every time someone sent me flowers. I was worried my ability to do my job in a courtroom would be adversely affected. In the beginning, I even suspected the low-level stuff, the slashed tires, the dead flowers, might be the handiwork of cops stung by the treatment they got in the witness box."

Ray emitted a low whistle. "Jesus, Suzannah. I'm glad Quigg talked some sense into you."

"Me, too. Anyway, I just wanted to say thanks."

"Just doing our jobs."

"I know. But I appreciate the professionalism with which you did it." Aware that every cop on the scene was following the exchange, she stepped back and gestured with a sweep of her hand to include all of them. "That goes for all of you. Thanks."

Before anyone could react to what they clearly perceived as an astonishing development, she marched to John's car and climbed into the passenger side. Immediately, she got a blast of dog breath down the back of her neck. Bandy.

"Hi, boy." He licked the fingers she proffered, then curled up on the back seat again. A moment later, John slid behind the wheel. Bandy didn't stir, and neither did she. She sat ramrod straight, eyes forward, waiting for him to start the car. Nothing. She felt John's warm gaze on her profile, felt his amusement, but still she refused to turn.

When the silence became intolerable, she said, "I think you have to put the square key in the ignition and turn clockwise."

He laughed. "Suzannah Phelps, you're an amazing woman."

That brought her head around. "What?"

"There's nothing a cop appreciates hearing more than, 'Sorry, I had my head up my ass.' It goes a long way in this business where all we hear are excuses, denials and defenses."

"Excuse me, I did not have my head up my ass!"

His teeth were a flash of white in the near darkness. "Sure you did. Briefly, anyway. And you were big enough to admit it. You earned a lot of respect out there just now."

"I didn't say it to earn anyone's respect. I just wanted them to know…. Oh, to hell with it. Yes, I had my head up my posterior. Satisfied?"

He answer was to lean over and kiss her.

It was just a meeting of lips. No wild mating of tongues, no hands grasping heads or angling chins. Just lips caressing lips in the sweetest, most innocent kiss Suzannah could remember ever sharing. Still, it was enough to light a fire in her belly. No, not her belly. Her heart? Her soul?

"You make me so proud," he said when he lifted his head.

The strange fire kicked higher, making her chest hurt and her throat ache. Suddenly, she wanted it to be easy again. Physical. Sexual. Body yearning toward body, flesh to flesh.

"That's nice, Detective, but what else do I make you feel?" She laid a hand on his thigh, felt the muscles there contract.

He groaned. "Happy?"

"What else?"

"Incredibly lucky?"

"That, too." She raked her nails gently over taut flesh. "But what else?"

He placed his hand over hers and drew it considerably north of his knee. "Horny. Hot. Needy."

She laughed. "Me, too. Let's go."

He fumbled with the keys. "Damn, how'd that go again?" he muttered. "Oh, yeah. Square one in the ignition, turn clockwise . . . ."

❧

Twenty minutes later, he covered her naked, sweat-slicked body with his own, pressing her into his extra-firm mattress as he ravaged her mouth for about the millionth time. He lifted his head, gazing down at all that passion distorting her normally cool, beautiful, self-possessed face.

He trapped her hands high over her head. "This isn't simple any more. You know that, don't you?"

She arched up, nipping at his throat. "I know."

"We're gonna have to talk about it, about what it means for both of us."

"I know."

She pulled him down again and he forgot about words. Instead, he let his body do the talking, making love to her with a reverence that left her eyes soft and damp and unable to hide the deep emotion there.

There would be plenty of time for the words, he thought later, as they lay spooned in the deep quiet of the night. They had their whole lives.

Chapter 12

SUZANNAH WAS TIRED. TIRED but happy.

The crime scene tape was still up when John dropped her home at eight o'clock to pick up her diaries. He wanted to stick close to her, but something had come up, something pretty hot to judge by his ill-concealed excitement. So she shooed him on his way, collected the diaries and drove herself to the station.

It didn't take long to confirm that the date on every last one of the receipts confiscated from Geoffrey Mann's vehicle matched exactly with dates of flower deliveries. She was a little troubled that there were no corresponding receipts for a handful of the X's on her calendar, but Ray indicated they had yet to search Mann's apartment. Who knew what that would yield? As for Mann, he'd lawyered up — maybe he wasn't as crazy as she'd initially thought — and would make an appearance this morning.

"Is that all for now?" she asked Ray.

"Far as I can see. We'll keep you apprised."

"Thanks." She turned to leave, then turned back again. "Is John expected back any time soon?"

"Any minute. But he's gonna have his hands full." Ray grinned. "Popped a local businessman on money laundering and conspiracy to import cocaine, plus a half dozen other fraud-related possibilities." He cocked his head. "Did you want me to give him a message for you?"

She wanted to invite John to supper. She wanted to cook something impossibly elaborate for him. She wanted to feed his every hunger. And she wanted to talk at last about that big unspoken thing between them that both thrilled and terrified her.

She felt a blush rise in her face. "No, it's okay. I'll catch up to him."

She did catch up to him, but not the way she intended to. On her way out of the station house, she caught a glimpse of him escorting a handcuffed prisoner. Instinctively, she shrank back into the shadow of the stairwell. Gilles DeBoeuf! Vince's client.

Dear Lord, it couldn't be happening.

But unquestionably it was. Ray had said a local businessman. Money laundering, conspiracy to import cocaine, fraud. She shook her head in disbelief. She'd always disliked DeBoeuf, but because of his sexual mores, which were on par with the average alley cat, not because she thought he was involved in anything shady, let alone downright criminal.

She risked another glance, to make sure she wasn't mistaken. No, that was DeBoeuf all right, with his Armani suit and hundred-dollar haircut. And oh, God, he was on his way to be paraded before the sergeant like a bar-room brawler or a petty thief. DeBoeuf would be livid at this humiliation.

She'd better talk to Vince.

Stepping out of the stairwell, she hurried out of the station, cell phone already in hand. Unlocking her rental, she jumped in and dialed the office, only to have Candace advise that Vince was already en route to the station. She hung up and dialed Vince's cell phone.

"I guess DeBoeuf called you already," she said without preamble.

"Yes, though he'd have done better to call Eddie Greenspan."

The foremost criminal lawyer in the country? Author of the "Criminal Code"? "It sounds bad, I know, but there are plenty of home-grown criminal lawyers who can do the job, don't you think?"

"From the sound of the case they've built against him, he might need to import OJ's defense team. And maybe I will, too," he muttered.

Suzannah's pulse jumped. "What do you mean?"

"According to DeBoeuf, they've got detail like you wouldn't believe. Every numbered company we've ever incorporated for him, every transfer, every asset we ever moved around." Vince swore, the uncharacteristic epithet sounding strange in her ear. "Can you believe DeBoeuf accused *me* of selling him out?"

"No." Suzannah's blood ran cold. *No, no, no.*

"Yes! The little prick. As if I knew, or particularly cared, what he was doing with those companies. Dammit, I just followed instructions. He knows that."

"Of course he does," she soothed automatically, her mind racing sickly. "It obviously came from another source, which will be established in due course."

Even as she spoke the words, the ice started invading her body, filling in the great yawning cavity that had suddenly opened up in her midsection.

She was the source. The conclusion was inescapable. She replayed it now, the night she'd surprised John in her den. He'd hidden his reading material, or rather intercepted her and distracted her before she could see it. She remembered it clearly because it was the only furtive vibe she'd ever got off him. Police stuff, he'd said, and she'd been only too ready to believe him. Or rather, only too ready to be distracted by an easy smile and a pair of skilled hands. Her skin burned with humiliation.

"Obviously, Gilles has already figured that out for himself, or he wouldn't be asking me to represent him now, though frankly, I'll try to talk him into hiring a good criminal specialist. But the thing of it is, no matter who represents him, I'm a little worried about going down right along with him."

"But you didn't do anything wrong."

"Come on, Suzannah. You know how it works. How many times does the client get on the bus in exchange for bringing his lawyer down?"

Oh, she knew, all right. He referred to the practice of an accused providing evidence — real or fabricated — against someone else in exchange for a lighter sentence. Or for a reduced term if the individual already stood convicted. It was a risk you took to practice criminal law.

"I think you can relax on that score, Vince. They'd never offer him a ticket, not for you." And not John, please God. Surely he wouldn't see Vince hurt. Surely he wouldn't do that to *anybody*. "You're not a big enough fish, Vince."

"Gee, I'm flattered. I think."

"Number one, you're not dirty. You've got an impeccable reputation, a respectable practice–"

"Present client excepted."

"Agreed. And you've never made yourself a thorn in anyone's side. Nobody's got even the smallest incentive to want to hurt you, with the possible exception of DeBoeuf, if he really does think you sold him out, and anything he's got to say will be taken with a bushel of salt."

Vince swore again, muttered something. She pressed the cell phone closer to her ear. "What's that?"

"I said, maybe you are. A big enough thorn in the side, that is. A big enough fish."

Oh no, oh no, oh no. This isn't happening.

"Suzannah? Are you there?"

"I'm here."

"I want you to go home right now, gather up all the DeBoeuf files and take them to the office. Put them on my desk. They never left my office, you understand? They never left my care, custody or control."

"It's too late."

A pause. "What do you mean, too late?"

"John Quigley. He's the arresting officer. I'm pretty sure he saw them. He's practically been living with me these last weeks, until the last day or so."

Another curse from Vince.

"I think he *read* the files, Vince. I think that's where he got all that detail."

"Okay, here's what you're going to do," Vince said. "Go home. Don't talk to anyone. Let me look into it. Presuming DeBoeuf retains me, I'll talk to the Crown Prosecutor as soon as I can manage it. We'll know what we're looking at then."

"Vince, this is all my fault. I've been so blind. I left those files laying around."

"Hey, sweetie, don't beat up on yourself. They were just corporate files. You didn't know — *we* didn't know — they could be of interest to the police."

"If anything happens to you —"

"Nothing's going to happen to either of us. No way can they use anything Detective Quigley might have gleaned directly from those files."

She made a strangled sound. "But he doesn't have to have the files. Now that he knows all the answers, he can go down to Corporate Affairs or Revenue Canada or the freaking Registry Office or wherever the hell he needs to go and ask precisely the right questions. It would be child's play to gather the information now."

"Exactly. So you have nothing to worry about. The clever detective put it together all by himself. You think he's going to dispute that?"

"Vince, I feel so awful."

"Of course you do, baby. That's love."

"No, that's naiveté." She wiped moisture from her cheek, amazed to find she was crying. "Look, Vince, I have to go."

"All right, but don't do anything rash. Let me look into this, okay?"

"Okay."

She pressed the button to disconnect, shut the phone off and tossed it on the passenger seat.

"Goddamn you, John Quigley."

She angled the mirror so she could examine her face. Ugh! She looked like a train wreck. Taking a tissue from her purse, she blotted her face, swearing they were the last tears she'd shed for that man.

Any man.

Slowly, deliberately, she took a compact from her bag and repaired the damage. Then she started the rental, backed out of her spot with exaggerated care and drove home.

Quigg opened the car door and let Bandy out. The squat little dog hit the pavement with a grunting exhalation, then trotted toward Suzannah's door, his tail windmilling furiously.

"I know how you feel, buddy."

Quigg stuck his key in the lock, let himself in and turned automatically to the alarm panel, ready to plug in the code to keep it from bleating. Dammit. It wasn't set.

"Suzannah?"

"Right here."

"Sorry, didn't mean to shout. I didn't see you there." He gestured to the alarm panel. "Honey, don't you think you should use this thing?"

"Not especially."

He frowned. The dog rushed her and she bent to pet it. Or maybe just to prevent it from gouging her legs.

"Ray says all Mann's receipts square with your deliveries."

"That's right," she said.

"And it's been confirmed Mann was at the Record Office the day you were attacked."

"So Ray said."

"Did you hear he got remanded for psychiatric evaluation?"

"Yes."

Something about her tone made him look at her, really look at her. Her face wasn't quite right. Fear, sharp and illogical, stabbed at his gut.

"Are you all right, Suzannah?"

She smiled serenely. "Of course. Why wouldn't I be? My stalker is behind bars. I can come and go again like a free woman."

"Amen to that."

"In fact, it's already feeling like it never happened. Like it was all a bad dream."

He frowned. "Yeah, a freaking nightmare."

"But the nightmare's over. I have my life back, now."

Fear again, tightening his midsection. "Suzannah, are you trying to tell me something, here? Because I feel like I'm missing something."

She twisted her hands together, the first sign that her cool composure wasn't perfect. "Yes, I guess I am."

"Then you'd better spell it out, sweetheart, 'cuz you know I'm not too good with this between-the-lines stuff."

He saw her draw a deep breath. "I don't think we should see each other anymore."

"What?"

"You know it's fraught with problems. For you, for me. Lord knows our jobs are hard enough as it is. Why make it any harder than it has to be?"

He eyed her sharply. "Have you been drinking?"

She laughed, a short, hard sound. "No, I'm dead sober, John. Maybe for the first time in weeks."

Jesus, God, no. "What's that mean?"

"Remember that little scene we choreographed for the staged arrest?"

He nodded curtly, and she continued.

"The reason the script came so easily is because it anticipated the truth. Mann is in custody and not likely to see freedom for a long time. Which means I don't need a live-in bodyguard anymore. And you — well, you must have enough fodder for a lifetime of locker room She-Rex tales by now."

He felt like every drop of his blood had drained away. "That's all it meant to you? You expect me to believe that? That you were paying for my protection with your … with your … Jesus!"

She had the grace to flush. "You're right. It was more than that. I had a little sexual dysfunction going on there, and you helped me with it. For which I will be eternally grateful."

The way she said it suggested she would be grateful, all right. Grateful to try out her newfound sexual ease with the next guy. A more suitable guy. A guy like the Armani-suited, Italian-shod, Rolex-wearing sonofabitch he'd collared today.

All the blood that had drained away seemed to rush back at once, straight to his head, a blinding red rush of fury. He wanted to shove her. He wanted to shout at her. He wanted to push her down and kiss her until she accepted him.

Oh, God, he had to get out of here, before he became what he despised. He cleared his throat, which felt like swallowing razor blades. "I guess we're square then, eh?"

"Yes, I guess so."

"I'd better pack my things."

"I've already done it." She produced his overnight bag seemingly from nowhere.

"Wow, how efficient of you."

She made no reply.

"Come on, then, Bandy. Let's go."

The dog hunkered down.

"Bandy, I'm not fooling. Come on." The mutt ignored his command. Quigg strode over, grabbed the mongrel by the collar and pulled. The dog refused to come to his feet, sticking to the Persian carpet like he'd been Velcroed there. "Bandy! Come on. Dammit, she wants us out of here."

"Don't drag him!"

"What do you suggest I do? Hire a crane? He won't get up and if I try to lift him, he'll freak."

"I'll drop him off. I still have a key. I'll leave it."

"Fine."

He wheeled and walked out, closing the door behind him quietly, though he would have loved to slam it hard enough to make the rafters tremble.

He didn't exercise quite so much control in reversing out her drive and shooting away in a squeal of protesting tires.

Damned traitor of a dog. He shoulda told her to keep the rotten mongrel.

Locker room fodder? That's what she thought he'd gotten out of this? He laughed bitterly. Yeah, that's exactly what he'd get. But not the kind she thought. He was screwed now, just as Ray warned. Just as his own instincts had warned. He'd stuck his neck out for this woman, ruffled feathers, antagonized Bruce Newman and anyone Newman might have spouted off to.

And forget about promotion. Even if he could earn it, how could he effectively supervise men who looked at him and saw a man who'd been ruled by his dick? Worse, a man who'd broken ranks with his colleagues.

Half way home, he pulled into a convenience store parking lot and killed the engine. He walked into the store, bought a pack of cigarettes, tore them open and lit up. Dragging the smoke deep into his lungs for the first time in eight years, he leaned back on the fender of the Taurus. He smoked the one cigarette, ground the butt out under his foot and tossed the rest in the garbage.

Then he got back in his car and drove home.

He let himself into the big, empty house he'd inherited from his aunt, hung the keys on a peg, grabbed a beer from the fridge, twisted the top off the bottle and flopped in his leather chair.

Yeah, he was royally screwed. He tipped the beer and drained half of it. The problem was, he'd do it all over again. Which made him a fool.

At least Suzannah was safe. He smiled grimly and took another swig of beer. After the way she'd slam-dunked him, he shouldn't give a rat's ass. Guess that made him worse than a fool. It made him pathetic. Well, so be it.

If he hadn't tailed her all those weeks ago, if he hadn't insisted she needed his help, Mann might have gotten to her. The thought had the power to twist his stomach into a painful knot. Even now, he couldn't believe their plan to lure Mann out had worked so well. Pity he hadn't confessed, though. Now they'd have to wait for the DNA comparison. He drained his beer and put the empty on the floor beside his chair.

No doubt about it, the DNA would be the clincher. If Suzannah hadn't jabbed the guy, the case'd be a lot harder to make. Amazing to think a few drops of blood .... .

Quigg leapt up, overbalancing the chair, which crashed to the floor. Mann should have had a pretty good puncture wound on the back of his right hand. Quigg couldn't remember seeing one, or even a dressing on his hand, for that matter.

He grabbed his cell phone and his keys. Seconds later, he was on his way back to Suzannah's. Fumbling with the cell phone, he finally managed to dial Ray's home number.

"Did Mann have any wounds on his hands?"

"Quigg? That you?"

"Quick, Ray. Did he have a puncture wound on his right hand? Or a bandage of any kind?"

Ray swore.

"Here's the thing," Quigg said. "I think there are two of them."

"Two stalkers?"

"One secret admirer — that's our mild-mannered, shy boy who liked to leave her pretty roses. And one stalker, who sent her those dead bouquets and did all that other stuff."

"Yes, dammit," said Ray. "He probably followed her, saw her dump the flowers, then retrieved them, delivering them right back to her once they were good and dead. We'd never find him through the florists because he never visited one."

"We got the wrong guy, Ray."

"Okay, stay there with Suzannah. I'm gonna call —"

"I'm not with Suzannah, but I'm on my way." Plenty of time to tell Ray later. "This guy won't wait long to go after her. He knows we'll tumble to the fact we got the wrong guy."

"I'll call for backup."

"Thanks, buddy."

Quigg stabbed the off button and tossed the cell phone. He took the corner with tires squealing and nailed the accelerator. "I'm coming, Suzannah."

⁂

Suzannah reclined on the couch with a cold compress across her eyes and Bandy by her side.

She'd sworn she wouldn't shed another tear over him, but there'd been no stemming the tide after he'd closed the door so quietly. Now she felt hollow, cried out, brittle.

And every time she closed her eyes, she saw his face, saw the way each cruel word she'd spoken sliced into him like hot lead into unprotected flesh. Which, dammit, wasn't fair! The point of the exercise was to hurt him like he'd hurt her. She should be taking a grim satisfaction from her success. She should be grateful that she never confessed her love to him. Glad that he'd never know how much his betrayal hurt her.

But all she felt was miserable.

Beside her, Bandy growled. She lifted the compress off her face and listened. Over the dog's low-throated, sustained growl, she heard a light tapping on her front door.

"Hush, Bandy. It's probably Vince." The dog stayed there on the couch as she got up to answer the door. A quick look through the security viewer told her it wasn't her partner. It was Renee LeRoy! Suzannah pulled back, then pressed her eye to the viewer again. Definitely her most un-favorite reporter, and she was looking distressed.

Another rapping on the door.

Sighing, Suzannah turned the knob and opened the door as far as the security chain allowed. "Renee? What are you doing here?"

Self-consciously hunched in the way of a woman who wanted to disappear, Renee cast anxious glances around. "I need to talk to you."

"I don't give interviews at home. No exceptions."

"It's not about an interview."

Of course. The hunched, anxious posture said it all. A domestic case.

"I don't see clients at home, either," she said. Which was perfectly true, and she wasn't about to make an exception now, when she looked and felt such a wreck. Especially not for a woman who'd made no secret of her disdain for Suzannah and her ilk. "Tell you what — if you'll call me tomorrow at my office, I promise I'll make time —"

"No! It has to be now. Please. It's important."

More anxious glances around the street, which as far as Suzannah could tell was deserted. Did this Amazon fear some man? Someone who dogged her footsteps as Mann had dogged Suzannah's?

Suzannah weakened. "Okay."

She removed the chain and opened the door again, allowing Renee to step inside. By the time she closed the door and turned back to her visitor, Suzannah found herself looking into the muzzle of a small handgun. Her heart leapt into overdrive. Great. A crazy woman. What else could possibly happen today?

"Take it easy, Renee." She held out a conciliatory hand. "Whatever your trouble is, I'm sure we can work it out."

"Lock the door."

Renee's voice sounded a few octaves deeper as she issued the command. Suzannah's face must have betrayed her shock, because Renee pulled off her wig of curly auburn hair to reveal short dark hair. "That's right, honey. Not a woman after all."

Not a crazy woman. A crazy man. Her pulse rate kicked higher. This was much worse. Then she noticed the bandage on the right hand. Flesh-toned and subtle, but unmistakable.

Not *a* crazy man. *The* crazy man. Her stalker.

"You're making a big mistake," she said. "My boyfriend will be right back."

"Oh, please, darling. I saw him leave here, this time for real. Although you did a pretty credible job last time. I actually bought it. You might have netted me if that imbecile hadn't blundered into your trap first."

"No, you're wrong. He's coming back!"

"I'll take my chances. Now, lock the door."

What were her chances of actually opening the door and getting away? Nil, probably. On the other hand, they weren't very rosy if she didn't make a break for it. A bullet in the back would no doubt be preferable to what she — no, not she — *he* had planned for her.

She'd do it, she decided. At least she could scream. Maybe that would alert the neighbors.

"Okay." She held up both hands. "I'll lock it." Fingers trembling, she turned to the door, pretending to deal with the lock. Now or never. She wrenched the door open and screamed, only to have her captor yank her back and slam the door.

Triggered by Suzannah's choked-off scream, Bandy launched himself at her attacker. All jagged teeth, bristling hair and slitted eyes, he looked like the fury of hell. Then the report of a gun shocked her eardrums, dropping the dog mid-leap. His growl turned to a yelp, and he hit the floor heavily. Horrified, Suzannah watched blood pool on the tiles from beneath Bandy's motionless body.

"You shot him." Her voice rang with disbelief. So much blood. She tried to rush to Bandy's aid, only to have her intruder restrain her.

"Forget him."

Susannah tried to pull her arm from his grip, but he neatly twisted her arm behind her back and marched her to the door.

"And don't imagine anyone heard that shot and is racing to the rescue. In case it escaped your notice, your neighbors haven't returned from their state-sponsored vacations." He twisted her arm a little higher. "Now, the lock, Ms. Phelps."

With her hand somewhere between her shoulder blades, she obliged.

"Well done." He looked around as though considering his options. "The kitchen, I think. It has all the tools." He gestured with his handgun, as though she had any choice with the grip he had on her arm.

Tools. Terror made her feet clumsy, but he half hauled, half frog-marched her to the kitchen, where he produced a set of handcuffs and cuffed her to a chair. Out of sheer reflex, she tested the bonds. Cold steel and solid oak. She'd never break free. Dear Lord, she was going to die. No one would ride to the rescue this time. She'd sent John away. Regret, sharp as the fear, pierced her.

If she died now, he'd think she really had used him and discarded him. His transgression seemed so insignificant now, her hurt so overblown, her need to save face so petty. Less than an hour ago, she'd been thanking God she'd never told him she loved him. Now, she'd do anything to have the chance.

Then do it. The thought cut through the numbing terror. *Stay alive so you can tell him. You're your only advocate here. Be smart. Think.*

She lifted her gaze and studied her captor as he closed the room's window blinds. Who was he?

Not a reporter, that's for sure. God, how had she missed it? As abrasive as 'Renee' had been in their contacts, Suzannah had never read any invective in the press. Why hadn't it occurred to her that the reporter never reported?

Because you were too cool to read your own press, came the answer.

She forced her focus back to his face, which was hairless enough to be a woman's, if somewhat square featured.

He returned to the table. "So, have you figured it out, Ms. Phelps? Do you remember me?"

"I will."

"Yes, you will." He opened her utensil drawer and picked up a black-handled knife. "Else what's the point?"

Her heart battered her ribs as he fingered the point of the blade. Every muscle stiffened as he passed behind her, but he merely pulled out another chair and sat.

Keep your wits about you, she counseled herself, willing her panic down. Keep him talking. You must survive.

"Do you think I make an attractive woman, Ms. Phelps?"

Oh, dear Lord, how to answer that one! She swallowed. "Better with the wig on."

He laughed. "Yes, better with the wig," he agreed. "Since the surgery, my skin has gotten smoother, but I just can't seem to do anything with this hair."

Surgery? Had he had a sex change? He turned to rifle through her utensil drawer again, and she took the opportunity to examine his face in profile. Dammit, who was he?

"Ah, these should do."

To her horror, she saw that he'd selected six bone-handled steak knives. A spurt of relief when he walked right past her with them, followed by a surge of sickness when he turned on one of her gas burners. Carefully, meticulously, he arranged the knives in a fan shape, steel blades resting in the blue flame, cool handles lying on the enamel range top.

Dear God, he was going to burn her.

She almost lost it then. It took every last shred of willpower she could muster not to panic. Her stomach wanted to revolt, her bowels to loosen, and her mind ... oh, God, her mind just wanted to take itself elsewhere. But if she succumbed to panic, she was as good as dead. She knew it.

Keep him talking. "Surgery." She caught at the subject like a drowning woman might grasp at a piece of flotsam. "You wanted to become a woman?"

He smiled, and she got a tantalizing flash of the same features, but more masculine. Think, Suzannah. Frantically, she tried to picture his lean, dark face stubbled by five-o'clock shadow.

"Become a woman? No, I can't say that was my aim."

"I don't understand. What kind of surgery do you mean?"

"A most unconventional surgery, and without benefit of anesthesia. More of a mutilation, I guess you'd say." He picked up one of the knives, tested it on the pad of his thumb without flinching, and put it back into the flame. "Castration."

Her mind was still reeling from the sight of him burning himself, her nostrils filled with the stench of singed flesh, but somehow the meaning of his words penetrated. *Sex crime*, her mind screamed. He must have committed a sex crime and the victim's husband or father availed himself of rough justice. "Someone castrated you?"

"Ah, I see where that clever mind of yours is going. Vigilante justice. But you're wrong." Another smile. "Or maybe no so far off the mark after all."

He turned away to adjust the flame on the burner. Suzannah trembled. "I don't understand."

"I did it to myself, Ms. Phelps. With a butcher knife."

Don't throw up. Don't throw up. She took shallow breaths to steady herself. "But why?"

"Because I'd become a monster, Ms. Phelps. The creature that inhabits parents' nightmares. And you helped me become that monster."

Oh, God, of course! She'd only defended a handful of men on sex crime charges, and only one on anything remotely pedophilic. "Remy Rosneau."

"Congratulations, Ms. Phelps. Move to the top of the class."

She searched her memory banks frantically. It hadn't been anything too horrific. Touching for a sexual purpose, the complainant being his twelve-year-old cousin. Suzannah had never believed her client was guilty. The circumstances were too convenient. The family feud between Remy's father and the victim's father, the fact that the victim admitted her testimony had been embroidered and heavily coached by her father, the fact that the victim's father hoped to gain financially by discrediting his brother's family to the extent that their ailing father might cut the disgraced branch of the family out of his will.

The provincial court judge had convicted Rosneau, but Suzannah had managed to persuade the Court of Appeal to overturn what she thought was a bad decision.

She swallowed. "Did you touch that girl, Remy?"

"Yes, I touched her."

"But you told me you hadn't, that it was just your uncle trying to smear your father through you."

"Of course I denied it." He looked genuinely insulted. "*Everyone* denies it."

Suzannah blinked. How could this be happening? "I don't understand. I successfully defended you against a charge you vowed was false, yet here you are blaming me for — wait a minute, what *are* you blaming me for?"

"I should have gone to jail. It wouldn't have happened if I'd just gone to jail."

Her mind reeled. "You wouldn't have … mutilated yourself?"

"I wouldn't have molested my niece. She visited that summer, from Montreal. If I'd been locked up, it wouldn't have happened."

Again, she fought down nausea. She had to keep a clear head. "The summer your conviction was overturned? That was over two years ago. I take it she didn't report your crime?"

"No."

"So you decided to punish yourself?"

"I had to stop the monster before it gained full control. Don't you see?"

"Yes, I see." She felt a reluctant respect stir in her numbed mind. It was extremely uncommon for a pedophile to seek treatment, let alone entertain a 'cure' as drastic as the one he'd opted for. Their pathology usually led them to cultivate victims in such a way as to allow them to continue to indulge their deviant compulsions.

"You *see*? Do you really, Ms. Phelps? Do you see that in getting rid of the monster, I created a freak? How am I supposed to live in this world? Where do I fit?"

"All you need is some help, Remy. You can have a good life, a rewarding life. But not if you harm me. It will only land you in prison, for real this time."

"Maybe that's where I deserve to be."

No, he deserved to be confined indefinitely to a mental institution, but she wasn't about to say that. "Do you really believe that, Remy?" she asked softly.

He lifted a knife, examined it. "Yes. Prison or worse."

"Then let me call the police. You can surrender —"

"Oh, I'll surrender, Ms. Phelps, but only after I've dealt with you."

He moved closer, close enough that she felt the heat emanating from the knife blade. "No, please —"

"I have to. Otherwise, another monster will just move in to take my place, and you'll help him do it."

"I won't. I promise. You don't need those knives."

"I'm afraid I do. You see, we have to drive the devil out. We have to fight fire with fire."

She couldn't restrain her fear any more. She screamed.

⁂

Beads of sweat sprung up on Quigg's brow as he squeezed the transmitter button on his radio. "He's inside the house with her. I repeat, inside the house. A single shot has been fired, but she's not hurt. He just led her to the kitchen in the south-east quadrant of the house and cuffed her to a chair." Quigg's words emerged calmly, dispassionately, even as his emotions threatened to slip the tight leash he'd imposed on them. Habit, he supposed. Training. Discipline. He called on all of those things now. "I'm going in. I have a key, so I should be able to slip in unnoticed. Tell backup to come in quiet. Repeat, no siren or lights. Front door will be open."

"Negative on entering the premises," came the dispatcher's voice. "Wait for backup."

"Sorry, no can do," he muttered, but he'd already replaced the radio. He climbed out of his car and eased the door shut. Drawing his 9mm from its holster, he sprinted across Suzannah's lawn and vaulted over a hedge of lilies, not slowing up until he'd gained the south-west corner of the house. The motion detector lights he'd insisted she install winked on, and he offered a silent thank you that it wasn't yet dark enough yet for them to attract attention from within.

He wanted like hell to barge right in her front door, but he had to survey the situation first, make sure they were still in the kitchen. He'd almost blundered into disaster once. Had Suzannah been able to get the door open far enough to escape, she'd have bowled him over on the doorstep. They'd probably both be dead. As it was, he'd nearly died when he heard the gun discharge. Then — oh, praise God — he'd heard Suzannah's voice again, reasoning with her intruder this time, and he'd known she hadn't been hit.

He'd wanted to storm the place then and there, more than he'd ever wanted anything in his life, but he'd restrained the impulse. Any rash action on his part could get her killed. So he'd crept to a window instead, in time to see a tall, slim figure half dragging, half marching Suzannah toward the kitchen. He'd slipped to another window with a view of the south end of her kitchen and dared another quick look. That's when he'd seen the intruder shackle her to the chair.

And that's when it occurred to him he'd better alert backup to roll in quiet. If they came in with lights and sirens, the only way Suzannah was getting out was through heaven's gates. He knew it in his soul. A man didn't stalk a woman so assiduously only to let her escape him at the eleventh hour. No, what they needed was stealth, not might.

Now, heart pounding like it might come right out of his chest, pistol at the ready, he inserted his key in her lock and turned the deadbolt as softly as he could. He held his breath for a few heart-beats, listening for any sound from within. Nothing. Muttering a Hail Mary, he opened the door. It swung inward silently, and he gave thanks for Suzannah's anal retentive streak. She would never suffer a chair spring to chirp, a floorboard to groan or a door hinge to squeak.

Then he saw Bandicoot's body lying in the vestibule amid a puddle of congealing blood.

The bastard shot Bandy!

For a few seconds, he literally saw red. Then he reined himself in. *He'll do a lot worse if you don't get a grip on yourself. Suck it up, Quigley. Do this right.*

Stepping over the threshold, he scanned the room, pistol leveled, but the room was empty. Leaving the door ajar, he skirted Bandy and headed straight for the kitchen. Just in time to hear Suzannah scream. By the time Quigg made the kitchen, the sonofabitch was standing behind her, the knife in his hand a glowing brand. For the second time tonight, his vision took on a distinct red tinge.

"Stop! Police!"

※

For a moment, Suzannah thought her terror-stretched mind had produced the ultimate mirage to comfort her — John crouched in her kitchen doorway, the muzzle of a deadly-looking handgun trained on Rosneau. She took in every detail of him, from the fire in his eyes to the disarray of his shirt; from the steadiness with which he gripped the pistol to the corded muscles standing out in his forearms.

Then Rosneau grabbed a handful of her hair and yanked her head back, hyper-extending her throat. "Just in time for the show, Detective."

"Let her go, buddy. There's no way out, and backup is on the way. Your situation will only get worse if you don't put that knife down."

He was real, not a figment of her imagination! John was really here.

Rosneau moved the glowing blade closer to her face. "Worse? How could it get any worse?"

"Maybe my putting a hollow-point bullet between your eyes?"

"Yes, but could you do it before I slit her pretty throat?"

Suzannah couldn't see Rosneau's face, but she heard the smile in his voice. What she could see was John's weapon lowering slightly.

"Don't listen to him, John! Don't surrender your weapon. He'll kill us both." Rosneau gave her hair another vicious tug, bringing tears to her eyes.

John lowered his weapon another inch, his eyes begging her to understand. "It's too risky. It's that bases loaded, three-two count again, honey."

What was he trying to tell her? Can't throw the fastball because Rosneau would be sitting on it. Can't afford to miss with the breaking ball. Throw him something off-speed. Something that looks like the fastball Rosneau was expecting . . . .

Of course!

John held up both hands, then started to lower his gun toward the floor.

Suzannah lifted one leg, planted a foot on the edge of the table and shoved backward in the chair as hard as she could. She felt Rosneau's surprise, heard him shout, felt the kiss of hot metal on her neck as she went down with the chair. Then the muzzle flash of John's gun, twice, so shockingly close, the reports deafening in her tiled kitchen.

As if in slow motion, she saw two crimson blooms appear dead-center of Rosneau's chest, one right after another, knocking him backward. She watched him hit her refrigerator. Incredibly, he stayed on his feet for a few seconds, looking as though he might roar right back with the blade he clutched. Why didn't John shoot him again? Then the knife clattered to the floor, followed a few seconds later by Rosneau. He landed right beside her, his lifeless eyes looking straight into hers.

Shuddering, she tried to roll away, but with her arms still trapped behind the overturned chair's back, she was pinned painfully in place.

"Suzannah, are you all right?" Hastily, he holstered his weapon.

"Get me up!"

Even as she spoke the words, he was reaching for her, lifting her chair and all, moving her away from Rosneau. Then his hands were moving over her as though to assure himself she was intact. "Thank God! The knife ... I thought he cut you."

"Just a burn."

He tipped her chin up, swore. "If I thought I could resuscitate the bastard, I think I might do it just so I could kill him again."

She shivered. "He *is* dead, isn't he?"

"Two rounds in the chest. Not much question about it, I don't think." Abruptly, he stood. She watched him press two fingers to Rosneau's neck. "Gone," he confirmed, then proceeded to rifle through the dead man's pockets.

"What are you doing?"

He held up a small key. "I'm gonna get you out of those bracelets before your shoulder sockets pop."

A few seconds later, he slid the cuffs off. She stood, rubbing her numbed wrists. Lord, her shoulders ached from going down backwards like that. Her right elbow stung, too, as did the burn on her neck. But she was alive. And Rosneau wasn't. She forced herself to look at the man.

"Should we try CPR or something?"

"The bastard tried to kill you. He killed my dog."

Her eyes filled. "I know. I'm sorry. When he came at me, Bandy leapt to my defense. Rosneau shot him point blank."

A muscle worked in his jaw. "I saw."

She drew a deep breath, wiped her eyes. "Still, aren't we supposed to do something?"

"Not to put too fine a point on it, I don't think we've got anything to work with. Paramedics will be here in a few minutes anyway."

"Backup, too, I suppose?"

"You know it."

"Three times inside of a week I've had a visit from you guys." She smiled. It was a weak, teary thing, but still a smile. "Four times within a month, if you count the time my car was torched. The *For Sale* signs are going to be sprouting up like dandelions on my neighbors' lawns."

"I'd laugh, but I'm using my remaining resources to combat the shakes." He exhaled, sounding just as shaky as she felt. "God, if I'd been any slower ... ." He allowed his words to trail off and sank down on a chair.

Suzannah remained standing. Not because her own legs weren't trembling with reaction, but because she couldn't quite bring herself to sit on one of those chairs yet.

"Not that I'm complaining about the timing or anything, but why did you come back?" she asked. "I didn't think ... I mean, after what I said ... ."

"No injury on Mann's hands. If he'd been the one you stabbed with your trusty Cross pen, no way could it have healed yet. That's when I finally tumbled to it — there were two guys, not one split personality. One a harmless admirer, the other, evil stalker guy. Speaking of which, who is our stalker guy?"

"A former client and mutual acquaintance, Remy Rosneau."

"Rosneau?" His voice rose on a note of incredulity. "The guy I popped for getting creepy with a young girl?"

She nodded, massaging her wrists. "His cousin."

He studied Rosneau's smooth-skinned face, now slack. "Doesn't look much like the guy I remember."

She bit down on her lip, lest she give in to the hysterical laughter welling in her chest. "It's a long story."

"But you got him off on that sexual touching charge. Eventually."

"Evidently that was the problem —"

John cocked his head, held up a hand. "Backup's here."

She frowned. "I don't hear sirens."

"Couldn't have them roaring up to the door while our friend Remy was still at the controls." He stood. "Stay here. I left the front door open, but the boys aren't expecting a warm reception."

Suzannah slumped against the table. A blue flame still burned low on her gas range, five knives fanning out from it. The air smelled like overheated metal and cordite and death, and Remy Rosneau's blood was seeping into her tile grout.

But it was over. It was finally over.

Quigg gave his statement to his Sergeant quickly, concisely and completely. None of which prevented him from eavesdropping as Suzannah gave her own statement to Ray Morgan, who'd arrived on the scene minutes after patrol response. A total pro, she gave her statement with an economy of words, while still covering the ground thoroughly. Seemed like everyone else was listening with more than half an ear, too, judging by the grimacing male reaction when she touched on Rosneau's act of self-castration. If she'd purposely set out to tighten the sphincters of a room full of men, she couldn't have done a better job.

What a freakin' whack job this guy was. He'd pleaded not guilty, cried a river to Suzannah about his innocence, then held her responsible for keeping him out of jail. He'd blamed her for everything. For not divining his true nature despite his lies. For not losing in court. For his reoffending. For his self-mutilation. And ultimately, for his unhappiness for what his handiwork with a Ginsu knife had wrought.

Meanwhile, in the background, the crime scene people worked away, snapping pictures and whatever else they had to do. Which would be pretty minimal, he supposed, since the perp was currently achieving room temperature on the kitchen floor.

When she finished her statement, he tried to talk her into going to her mother's for the night, but she insisted on staying put. He would have suggested his place, but he wasn't dumb enough to imagine anything had changed. Four hours ago, she'd said she didn't need a cop in her life. Now, she *really* didn't need him. All the cockroaches had come out of the woodwork. It would be free sailing from here.

Still, he figured he'd hang around until the other guys left, if only to make sure she realized what a total crock Rosneau had spewed.

In shorter order than he would have imagined possible, they lifted Rosneau's corpse onto a gurney and wheeled him out to the ambulance that would transport him to the hospital's morgue. One of the ambulance attendants came back, gesturing to Bandy's blanket covered body. "Would you like us to remove the dog?"

Quigg felt his throat close. Poor sonofabitch. Kicked around half his life, only to wind up bleeding out on Suzannah's floor. *My fault, too. If I'd noticed Mann's hand .... * Dammit all to hell. He swallowed with difficulty. "You can do that? Hold him in the morgue?"

"Don't see why not."

Quigg cleared his throat, grateful for the EMT's awkward kindness. "Okay, then. Let's do it. I'll be around early tomorrow to pick him up."

The attendant bent to uncover Bandy, arranging the blanket beside the dog. Quigg knelt to help him transfer the blood-soaked dog onto the makeshift carrier. On the count of three, they hefted Bandy's substantial, barrel-like body onto the blanket. When Quigg would have folded the fabric over his pet, the EMT stopped him.

"Shit, look at that."

Quigg looked down at his motionless dog. "Look at what?"

"Fresh welling of blood, when we moved him just now." Whipping the stethoscope from around his neck, he fitted it to his ears and applied the business end to the dog's chest. "Holy cow." He tore the stethoscope off. "This dog's alive!"

"Get a vet on the phone!" Quigg shouted.

Thirty seconds later, Suzannah handed him a cordless phone. "Dr. Orser," she said.

"Dr. Orser, this is Detective John Quigley of the Fredericton City Police. We got a civilian dog down, with a point-blank gunshot wound to the chest. We thought he was dead. In fact, he's been lying here unconscious for almost an hour. Big-time blood loss. Can we bring him in?" He looked up at Suzannah, whose eyes were bright with hope. "Good. In the meantime, I just happen to have an EMT here who's pulling for this guy. Is there anything he can do to stabilize the mutt before transport?"

"Let me talk to him," the EMT said.

Quigg passed the phone.

Twenty minutes later, with the dog wrapped in blankets in Quigg's back seat and Suzannah sitting beside him squeezing an oxygen mask over his muzzle, they rolled into Dr. Orser's parking lot. The vet met them in the parking lot. With the help of his anesthetist, Dr. Orser transferred the dog onto a gurney. He took the portable oxygen from Suzannah and laid it beside Bandy on the stretcher. From there, they whisked the still unconscious dog away.

Suzannah sank into a chair in the empty waiting room; it was after hours — they'd opened specially for this emergency. Quigg paced, scowling around at the hospital-quality veterinary operation. "Look, they offer health insurance for your pets." He gestured to a sign on the wall. "This is going to cost four figures if it costs a dime."

"I'll pay it," she volunteered. "It's my fault. I let Rosneau in, and Bandy was just trying to protect me."

"It's not your fault and you will not pay for it. I was just yakking for something to say. He's my dog and he did just what I'd have done in his place." He rolled his shoulders to try to ease the incredible tension there. "Except I wouldn't have got shot."

"Come here and sit down."

Because he didn't know what else to do, he obeyed.

"I'm sorry, Suz." He raked a hand through his hair. "None of this would have happened if I'd been doing my job. Geoffrey Mann just fell into our trap so neatly. He admitted sending you flowers, his receipts matched up perfectly with your deliveries, he was at the Record Office the day you were attacked. Dammit, he just fit the bill so bloody well, we didn't even bother to look at his goddamn hand. We were too busy arranging for DNA warrants and anticipating a slam dunk. Our bad."

"Mine, too. I'm the one who supposedly marked him. I should have looked for that confirmation. Besides which, I'm supposed to be the guardian against wrongful conviction. I should have looked harder, been less ready to accept the prima facie evidence." She grimaced, and his heart turned over. "I guess it's a lot easier when you're not emotionally involved, huh? A lesson I'll remember for the future."

Quigg shifted in his chair, looked at the clock. How long did dog surgery take? He cleared his throat. "I hope you realize what a crock Remy Rosneau was spouting, don't you? I mean, nobody could possibly hold you accountable for any of that stuff. He hired you; you represented him with integrity and vigor, in good faith, and you prevailed. End of story. He's responsible for every damned thing he did, before and after that."

She shuddered beside him. Her chair abutted his chair, and he felt the delicate vibration. Damn, he wished she were his to comfort, to hold.

"He was sick, John."

John. No one else called him that, except his mother. After tonight … . Dear God, he was going to miss her. He didn't even have the cloak of anger that had protected him earlier when she'd sent him on his way.

"Yes, he was sick. And that wasn't your fault, either."

She sighed. "I know. I know all those things, John. But the fact remains he raped his thirteen-year-old niece because I helped him evade conviction."

"Yeah, and I failed to make a compelling enough case to convince the superior court of his guilt. If you want to look at it that way, it's my fault. I'll have to live with it. And keep trying. And so will you."

She blinked rapidly and looked away. "Yeah. You're right. So much to think about. I helped a guilty man escape punishment, and I helped put an innocent one behind bars, if only for a matter of hours. Only you know what? I don't want to think about it now."

"Then don't." Oh, God his heart was so bruised. He sank back in his chair and closed his eyes.

"Don't you want to know what I *do* want to think about?"

"Sure." Anything to keep him from examining these love contusions too closely.

"Us."

His eyes sprang open. "Us?" He took refuge in flippancy so his shock wouldn't show. "Honey, unless I misunderstood you earlier, there is no us. Bad guy collared. Princess no longer requires live-in bodyguard, goes back to glamorous life. Detective goes back to drinking Moosehead Dry out of a can in front of the Expos ball game. End of interlude."

"I'm sorry about what I said. I didn't mean it."

He blinked. "Which parts?"

"Any of it. I didn't mean a single word."

He surged to his feet. "Are you crazy, woman? Or just sadistic? Does it give you pleasure to jerk me around like this?"

"Jerk *you* around?" She came to her feet then, too. "What about what you did to *me*? I was just trying to save some face."

"Face! Cripes, I never saw a woman so concerned with face. You should have been born a goddamn man."

"Maybe I should have! Then I wouldn't have jerks like you who think it's your God-given right to run roughshod over me."

"Wait a minute. What are you talking about? What did I ever do to you?"

He watched her draw a couple of deep breaths, watched her rein in that temper of hers. When she spoke at last, it was her best reasonable voice.

"I know about your arrest today."

Quigg shook his head, as though that might rearrange the words she'd said into an order that actually made sense. "Gilles DeBoeuf? What the hell has he got to do with us?"

"I know where you got your information, John."

She represented Letitia Woods? Before he could pin her down, she held up a hand to stop him.

"I don't care, okay?" She dropped her gaze, started twisting the gold tennis bracelet on her right wrist. "I was mad enough before to blow you off, but I've have time to put things in perspective. That whole thing with Rosneau really underscored how insignificant a thing it was. The upshot is, I don't want it to stand in our way. I can get past it."

Quigg just goggled at her.

"Dammit, I just said I don't want it to spell the end for us. What more do you want me to say?

"Have I stumbled into the *Twilight Zone*?"

"Excuse me?" She lifted her nose in that haughty way she had. "I think you know what I'm talking about."

"Suzy, honey, you can get as huffy as you like, but it won't change the fact that I don't have the first clue what you're talking about. You might as well have delivered that speech in Swahili, for all it means to me."

"For goodness sake, I know you read the files!" she flared.

When he just looked at her blankly, he thought she'd go ballistic. "The DeBoeuf files. In my study. I practically caught you red-handed that night, but I let you distract me."

He felt his face go slack, knew he must look stunned. "What?"

"John, I *saw* you hide what you'd been reading. Then, if I remember correctly, you developed a sudden fascination for my earlobe and we retired to bed."

"You gotta be kidding me."

"Haven't you been listening? *I. Don't. Care.* If DeBoeuf is involved in organized crime, if he's importing drugs and laundering money for the big guys, he deserves whatever he gets. Please, just don't drag Vince into it. He didn't know anything of DeBoeuf's master plan. He was just following very narrow, very specific instructions. He wasn't privy to the big picture."

Full realization dawned. *Oh, Suzannah, you wonderful, foolish, proud woman.* He grinned. He knew it wasn't wise, but he couldn't help it. He felt it spreading across his face, slow and inexorable as dawn breaking.

She gaped. "You're laughing at me? Laughing?"

"No, not at all." He tried to wipe the smile away. "I'm just trying to come to terms with this. I mean, you've always been such a stickler for us cops observing proper evidentiary protocol —"

"You ungrateful —" Her chest heaved, rather nicely, he thought, as she searched for an adequate word. "— pig!"

"Whoa, careful. I'm sensitive about names like that."

"That's it. Forget it. I'm calling Gilles DeBoeuf in the morning to tell him where you got your information. The Crown Prosecutor, too."

He did laugh this time. "You're gonna have one confused client, then, sugar. 'Cuz it was his executive assistant Letitia Wood who dished the goods on friend Gilles. Seems he was sleeping with the fair Letitia, whilst stringing her along with promises that he'd divorce his wife and marry her. Unfortunately for Mr. DeBoeuf, someone snapped some pics of him and the missus renewing their vows in a posh backyard ceremony to which Letitia had not been invited."

She groaned and hid her face in her hands a few seconds, then raked her fingers back through her hair. "Oh, hell."

"Precisely."

"His EA?"

"Yep."

She chewed her lip for a few seconds. "So, what the devil were you reading that night in my study?"

His grin faded as he considered his options. He could sluff her question off, claim general police stuff. Confidentiality and all that. They could carry on from there, feeling their way as they went.

Or they could start fresh. She'd just demonstrated the lengths to which she was capable of going to maintain this relationship. He could do the same.

"I was studying for my Sergeant's exam."

"Sergeant? Of the detective bureau?"

"They'll put me wherever they want me, if and when the time comes, but yeah, I'd like Major Crimes. There'll be an opening coming up, but I'm not fooling myself it'll be mine for the asking. Hell, I don't even know if I'll pass the damned exam."

She laid a hand on his cheek. He couldn't help it. He turned his face into her palm.

"You'll pass," she said. "But is this what you really want?"

He shrugged. "It'd keep me behind a desk more. And it would certainly minimize the possibility that I'd ever be a witness in one of your cases. That can't be a bad thing."

She dropped her hand from his face, but only to find his hand. He readily twined his fingers with hers.

"Are you doing this for me, John Quigley, because you think it's what I want? Or are you doing it for you?"

He snorted. Christ, did everyone have to ask that question? At this point, he better just assume it would be on the exam.

"That wasn't a very erudite response."

Erudite. God, he loved what came out of her mouth. Come to that, he loved her mouth, period.

"John?"

"I don't know how to answer that. Both, I guess. For you, for me. For us." He looked down at their clasped hands, hers so white and elegant, his so big and clumsy. "You make me want to *be* more. That's why I started looking into promotion opportunities. Then I found I kinda liked the idea of having my finger on the pulse of everything. And I think I could bring some decent skills to the job."

"Of course, you could."

"Thanks." Suddenly, the talk petered out. Not because there was nothing left to say, but because what was left was hard. He rolled his shoulders. "So, does this mean we can keep seeing each other?"

He risked a look at her face, but it seemed it was her turn to contemplate their joined hands.

"I was hoping for something more."

His heart jumped. "Me, too. I want you to move in with me, in my giant, rambling two-story mausoleum. I want us to make a home out of it, like it once was."

"Okay."

"Okay?"

She lifted her gaze then and her eyes were bluer than he'd ever seen them.

She smiled. "Yeah, I said okay. I'd love to live in your Aunt Charlotte's house and plant perennial beds and herb gardens and strip that gorgeous hardwood floor in the entryway. But I was hoping for still more."

He swallowed hard, hoping that would get his heart out of his throat. "More?"

"Un-huh. More."

Dammit, just ask her!

"Suzannah Phelps, will you marry me?"

She looked like she might cry, but the corners of her lips kicked upward. That had to be a good sign, didn't it?

"I'd very much like to marry you, John Quigley. But you have to give me that something more first."

His heart tumbled and rolled in his chest like a stone being churned by a white water cataract. "What more do you need?"

"I need the words, Detective."

His jaw dropped. "Is that all?"

"*All?* John, that's everything."

"Of course I love you." He shook his head in wonder. "How could you not know that? I think it started the first time I sat in the witness box and watched you work. All that passion and purpose on the inside, and all that self-possessed composure on the outside. How could I not fall for you?"

She blinked rapidly, but not in time to stop a couple of tears from sliding down her cheeks. "Most men in that witness box had a distinctly different reaction."

"I'm a lot smarter than most men."

She laughed, knuckling away the moisture on her face. "Yes, you are, Detective. I guess that's why I love you."

He kissed her then, with all the tenderness swelling his heart.

Quigg came to his senses at the sound of someone clearing his throat. Pulling back, he found Dr. Orser standing there looking weary but amused.

Suzannah gripped his hand tight enough to grind bones.

"What's the news, doc?" he said.

"He's critical, mainly due to blood loss, but stable. My money's on him pulling through just fine."

"Thank God!" breathed Suzannah.

"Cosmetically, he's going to look pretty rough for a while," the vet warned.

"Dang," Quigg said. "Guess I'd better phone that Hollywood agent and cancel his screen test."

"Screen test?" Dr. Orser looked skeptical. "Forgive me for saying so, but that dog has to be one of the homeliest mutts I've ever laid eyes on."

Suzannah looked at her husband-to-be and saw their future stretching out in front of them, bright and full of possibility. And homely dogs. She beamed. "Yes. Yes, he is, isn't he?"

Epilogue

SUZANNAH GAZED AT HER husband of one year across the linen-draped patio table in the back yard of their York Street home. Between them sat the remains of the elegant meal he'd arranged, courtesy of a gourmet caterer, for their anniversary. From the CD player hidden somewhere, Mark Knopfler's understated vocals and achingly beautiful guitar caressed the evening air.

"I can't believe you planned this all yourself."

He grinned. "Thought I'd forget, didn't you?"

"Not a chance, Detective Quigley. After all, I started dropping clues last month."

"That's Sergeant Quigley, thank you. Major Crimes, no less."

Her jaw dropped. "It came through?"

"It did."

She flew around the table and into his arms. He caught her lightly, easily, pulling her onto his lap and covering her laughing mouth with his. A moment later, the laughter and joy had segued into pure need. She pulled back a few inches.

"I have a present for you, too."

He groaned. "Honey, you don't have to remind me. I've been thinking about nothing else all day."

He insinuated a hand into the bodice of her gown to cup a breast, much fuller since their daughter had arrived. She dug her nails into his biceps and let desire heat her blood and curl her toes. This time she could have him. The doctor had given them the proverbial green light. Tonight, after the baby went down. She shivered and pulled back another fraction.

"Not *that* present, dummy."

"Then what'd you get me? Another hundred-dollar tie?"

"Not even close." But speaking of ties, she adjusted the muted charcoal silk number she'd picked out for him last week. "No, I took a new job."

She felt him tense under her. "What do you mean? What kind of new job."

"Teaching."

"Law?"

She rolled her eyes. "No, basket-weaving. Of course, law, right here at the university."

"You're not giving up your career for our family, are you? 'Cuz we talked about this. I won't have you sacrifice more than me. You've already given up your practice for these past few months —"

"So competitive, Sergeant." When he didn't laugh, she sobered. "No, that's not what it's about. My teaching schedule will definitely make motherhood more manageable than my law practice did, but that's just an incredibly wonderful bonus."

He still looked suspicious. "And it's not about me, or my job? Potential for conflict? Perception that it might hold me back or compromise me to have a wife in the criminal defense trenches?"

She shook her head. "Nope. If that's what it was about, I could drop the idea, couldn't I? You already got the promotion."

He watched her with those steady, patient brown eyes. She knew there'd be no more questions. He'd just wait for her to expound on her reasons. He knew her too well.

"It just feels right for me now. I needed to do what I did for all those years, and I feel like I honored the spirit of the system, always. But it's time to do something different."

"You could cross the floor and work for the Province. You know how badly they're hurting for Crown Prosecutors."

She smiled. "You think we have potential for conflict now? I can just see every decision I made being second-guessed, people always wondering how heavily influenced I was by my husband, the detective bureau sergeant."

He shrugged. "It wouldn't be fatal."

"I know. If I wanted it badly enough, we could work it out, I expect. But what I really want to do, Sergeant, is indoctrinate a whole crop of bright young minds. I want to send them out there

to safeguard the rights of the disadvantaged and the socially marginalized —"

"Dear God, an army of them!"

"— to prosecute accused persons in the right spirit, a spirit of
seeking truth. To uphold our laws from the bench as judges. I want
to do my part to make it a better system."

"Okay. Works for me. Now, get up."

"Huh?"

"Our song's coming on. Plus, by my calculations, I have about
one more minute before this nicely pressed, beautifully tailored
suit I put on for this occasion starts looking like I slept in it. So
let's dance."

Smiling radiantly, she moved into his arms and they swayed
together, their silhouettes merged in the twilight.

Lifting his head, Bandicoot whined softly. He should go over
there and take a chunk out of his master for manhandling his
mistress like that. On the other hand, she didn't seem to mind too
much. Besides, he had a new job now. Dropping his head onto his
paws, he went back to watching the infant kicking happily in the
mosquito-netted bassinet.

⁂

Thank you for investing that most precious of commodities — your time — in my book! If you enjoyed *Guarding Suzannah*, I would be thrilled if you could help me buzz it. You can do this by:

Recommending it. Help other readers find this book by recommending it to friends, readers' groups and discussion boards.

Reviewing it. Please share with other readers what you liked about this book by reviewing it wherever you purchased it, or at readers' sites such as Goodreads. If you do choose to review it, I would be delighted to gift you with an electronic copy of your choice of any of my other titles. Simply email me to alert me to your review and let me know which of my books you would like to have and in what electronic format. My email address is norahwilsonwrites@gmail.com.

Read on for an excerpt from *Saving Grace*, the next book in my Serve and Protect Series.

Also available from Norah Wilson:

Sensual Romantic Suspense
SAVING GRACE, Book 2 in the Serve and Protect Series
PROTECTING PAIGE, Book 3 in the Serve and Protect Series
NEEDING NITA, a novella in the Serve and Protect Series

Sensual Romantic Suspense w/Paranormal Element
EVERY BREATH SHE TAKES
(coming soon from Montlake Romance)

Sensual Paranormal Romance
THE MERZETTI EFFECT: A Vampire Romance
NIGHTFALL: A Vampire Romance

As N.L. Wilson
(writing partnership of Norah Wilson and Heather Doherty)
Dix Dodd Mysteries (humorous)
THE CASE OF THE FLASHING FASHION QUEEN
FAMILY JEWELS
DEATH BY CUDDLE CLUB (coming soon)

As Wilson Doherty
(writing partnership of Norah Wilson and Heather Doherty)
YA Paranormal
THE SUMMONING: Book 1 in the Gatekeepers Series
ASHLYN'S RADIO

About the Author

Norah Wilson lives in Fredericton, New Brunswick with her husband, two adult children, her beloved Rotti-Lab mix Chloe, and numerous rats (the pet kind). Norah has had three of her romantic suspense stories — including this one! — final in the Romance Writers of America's Golden Heart® contest until she sold her first story in 2004. She was also the winner of Dorchester Publishing's New Voice in Romance contest in 2003.

Norah loves to hear from readers!

Connect with Her Online:
Twitter: http://twitter.com/norah_wilson
Facebook: http://www.facebook.com/norah.wilson1
Goodreads:
http://www.goodreads.com/author/show/1361508.Norah_Wilson
Norah's Website: http://www.norahwilsonwrites.com
Wilson Doherty's Website: http://www.writersgrimoire.com

Excerpt from Saving Grace
(Book 2 in the *Serve and Protect Series*)

After wrecking her car and waking in hospital with amnesia, fledgling reporter Grace Morgan has no idea why she'd been in the process of leaving the husband she loves so dearly. Her husband, Police Detective Ray (Razor) Morgan tells her she was leaving him for another man, but that just can't be so. Can it? She's determined to remember, even if it kills her. And it just might. When bullets start to fly, Ray is forced to take the wife he believes faithless on the lam until they can figure out who is trying to kill them.

Saving Grace

BEING DRUNK SLOWED RAY Morgan's reaction time. The telephone managed a full ring before he snatched the receiver.

"Grace?" To his own ears, his voice sounded like someone else's.

A second's silence, then a man's voice. "That you, Razor?"

Ray sagged back into the depths of the couch. John Quigley, from the station.

Not Grace after all. Never again Grace.

"Yeah, it's me." Ray dragged a hand over his face. "'Fraid I'm no good to you tonight, though, Quigg."

Another pause. "You okay, Ray?"

"Sure. Been keeping company with Jim Beam, is all." Ray's lips twisted at his own wit. Okay, so maybe he wasn't that witty, but it was either laugh or cry. "S'okay, though. I'm not catching tonight anyway. Hallett is."

"Just a sec, Ray."

Quigg must have covered the mouthpiece, because Ray could hear muffled conversation in the background.

"Okay, I'm back," Quigley said.

"I was sayin' to call Gord Hallett. He's your man tonight."

"I don't need a detective, Ray. I was looking for you."

"Huh? You're looking for me at, what …?" He squinted across the room at the glow of the VCR's digital clock. Grace's VCR. She hadn't slowed down long enough to take anything. What had he been saying? Oh, yeah, the time. "… eleven o'clock at night?"

"It's Grace."

At the mention of his wife's name, Ray felt the hollowness in his gut open up again, wide and bottomless as ever. Guess the bourbon hadn't filled it after all.

Leave it to Grace to get stopped on her way out of town, in her red Mustang the boys in Patrol had come to know so well. Had she explained why her foot was so heavy tonight? His grip on the phone tightened. Had she told the uniform — a guy Ray would have to face every day for the next ten years — that she was rushing off to meet her lover and couldn't spare the horses?

Her lover.

"You got her downtown?" he asked evenly.

"Downtown? Hell, no. They took her to —"

"'Cuz you can keep her. You hear me, Quigg? I don't care."

"Dammit, Ray, listen to me. She's been in an accident."

Ray shot to his feet, dragging the telephone off the table. It hit the floor with a crash, but the connection survived. "What happened?"

"She missed a bend on Route 7, rolled her vehicle."

He felt his stomach squeeze. "Is she hurt bad?"

"Hard to say. By the time I got there, they were already loading her into the bus. But she didn't look too bad, considering she rolled that puppy like the Marlboro man rolls a cigarette. Paramedic said he thought she might have lost consciousness for a bit, but she seemed pretty with it to me."

Wait a minute, Quigg was off duty. Why'd they call Quigg?

Unless Grace was hurt so bad they thought his best friend should break the news.

Ray gripped the receiver so hard now his fingers hurt. "Why'd they call you?"

"Nobody called me. Suz and I were on our way home from visiting friends when we came on the scene. I stopped to see if our Mountie friends could use a hand. When I saw it was Grace, I offered to make the call."

Okay, relax, man. Breathe. Maybe it wasn't that bad. *But she'd rolled the car.*

Pressing a thumb and forefinger to his closed eyelids, he pushed back the images from every bad wreck he'd seen in his twelve years on the force.

"They taking her to the Regional?"

"She's probably there already."

"I'll be there in —" Ah, hell, the booze. *Morgan, you idiot.* "Quigg, I'm in no shape to drive. Can you send a car?"

"Way ahead of you, buddy. Stevie B will be there in about four minutes."

⁂

Four hours later, Ray sat across the desk from Dr. Lawrence Greenfield, the neurologist who'd just finished Grace's workup.

The six cups of coffee he'd downed had sobered him up, but his stomach lining felt like he'd been drinking battery acid.

"So she's going to be okay?" Ray had been through such a wild range of emotions in the five hours since Grace had dropped her bombshell, he didn't know how he felt about this news. Christ, he didn't even know how he was *supposed* to feel. He eyed the doctor, who looked way too young to be fooling around with anyone's grey matter. "She'll walk away with no real injury?"

"I wouldn't go that far. At least not yet. She did suffer a Grade Three concussion." Dr. Greenfield leaned forward in his chair, steepling his hands. "Brain injury is more of a process than an event, Detective. It can escalate over as much as seventy-two hours, so we'll have to wait and watch for the next little while. What I *can* tell you is she has no focal injury we can pinpoint with conventional imaging."

"Focal injury?"

"No concentrated damage in any one area. The scans were clean. On the other hand, any time a patient loses consciousness, we have to be suspicious."

"What do you mean, suspicious?"

"She could have a diffuse injury, where the pathology is spread throughout the brain, rather than focused in a specific spot. We'll have to follow her for a while to rule out more subtle brain injury."

Ray slouched back in his chair, kicking a leg out carelessly. "She's conscious now?"

"Yes. And anxious to see you."

Ray rubbed a hand over the back of his neck. "Then I think I'd go back and look at those scans again, Doc."

"I'm sorry?"

"She can't possibly want to see me." He congratulated himself on how matter-of-fact he sounded. "She left me tonight. She was on her way to join her lover when she had her accident."

Dr. Greenfield blinked. "She told me she was coming home from an interview with a man who raises miniature horses, and that you'd be worried that she was late."

The pony interview? "Doc, that interview was a week ago. The story ran on Monday."

"I see." Dr. Greenfield leaned back. "Well, this puts things in rather a different light."

"What are you saying?"

"I'm saying we could be looking at a retrograde amnesia."

Amnesia? Oh, Christ, he was in a bad novel now. "But you said she'd escaped injury."

"Amnesia can accompany any loss of consciousness, however brief, although I thought we'd ruled it out." Greenfield removed his glasses and polished them. "She identified the date and day."

"Couldn't she have picked that up from the EMTs or the hospital staff?"

"Absolutely. Amnesia victims can be very good at deducing such things from clues gleaned after the accident. But she correctly answered a whole host of other questions for me, including the results of Tuesday's municipal election."

Ray digested this information. "Is it possible she remembers some things, but not others?"

"Oh, yes. In fact, it's quite probable." Dr. Greenfield replaced his glasses. "Amnesia can leave holes in the memory, with no predicting where those holes will appear. The location of the gaps can be as random as the holes in Swiss cheese. In fact, we call it Swiss cheese memory."

Terrific. Freaking wonderful. "So she might remember the election results, but not the fact that she's taken a lover??

"I suppose it's possible."

To his credit, Greenfield's gaze remained steady, but Ray could read eyes. Faint embarrassment, carefully masked empathy for the cuckolded husband.

"Or she may not have forgotten Romeo at all, right, Doc?" he rasped. "Just the fact that she told me about him."

"That's also a possibility," the neurologist conceded. "Whatever the case, Detective, I can vouch for the fact that she seems genuinely anxious to see you. She's very much in need of some sympathy and support."

Ray made no comment, keeping his face carefully blank.

"I should add that new memories are especially vulnerable, since it takes a few days for your brain to move them into permanent memory." Dr. Greenfield hunched forward again. "Do you use a computer, Mr. Morgan?"

Ray struggled to follow. "Of course I do. Who doesn't?"

"Well, to make a very crude analogy, fresh events, whatever might have happened in the last couple of days, are to your brain what random-access memory, or RAM, is to your computer. If the computer unexpectedly loses power before a bit of data gets stored on the hard drive, it's lost. You can boot up again, but whatever was in the RAM has been wiped out. Thus, with any loss of consciousness, it's possible to lose memories that were in transition."

Great. She'd probably forgotten she'd dumped him.

Ray stood. "Well, no time like the present, is there, Doc? Let's go see my darling wife."

Dr. Greenfield's eyes widened. "Surely you don't plan to tell her … I mean, you won't —"

"Won't what? Suggest she call her boyfriend so she can cry on his shoulder instead?" Ray drew himself up, growing in height and girth, and let his expression go flat in the way he knew inspired fear. *Bad cop to badder cop.* "Why shouldn't I? She chose *him*."

Dr. Greenfield looked singularly unintimidated, no doubt because he'd already seen the raw edge of Ray's anguish.

Damn you, Grace, how could you do this to me?

"The fact remains that she seems to need *you* right now. She's quite distraught. The last thing she needs is to be upset any further. If a diagnosis of retrograde amnesia is confirmed, I'd like to give her a chance to recover her memories on her own." Dr. Greenfield's intense gaze bored into Ray. "Can I have your cooperation on that point?"

Ray stared back at the doctor, unblinking. "I hear you, Doc. Now, take me to her."

⚜

Grace Morgan felt like a dog's breakfast.

Despite the painkillers the nurse had given her, everything she owned seemed to hurt, albeit in a distant way, and her head ached with a dull persistence. But she hadn't cried.

In fact, she seemed unable to cry. Instead of tears, there was just a hot, heavy misery in her chest. If only Ray would come. If he were here with her, she could cry rivers.

She'd cry for her beloved Mustang, shockingly crumpled now, a red husk of twisted metal they'd had to open like a sardine can. How had she come out of it alive?

She'd cry for her carelessness.

She'd cry for scaring Ray, and for scaring herself.

Ray. He would gather her close and soothe her while the pain seeped out, soaking his shirt. He would lend her his strength, his toughness. He'd kiss her so carefully and sweetly .... .

She could almost cry, just thinking about it. Almost.

Ray, where are you?

On cue, the door swung open to admit her husband. Her heart lightened at the sight of him, so strong, so solid. His shoulders seemed to fill even this institutional-size doorway.

If she felt bad, he looked worse. Haggard. And for the first time she could remember in the six years she'd known him, he looked positively rumpled, and his face was shadowed with stubble as though he'd missed his second shave of the day.

Poor pet. He must have been so worried.

"Ray." Her right arm hindered by IV lines, she reached across her body with her left arm. He took her hand, but there was something wrong. He looked ... funny. Guarded. Wrong.

Oh, Lord, was she dying after all? Was her brain irrevocably damaged and nobody wanted to tell her? She could be hemorrhaging right now, her brain swelling out of control. Maybe that's why her head hurt. Maybe .... .

Then he touched her forehead, brushing aside the fringe of hair peeping out from under the bandage, his gentleness dispelling her crazy impression.

"You all right?"

She would be now. "Yeah, I'm all right. Unless you know something I don't."

That look was back on his face again. "What do you mean?"

"They didn't send you in here to tell me they mixed up the charts, by any chance? That my brain is Jell-O after all?"

He smiled, but it didn't reach his eyes. "No, your head is fine, as far as they can tell."

She drew his hand to her cheek, pressing it there with her own palm. Some of the pain abated. "That's what they told me, too, but you'd never know it from the way I feel."

"Do you remember what happened?"

She swallowed hard, her throat tight with the need to cry. "I rolled the Mustang."

"Like a cowboy's cigarette, to quote Quigg." Another ghost of a smile curved his lips. Lips he hadn't yet pressed to hers.

She smiled tremulously. "I guess I'm lucky, huh?"

"Very lucky."

The tears welled, scalding, ready to spill. "I really loved that car."

"Something tells me you could love another one."

Again that twisting of his lips. It wasn't humor that lit his eyes. What? A vague, formless anxiety rose in her breast.

"A newer model, with fewer miles on the odometer. Or maybe something faster, flashier."

She wasn't imagining things. His tone was … off. What was it she was hearing? Accusation? Grace blinked. "Are you very angry? About the car, I mean?"

He seemed to swallow with difficulty, and his hand tightened on her chin. "Grace, I don't give a damn about the car."

For the first time since he entered the room, she finally saw what she expected to see in his face. *To hell with the car. You're okay. You're safe,* his eyes said. Her sense of strangeness dissipated.

"I was so scared."

He pulled her into his arms. The dam broke and her tears spilled over at last.

⚜

They kept Grace overnight for observation.

Ray stayed, planting himself in the single chair by her bed. Once he dozed off, waking when the night nurse came in for yet another check. At eight o'clock, he left Grace to her breakfast and went down to the lobby to find a pay phone.

He was a fool, plain and simple. He knew it, but knowing didn't seem to help. He was going to take her home anyway.

Of course, it wasn't like he had a helluva lot of alternatives. He couldn't send her home to her mother, that frozen excuse for a human being, even supposing Elizabeth Dempsey would take her daughter in. Grace's father had died two years ago, completing the retreat from an imperious wife which Ray figured must have begun minutes after Grace's conception.

No, there was no place for Grace to go. Not in her current condition.

Ray dropped his quarter and punched in the number, kneading the tense muscles at the back of his neck as he waited for his Sergeant to answer. It was likely to be a short-lived arrangement anyway, having Grace back home. When she didn't show up for her rendezvous, no doubt lover boy would come looking —

"Quigley."

"Quigg, it's me."

"About time you checked in. How's it going?"

"Grace is good. Concussed and sore as hell, but okay."

"Yeah, I've been getting regular updates. But that's not what I meant."

Ray bit back a sigh. "Is this where I'm supposed to ask what you *did* mean?"

"Last night you were ready to let her rot in the lockup."

"What's wrong with that?" Pain shot up to the base of his skull, and Ray massaged his neck again. "Biggest favor I could do for the motoring public, with that lead foot of hers."

"Except you don't know how to be mean to Grace. Leastways, not before yesterday."

"Yeah, well." Ray rubbed at a scuff on the tiled floor with the toe of his Nikes. There was a pause at the other end of the line, no doubt so Quigg could digest that pithy comment.

"I think you should take some time off," Quigg said at last.

"That's actually why I'm calling. I'll need a day or so to get Grace settled."

"I was thinking more in terms of weeks."

"Weeks?" The idea of spending days at home with Grace as she recovered her mobility — and her memory — filled him with cold dread. Not that it would take long. Even if nature didn't cooperate, Grace's paramour was bound to show up to hurry the process. Ray had been counting on putting in long days on the job, both before and after Grace's veil of forgetfulness fell — or was ripped — away.

"I can't take time off. You'll be short-staffed."

"Not for long. Woods is three days away from rotating in."

"He'll need orientation … ."

"He's been here before," Quigg said. "Couple of days, it'll be like he's never been gone."

"But what about Landis?"

"I'm pretty sure our small-town bad guy will be here when you get back."

"There's nothing small-town about that bastard, and you know it." Ray knew he was letting the simmering fury of his domestic disaster leech into his voice, but he didn't care. That puke Viktor Landis was a worthy target for it. "He's got his fingers into every dirty deal that goes down in this town."

"And some day you'll catch him at it, but not this week. And not next week." Quigg's agreeable tone turned hard. "Compassionate leave, Razor. Two weeks, starting now. The work'll be here when you get back. It's not going anywhere."

"But I only need a few days, not weeks."

"Take 'em anyway."

A definite command. Ray gripped the receiver tightly. Dammit, how could his friend do this to him? He *needed* to work.

"Get away from the station house," Quigg said, his voice softer now. "Spend some time with Grace. Chrissakes, Ray, you haven't taken a real break since your honeymoon."

Quigg's words stopped the retort on Ray's tongue. Had it been that long since he'd taken a vacation? He was passionate about his job, but *four years?* Why hadn't Grace said something?

"What do you say, buddy? You gonna take the time or do I have to suspend you?"

Before his promotion last year, Quigg had worked right alongside Ray in the detective bureau. Hell, he was the best friend Ray had in the world. But it wasn't going to make any difference here. Quigg meant business.

Ray put his hand on the phone's switch hook, ready to break the connection. "A week."

"Two." Another command. "And Ray? I know you're not in the market for unsolicited advice, but I'm gonna give you some anyway. Whatever you need to do to get straight with Grace, do it. She's a keeper."

"You're right."

"Of course I'm right. She's a good —"

"I meant about the unsolicited advice." With that, he replaced the receiver.

He stood staring at the telephone for a few minutes. Then, feeling like a man condemned, he turned on his heel and went in search of the doctor to see about Grace's discharge.

⁂

Six days later, Grace sat in her bedroom, battling tears.

Her headaches had receded, and her bruises were resolving nicely. The total body agony she'd come home with had faded to mere muscle pain, easily tamed by a couple of Ibuprofen. In fact, she had everything a recuperating patient could wish for.

Ray had taken time off to nurse her. He'd fixed her meals, bought her medication, ferried her to and from the doctor's office, and generally anticipated whatever she needed before she asked for it.

In those first days, he'd massaged her sore muscles and changed the bedding regularly. He'd helped her in and out of the bath until her soreness abated enough for her to manage by herself. He rented videos for her, most of which they watched together.

He talked to her, too. Did she remember the bird-watching trip they'd taken to the Tantramar Marshes last year? The Christmas they spent in their first apartment, before they'd bought this house? He even pulled out the photo albums she'd lovingly constructed over the years, and which he'd largely ignored, and got her to narrate each snapshot.

Yes, her husband was the perfect companion.

And she was thoroughly, completely miserable.

Oh, he was the soul of kindness, but his kindness was platonic, his touch devoid of anything remotely sexual. Even with their heads bent together over the photo album, she hadn't managed to strike a spark off him. And she'd tried. Somewhere along the way, she seemed to have gained a caregiver and lost her lover. He even slept on the couch at night, claiming he didn't want to jar her sore body.

That last thought had her knuckling her eyes like a kid.

Oh, grow up. He just doesn't want to hurt you. It's up to you to show him you're better, that you're ready to be treated like a woman again, not an invalid.

Though she thought she'd been pretty eloquent on the subject last night when he'd given her the back rub she'd requested. Or at least as eloquent as she could be in a non-verbal way. She squirmed as she recalled the way she'd purred and stretched under his hands, but none of her signals had slowed his firm, clinical strokes or brought that fierce light to his brown eyes.

Why, oh why, couldn't he see how desperately she needed this connection with him, the reassurance of physical closeness?

She chewed at her lip. Maybe men really did need things spelled out. They were always complaining women expected them to read their mind. Maybe she had to be more direct about it. Except he'd never had any trouble reading her body language before the accident. She'd never had to ask for *that*. The very idea made her face flame.

She'd come to Ray a shy virgin, and while he'd carefully and skillfully relieved her of that state, he'd seemed content for her to keep her demureness. More than content, she suspected. He'd grown up with a mother who prized ladylike decorum above all else. Grace grimaced, thinking how often her own nature fell short of that saintly mark, at least in thought if not in actual deed.

But in the five years they'd been married, Ray had never avoided their bed before. His disinterest *had* to stem from the accident, and his reaction to her injuries.

Her spirits revived as she warmed to the idea. Really, it made perfect sense. He'd always treated her gently, so careful not to frighten or hurt her. So much so that she sometimes want to scream. Obviously, he needed her to affirm her return to health more forcefully.

She'd do it, she decided. She'd do it tonight.

⋆⋆⋆

This was sheer, unmitigated hell.

Ray leaned against the cupboard as he waited for the kettle to boil. He'd been in some tight spots in his time. Hell, in the four years he'd put in on the Metropolitan Toronto force before coming to Fredericton, he'd seen some truly bad shit. But nothing had tested him quite like this.

Six days, and still she acted like everything was normal.

As far as he could tell, Grace's recall was perfect, except for the last day or two before the crash. Which meant she must remember the fact of her lover's existence. Much as he'd like to, he couldn't believe those random Swiss cheese 'memory holes' Dr. Greenfield alluded to could excise the bastard so neatly.

Clearly, though, she had no memory of telling him.

And equally clearly, she was in the mood for sex.

Sex.

The word brought down the cascade of visuals he alternately tortured himself with and ruthlessly suppressed. His wife, another man. Grace welcoming another man, opening her arms for him, parting her legs —

The shrill scream of the kettle dragged him back from the edge of madness. Cursing, he shut the burner off, forcing the images back into the dark place from which they'd escaped.

Back to the problem at hand. What to do about Grace's amorous urges? He threw two tea bags in the pot and added boiling water. He sure as hell wasn't going to oblige her. Thank God for that puritanical streak her mother had instilled in her. She wouldn't ask him to make love to her, at least not in so many words. As for her non-verbal invitations, he'd continue to let them sail over his head.

How long would it take for memory to return? Greenfield had urged him not to force the matter, allowing Grace to remember it herself. But there was a limit to how much a man could take, a limit Ray feared he was rapidly approaching.

And where was this jerk? It'd been *six days*. What kind of man wouldn't come looking for a woman like Grace when she failed to show up?

The smart kind. The kind who fears the righteous wrath of a man who carries a gun for a living.

With a fierce oath, he drove the violent fantasy from his mind. Satisfying as it was, it was only fantasy. If Grace wanted to walk out that door with another man, he wouldn't detain her.

Grimly, he put the teapot on the tray, along with the weekly rag containing the story he knew she was going to hate. Willing his face blank, he lifted the tray and headed to the bedroom.

⁂

Where was he? She'd heard the kettle whistle minutes ago.

Grace lay on the bed pretending to read, wearing nothing but one of Ray's good white shirts.

Well, okay, Ray's shirt and a pair of bikini panties. She wasn't brave enough to dispense with that bit of covering. But it was literally a *bit,* a barely-there scrap of lace.

She flicked back her hair, lustrous from the oil treatment she'd used on it earlier. Smooth and touchable as silk, straight as a waterfall, it was her one vanity. She tossed it back again and drew one knee up, striving for a sexy pose.

Striving and failing. Shoot. She was far too jittery to pull this off. Ridiculous to get so twisted out of shape over the prospect of seducing her own husband. It's just that he'd been so … distant.

While he accepted her touch, she sometimes got the soul-shriveling impression he had to fight himself not to shake her off. And he sure as heck hadn't initiated any touching of his own, at least nothing that wasn't related to her care. Now that she was so much better, he hardly touched her at all.

Oh, God, what if his distance sprang from more than concern about her injuries? What if he didn't want her? What if he found her efforts at seduction crass? What if he turned her down?

Grace pressed a hand to her stomach. It felt like she'd swallowed a dozen Mexican jumping beans, like the ones her father had given her when she was six. Jumping beans her mother had discarded with the trash despite Grace's protests that the caterpillars inside would perish before they could emerge as butterflies.

She groaned. Way to go, Gracie. When he comes in, you can be wearing that whipped puppy look you get when you think about Mama. That'd be real seductive.

No, she needed to think positive thoughts. She needed to show Ray she was a well woman. Strong. Lustful.

Very lustful.

Abandoning the magazine, she rolled onto her back. Closing her eyes, she imagined Ray approaching the bed, looking down at her with those smoldering, hooded eyes. He'd bend down to kiss her with exquisite delicacy, and his hand would go to her waist, careful not to rush her. Then, as she grew ardent beneath him, he'd lift his hands to her breasts.

Her breathing grew short. With one hand, she cupped a tingling breast, using her other hand to skim her thigh where the hem of Ray's shirt left off. Next, he'd slowly unbutton the shirt —

Something — not noise, for Ray always moved soundlessly as a cat — made her open her eyes.

He stood in the doorway, a tray clutched in his hands, looking like he'd been turned to stone. *Which, I guess, would make me the Medusa head.*

Grace shook the dismal thought away. At least she'd captured his attention. Even as a blush warmed her face, she drew herself up on her elbows.

"There you are." Her shallow respirations made her sound breathless as a schoolgirl, but she couldn't help it. "I was going to come looking for you in another minute."

Her words had the effect of unfreezing him. His movements jerky, he approached the bed, putting the tray down on the night table.

"I brought you the weekly paper." Keeping his eyes firmly fixed on the tray, he poured the tea "You better read it."

Grace's shaky confidence took a plunge. He hadn't even spared her a sideways look after that first eyeful. To counter her flagging assurance, she reminded herself how much he loved seeing her in his shirts. He'd said so dozens of times, proved it dozens of times.

She took a deep breath, drew herself up on her knees. "I can think of things I want more than the paper," she said, running her index finger along his bare forearm.

Ray sloshed the tea he was pouring. With a muffled oath, he put the teapot down and snatched the newspaper up before it could become totally saturated. Grace shrank back as he shook droplets off the newspaper.

"Here," he said gruffly, thrusting the paper at her while he mopped the tea up with a napkin. "Front page, bottom right."

Her face burning, she took the paper, more as a physical shield to hide her humiliation than anything else, but the photo at the bottom of the page drew her eye. The sight of her crumpled Mustang, its roof peeled back grotesquely, struck her hard. Without warning, her mind lurched backward.

She was in her car, hurtling through the night, the road black, unwinding in her headlights like a shiny snake. Her hands gripped the wheel, and her heart was heavy with misery. Oncoming cars, their headlights brilliant blobs through the prism of her tears. Tires catching the graveled shoulder. That sick feeling when she started to lose it. Then … nothing.

"You okay?"

Grace lifted a hand to her head.

"It's not like you didn't expect this, right?" Ray swiped the bottom of her teacup with a cloth napkin and handed it to her.

She accepted it automatically. "It's one thing for your own paper to give the story a pass, but you had to know this other rag would run with it."

She looked up at him, seeing black road, headlights. "My accident — what time was it?"

His gaze slid away. "Ten thirty. Ten forty-five."

Almost eleven o'clock! That couldn't be right. She'd been coming home from an interview with the horse guy. Garnet Soles.

The idea seemed somehow both right and wrong. She'd started home from that interview well before five o'clock. It just didn't add up. And what was she doing out that late?

"Ray, where was I going?"

He lifted his gaze to meet hers, his expression guarded. "I don't know."

She searched his face for long moments. He spoke the truth, she decided at last. But he also lied. If he didn't know *where* she was going, he most certainly knew *why*.

"I wasn't coming back from the horse interview."

She swallowed when he shook his head.

"I've forgotten something important, haven't I?"

He nodded.

"That's why Dr. Greenfield kept asking me those questions."

"Yes."

Her stomach took a plunge. That's why Ray had poured over the photo albums with her. Testing her memory, not reminiscing.

Ask him. Ask him why you were flying down that rain-wet highway after dark.

No! Whatever it was, she wasn't ready to hear it.

Something scalded her thigh. She looked down to find she'd spilled most of her tea on herself.

Ray swore, taking the china cup from her trembling hands.

"Your best shirt," she said.

He cursed. "It's my fault."

"It's the one I bought you for your birthday last year."

"Forget the shirt." He strode to the bathroom. She heard the splash of water, then he was back, wet cloth in hand.

"Egyptian cotton." She examined the brown splotch. She'd bought it at a men's luxury store, spending the better part of a paycheck on it. Ray appreciated a really fine shirt.

"Here, put this on your thigh."

Suddenly, it seemed imperative that she save the shirt. If she didn't deal with the stain immediately, it would set, and she couldn't use bleach on the fine fibers. "I'll wash it now."

Her fingers fumbled with the buttons, but he brushed her hands away.

"Forget the shirt, dammit. Just lie down and let me put this cold cloth on that burn."

She lay back. He was right; it was just a shirt.

Ray perched beside her on the edge of the bed and gently applied the cold cloth to the red flesh at the top of her thigh.

As he bent over his task, Grace studied his lean face, so infinitely dear to her. Deep grooves bracketed a sensual mouth, and sandy brown hair sprang back from a high, smooth forehead. His downcast lashes lay sooty against his dark skin, shielding warm brown eyes.

Oh, God, why did it feel like she was losing him? It made no sense. Nothing made sense.

He glanced up. "Better?"

"I'm scared."

A muscle leapt in his jaw and he lowered his gaze again. "It'll be okay," he said, his voice gruff as he flipped the cloth to the other, cooler side.

Would it really? Something terrifying loomed at the edge of memory, just beyond her grasp. Would it ever be okay again? A shudder racked her.

"Hold me, Ray." The words were out before she knew she was going to say them. His head came up again and she met his eyes, realizing with a shock that they were as pain-filled as hers must be. Her fear took another leap. "Please."

He groaned, pulling her into his arms. She pressed herself against him, seeking to obliterate the fear bleeding into her soul from that dark, shrouded corner in her mind. *Love me*, she begged silently, her hands roaming his back.

He crushed her against his chest, trapping her arms and burying her face against his neck. Oh, Lord, he was going to rock her like a baby. He planned to comfort her in that same sexless way he'd treated her all week.

No! She wouldn't let him do this. Her arms might be pinned by his embrace, but she still had options. She opened her mouth on his neck, tasting him with her lips and tongue.

"Grace."

Her name on his lips was a growl, a warning she was past heeding. She needed this, needed him. Wriggling on his lap, she inched higher, kissing the underside of his clenched jaw, inhaling the clean scent of the lemongrass soap he used.

"No, Grace." He grasped her upper arms. "Your leg."

"It's fine. *I'm* fine. I have been for days."

He eased her away, holding her at arm's length. A few days ago — shoot, maybe a few minutes ago — she'd have let him put her aside. But not now. She couldn't let him retreat to that place he'd been these past days.

She dipped her head as though giving up, and he slackened his grip. The instant he did, she leaned into him, using her full weight. Had he anticipated such a move, she never could have budged him, but as it was, she overbalanced him easily. The next instant she sprawled atop him. The look of astonishment on his face would have been funny, under other circumstances.

Oh, my God, I'm on top! What now?

Quickly, before he could recover his wits, or maybe before she recovered her own, she bent and kissed his slack mouth.

For a few heartbeats, he lay there, unresponsive. Fueled by equal parts of fear and need, she kissed him with renewed desperation. Then, just as she began to despair, she felt him catch fire beneath her. In a single heartbeat, he was right there with her. Trapping her head, tangling his fingers in her hair, he kissed her back.

Giddy, she slid her hands over him, glorying in the way he arched up into her. Could she take him like this, claim him as thoroughly as he'd claimed her so many times? The idea sent bolts of excitement zinging jaggedly along her nerve endings. Did she dare try?

Deciding she had nothing to lose, she broke the kiss and sat up so she could tackle his belt. He groaned and pulled her back down. Wrapping an arm around her, he rolled her swiftly onto her back, pinning her beneath him. She wanted to protest, but then he was kissing her again, deep and hot and insistent, and she couldn't think of one single thing to complain about.

Besides, it was probably best this way. She needed him to take her with an authority that left no room for doubt.

"Love me, Ray," she urged against his ear. "Love me like you've never loved me before."

His body stilled. Cursing, he levered himself off her and strode out of the bedroom.

Grace was still trying to process what had happened when she heard the front door slam. A few seconds later, Ray's truck roared to life, reversed out of the driveway and accelerated off. As she listened to the sound of his engine growing fainter, she realized she'd felt this same black despair before.

At the wheel of her car as she sped away from her husband on a ribbon of wet blacktop.